Ripples in Time

Ron Mueller

Ripples in Time

Books and Stories by Ron Mueller

The Taelo Series
Taelo: The Early Years
Taelo: The Golden Feather
Taelo: Journey of Discovery
Taelo: Dangerous Passage
Taelo: Condor Clan Slingers
Taelo: Circumvention
Taelo: The Journey of Sages
Taelo: Collection
Taelo: Future Leaders Journey

A Taelo Story:
White Swan and Quiet Pheasant
The Child's Name
Floating Cloud
Quiet Rabbit
Busy Bee
Little Otter & Talking Wren
Broken Spear
Burley Bear & Meadow Flower

Science Fiction
The Savitar Series:
  Journey's End
  Savitar
  Confluence
  Savitar Collection

Bram Nielson Series
  The Fold
  The Message
  Fold Wormhole
  Negative Fold
  Ripples in Time
  Bram Nielson Collection

Single Science Fiction Books
  Current Past and Future
  The Event
  The Door
  Viajante 7

Ron Mueller

<u>Fiction Series</u>

The Alex Evercrest Series
  The River Front
  The Girl on The Grill
  Missing
  Maggot
  Racist
  Votive Candles
  Windy City
  Country Road
  Pool of Blood
  Sins of the Daughter
  Body Parts
  The Skull Collector
  The Vanishing
  The Shadow Fighter
  Moonshine
  Grief's Trajectory
  The Magic Touch
  Northern Lights
  Alex Evercrest Heroin Collection
  Alex Evercrest Collection Two
  New Direction

A Brian Oneil Novell
  Hawaiian Phoenix
  Moon Curser
  Death Broker
  Hawaiian Princesses

The Problem Solver Series
  Solutions
  Drug Lords
  Border Crosser
  Problem Solver Collection

Imagination by Courtney Huynh and Chloe Parker

Ripples in Time
By: *Ron Mueller*

Around the World Publishing LLC
4914 Cooper Road Suite 144
Cincinnati, Ohio 45242-9998

ISBN 13: 978-1-68223-279-8
ISBN 10: 1-68223-279-4

Distributed by Ingram
Cover Picture by: Onyx @ShutterStock
Cover Design by: Ron Mueller

Ron Mueller

Dedicated to those that accept

that nothing we understand

is exactly how we perceive it.

Ripples in Time

<u>Table of Content</u>

Ron Mueller

<u>Chapter 1: Transition Plans</u>

As the saying goes, all good things must come to an end. It was clear to Bram that it was time to end the presence of the Fold effort on Earth. He had mixed feelings about the ability of everyone making the transition to another planet, in another solar system in another galaxy. Mataia, the destination planet was equivalent to what earth would have been before more than plant life had begun. It was less stressed and had less tectonic plate activity but otherwise it had a similar proportion of water to land mass and the atmosphere was almost a duplicate of what the Earth had.

The ability to Fold between Earth and Mataia had made the transition a reality.

Bram met Eric, Jeffrey, and Elizabeth to discuss the transition of the Fold effort to Mataia. The four of them developed an initial transition plan that was as flexible as possible.

Bram pointed out that it would take several years to fade out the Fold project from Earth in a manner that it would draw no attention. The Fold program had never become public but there were influential individuals who had been aware of it. He pointed out that Olivia Newton a member of the now dissolved Senate Oversight Committee was coming out to meet with him in a desire to be part of the Fold project. He added that he hoped that Jeffrey and she would work together to establish the Mataian government.

Jeffrey smiled and replied that he would love that assignment from his new boss.

Bram shook his head and replied that his head would remain in the world of science in an effort to move the Fold capability forward.

He then asked Erica whether she would lead the move of the Fold project from Earth to Mataia.

Erica nodded and said that she was pleased to be the one to help get Mataia going. She felt that it would be a high point of her work life.

Bram said that his objective was to leave Earth in such a fashion that no one would know they were gone.

Elizabeth spoke up and asked what an old lady like her could possibly do to help make it all happen.

Ripples in Time

Bram said that she should think about setting up the education system on Mataia. She would need to recruit top talent to be the teachers and instructors of a system that began at the lowest grade and went through to where PhDs were graduating.

Elizabeth asked if there were school buildings on Mataia.

Bram smiled and said that she should get together with Amy and Pat to lay out the buildings and then work with Erica to figure out how to outfit the school system. He added that her question highlighted the monumental undertaking that the move to Mataia represented.

He said that he had done a little thinking on the details but was certain that there would be several areas that he felt would be challenges.

One was the logistical arrangements that were necessary to support a functioning Einstein City. Supplies from Earth would need to be constantly Folded in. He felt that they needed a facility separate from the current Arrival Terminal to accommodate the arrival of the logistical materials.

He went on to point out that there most likely were additional facilities that they had not thought about that would need to be built and then transported to Mataia. He was planning on having Amy and Pat be the two who would lead that effort.

The second challenge would be to vet the personnel that would make permanent moves to Mataia. Their selection needed to be carefully considered. They should be vetted as to their love for the work they were currently doing in the Fold project and to seeing a future for themselves in living on Mataia in the long term. He added that for all their lifetimes return to Earth would be possible but at some point, that would become a rare occurrence.

Erica suggested that she spend time with each of the other team members and develop the details of a transition plan. She pointed out that sometime in the future the Fold facility at Dallas would need to be slowly erased. She did not think folding the existing buildings to Mataia would be practical nor desirable because Amy and Pat had improved the way homes and other structures were built for Mataia. However, she pointed out that the homes at the site could be Folded to various countries to establish very nice communities for people needing homes. She thought that the industrial buildings could be relocated to a strategic location where they could continue to be used as part of the logistical material handling facility for things going out to Mataia.

Bram thanked Erica for taking the lead in that area.

He said he wanted to work with Elizabeth and Jeffrey on selecting the personnel that would be emigrating to Mataia.

Ripples in Time

He added that he also wanted to work with Melisa and Marcus to set up vacation spots on Mataia as well as a way to maintain the Earth vacation spots. He said that he felt that the transition would be much less stressful on everyone if their leisure time could be spent on both planets. In that way, leaving Earth would not be so dramatic.

Jeffrey asked whether the members of the Stetson family were in line to move to Mataia.

Bram shared that he had talked with Lacy and Linda and the two definitely were eager to be included. The rest of the Stetson family were on the fence. They were quite willing to aid in the transition, but they felt that they were going to remain on Earth. Linda had let him know that her brother Luke was eager to set up the transport manufacturing center on Mataia or do whatever was needed. He thought that his future was going to be there.

Bram later met with Pat and Amy to discuss what they thought the transition needed to include.

Amy pointed out that it would take years to slowly change the Mataian environment to at least make it able support life like Earth.

Amy pointed out that they needed to keep everything in balance and that the transition should move slowly forward over their lifetime and perhaps beyond, in short it would take time.

Bram said that he would love to take part in some of the Mataian transformation details of moving as time permitted but they would all be very busy for as far into the future that he could see, and they should continue to default, to taking it slowly and Fold plants and animals to Mataia in a controlled and well managed manner. He added that he was counting on the two of them setting up a team that would manage and oversee that effort.

He then met with Marcus to discuss the transition to work on Mataia.

Marcus said that he was eager to make the move and would plan to work there each day. He needed to get his home there organized. He pointed out that he was taking mini vacations with Mylan and Marcus Jr. on almost all the upcoming weekends for the next several months. He had been outfitting his house on Mataia and had taken one mini vacation there with the two and they were now enthused about the move. The two had really enjoyed the beach that they had gone to and the hike in several of the valleys.

Bram reminded Marcus that there was a naming contest for all locations on Mataia and as well as for naming the stars visible from the planet's surface. He suggested getting the two into those contests as a way to enthuse them about their move. He also made the point that they could move into their new home and still attend classes in Dallas or on weekends do mini vacations on Earth.

Ripples in Time

Marcus smiled and said that the discussion had solved his concern about their safety at his current home at the Fold housing complex. He would be making the move as soon as possible.

Bram shared that he and Pat had started to live on Mataia and Folding to work in the Morning and that his FBI bodyguards were doing the same. He was hoping all of the inner circle would soon be doing something similar.

He pointed out that doing so had already surfaced several life activities that were not significant but that needed to be addressed as they transitioned.

Marcus asked for an example.

Bram said that setting up the materials and supply chain logistics was the area that had been exposed when they had to take up a supply of toilet paper and paper towels. That simple need had clarified the fact that there were no trees to supply the fiber to make paper. So, both those items needed a replacement or a long-term logistical plan.

Marcus laughed and said that they would certainly have to solve many such weighty and critical problems.

Bram's next meeting was with Mallica in person and Orlando on screen. They discussed getting Mallica focused on working with him on exploring both the positive and the negative Fold environment. He shared that she and Marcus would be central to that effort.

He asked Orlando if he were willing to establish a way to keep order on Mataia.

Orlando commented that he thought he would enjoy such a role.

Bram challenged him to do it in a way that would require no weapons and would fundamentally be based on the philosophy of treating others the way he wished to be treated. He challenged Orlando to make the way to keep order a friendly embrace.

Orlando laughed and asked if he should wear a Santa Clause outfit.

Bram shook his head and said that he wanted Orlando to be the Marine that he was and to see if he could set up a system that would make Zuri proud.

Orlando nodded and in a more serious tone said that he now understood how serious Bram was.

Orlando smiled and said he understood perfectly what Bram expected.

Bram suggested that he enroll Castor and Donna in that effort.

Bram realized that Mallica had tears in her eyes and asked what was up.

Mallica shook her head and commented that she had just thought through all the things that had transpired since hanging on out in the desert compound where they had all started. She was glad that Elizabeth had convinced her to stay on.

Bram nodded and thanked her for staying. He felt bad about that time but felt great about everything that she had contributed. He added that she was a big part of the success of the Fold effort and Orlando was a big part of having kept him alive. They were both more than just his good friends, they were now more like family.

His final discussion for the day was with Remi and Lori.

Remi commented that he was eager to make the move to Mataia and to get his lab functional there. He said he and Lori had reviewed the people in the lab and agreed that they had a group of very hard-working people who were eager to be a part of the continuing Fold effort. The research and analysis of the Mataian environment and any samples that would be gathered from somewhere in the universe would be something they would never be able to experience in any other work environment.

Lori added that she had met with each of their current staff members, and everyone had said they definitely wanted to stay with the Fold effort.

Bram asked the two to work with Pat and Amy to make sure that housing would be available, and that the logistics group be kept appraised of the number making the move.

He commented that the pace of transition was going to be limited by how quickly they could establish a place for everyone to live and to adjust the quantity of materials logistics to support Mataia and to obtain equipment to handle and store the materials.

He said that he would need to make sure that Erika had a handle on world building at a fast forward mode.

That evening he discussed the situation with Pat as they sat on their two person recliners.

Zoe and Eric were having a cup of tea in one set of easy chairs and Bob and Thomas in the other set. In the past only two of the four had been in the office at the same time lately the four had often sat in at one time.

Zoe commented that the four of them had discussed the mountain of effort that faced them all for the move and had decided that they should figure out how to jump in to help and in the short term do whatever was needed during the initial transition.

Bram thanked them and said that they should get with Erica, Amy and Pat and see where the help was needed. He said that he was sure they would be taken up on their offer to help.

Zoe commented that she was excited about the move, but she also wanted everyone to remember that the role of the four was first as the bodyguard for their loveable and zany mad Fold scientist.

Bram said that he hoped that in the near future, they would think of each other only as very good friends.

The next morning Bram asked Linda to see if Ray could join in on the meeting that he was planning to have with Olivia Newton in the afternoon.

Linda smiled and asked if Bram was going to make Lacy's new husband an offer he could not refuse.

Bram smiled and asked if Ray had any legal and organizational skills.

Linda replied that she had no clue how good he might be, but he had impressed her sister enough to marry him and that spoke highly about his character.

Bram said that Lacy's acceptance was good enough for him and yes, he would make him an offer that he hoped was a big enough net to pull him in.

Linda asked if it was OK to share with Lacy that Ray would be in the meeting with Olivia Newton.

Bram said it would be fine, but he did not know exactly what the offer was going to be.

Linda said that any offer would be acceptable, and that Ray had been worried about not being able to get on the Fold staff.

Linda then asked what he might have in mind for Rafael.

Bram asked Linda to give him several suggestions about where Rafael would be most interested in working. Then she could set up a meeting with him so that he could get to know him better. He commented that he had spent time with him before and after the wedding, but they had not discussed work.

Linda smiled and said the Evenders, and the Tailors would be the Stetson replacement on Mataia.

Bram thanked her and said that he wondered when fishing on Mataia would be as good as the Stetsons had shown them in Dallas.

He asked Linda to let him know when Olivia arrived and to make sure there were overnight accommodations ready as well.

Bram then went into his office after Zoe and Eric had declared it clear. He went straight to the bookshelf and opened the tiny door and took Isaac and Ada into his hand and carried them over to his desk.

He asked them whether he should move the boulder in the desert to Mataia and laughed when both of the mice nodded their heads up and down.

Zoe came over and asked whether they should make sure that their father, Einstein, also made the trip. She pointed to them as they bobbed their heads up and down.

Eric asked whether there was a desert-like area on Mataia.

They all looked at each other and said that they could not remember seeing a desert in any of the videos they had seen. Zoe said she would follow up and go searching for the right place to move the boulder.

Bram said that Marial had mentioned that one of the many unexplained artifacts was a large boulder located on one of the few desert islands on Mataia. There seemed to be no explanation of how it had gotten there nor why the island was the only place where mice were the dominant species. He suggested that Zoe look for that island.

Linda buzzed in and said that Olivia would be at his office in fifteen minutes, and she had Ray standing by.

Bram picked up Isaac and Ada and carried them back to the bookcase and closed it after the two went in.

Linda knocked and brought Olivia in.

Bram greeted her and made the point of recognizing Zoe and Eric as part of the meeting. He had Olivia sit next to him at the table and with Ray on the screen across from them.

After introducing Olivia, Bram stated that the objective of the meeting was to establish the leaders of the group that would write the constitution for a new world government.

Ron Mueller

Chapter 2: Mataia Constitution

His statement was met with silence. It was clear to him that he had surprised everyone in the room.

He looked at Olivia and then over to the screen at Ray and asked if there were any questions.

Olivia asked where he was planning to set up his government. Ray asked if it would be on Earth.

Bram said he was asking them to write the constitution for a world government, for the world of Mataia. It would be the planet that everyone associated with the Fold effort would move to.

Once again Bram was met with silence. He asked Linda to que up the Mataia video.

He then explained what the two were about to see was something that only his inner circle had seen before. They would see a world that had been named Mataia.

The tour of Mataia began and for the next hour they watched the presentation. Both Olivia and Ray would periodically comment on the splendor and the beauty that was shown. At the end, Bram said that they had taken a quick tour around a new world. It was a world located several light years away in a solar system similar to Earth's solar system. This new world would be home to those who were willing to leave Earth and live there.

Bram then turned on the tour of Einstein, City and declared that it was the first city on the planet and was already being used by about twenty of the Fold personnel, including himself. It needs many small items to make it a fully independent functioning city and it would take time to make that happen.

After the brief arial tour Bram stopped and suggested they all get a cup of tea, coffee or other refreshments and then continue the meeting.

While they were getting coffee Olivia asked if what she had just seen was real. She had been blown away when they had gone on the Fold Vacation in Greece but to be shown a full city on another planet seemed to be impossible. How had he achieved it in such a short period of time and how had the buildings been built in such short order? She said she saw no construction equipment or ongoing construction. She commented that it seems so polished and perfect that it was hard to believe.

Bram sat down at the table and nodded and said that he had his team of super people to thank. They had accomplished what she had seen in record breaking time. He went on to share that everything that she had seen was built on Earth and Folded into place on Mataia.

Ray mentioned that Lacy had told him that he would be blown away by what he was going to learn in the meeting.

He knew she had been dying for him to learn more about the Fold effort. She said that he would learn it from Bram or not at all. He asked what he personally had to do to be an integral part of the Fold effort and that he wanted to be as passionate as Lacy was about it.

Bram asked Olivia if she was ready to commit to the Fold effort.

Olivia nodded and said that she had some family-oriented questions before jumping in, but she did want to jump in. She wanted to make sure about the short- and long-term education of her children. She also wanted to know what her husband could do. Finally, she wanted to know how the transition would be handled. How would the family stay connected with friends and other family members?

Bram liked her questions. He made a point that he was working on Mataia during the morning and finishing the day at his office on Earth. Other than having to keep the Fold technology invisible it was in fact no different than commuting to work in the morning and going home in the afternoon.

He said that how one handled the day and how the transition would be handled would need to be tailored to each individual. She would only need to set up an isolated location where she and family could be picked up and then return via Fold. She and family could design the transition as it fit their needs. The only difficulty would be making sure everything was kept secret.

Olivia shook her head and commented that it was hard to grasp the flexibility that was available in going to and returning from a place several light years away. She had not envisioned the Fold capability to the extent that she was now getting exposure to.

She asked why Bram was isolating the Fold capability from the rest of the Earth's population.

Bram shook his head and asked her to think about the impact to the current social, economic, and military situations that she knew about. If she came to a different conclusion and had the means to manage making the Fold capability part of Earth's current situation, he would like to hear about it.

Olivia thought for a moment and said that she did not have a clue how that would be possible.

Bram said that he had come to that conclusion, but he had also asked those on his team the same question and they did not have an answer either.

He shared the fact that the Fold effort had suffered many physical attacks that included military action, rocket attacks from both the current time and had suffered attacks from the future as well.

He pointed out that Fold was a capability that had yet to be fully understood and it was a threat to a reality that everyone had come to believe was fixed but was in fact malleable.

Olivia asked how he was going to manage that from Mataia.

Bram replied that Fold was being disappeared on Earth and he was working on how to put barriers in place that would help contain how Fold got utilized on either planet. He admitted that he was not sure how it would all get done and whether he would be successful. He commented that he had no clue if the attempt to contain and control the Fold capability would be successful.

Olivia said she had one final question and that was how long the transition would take.

Bram replied that it would most likely be longer than any of them would live and that their children or grandchildren would be the ones that would live in a completely independent Mataia.

Olivia said she like the tenor of his answers. She said that she would definitely embrace the effort. She would do her best at creating a government that would last through future generations and would produce a society that focused on embracing and honoring each other.

Bram smiled and said that he looked forward to her leadership and in being part of setting up the Mataian government.

Zoe had expected that Bram would convince both Olivia and Ray to be part of the effort. She had previously had her friend in the FBI do extensive checks on both of them and had been please to find out that they had no blemishes other than some speeding tickets.

She had learned that both of Olivia's kids, though very good in school, were heavy party drinkers. She felt that this would be a risk to the Fold effort.

Ray was the one with the speeding tickets, with the most recent being in the last month.

She spoke up and asked if they could openly discuss a few issues that were personal and involved other family members.

Bram let Ray and Olivia know that he had asked Zoe to dig into both of their personal and family backgrounds. He followed up by saying that he wanted to make this a positive move and not a punitive one.

He suggested that they tackle Ray's issue first and then after that ask him to sign off. They would then address the issue associated with Olivia.

Ray put up his hands and said he was guilty. He shared that he received the official notice of his speeding ticket in the mail just that morning.

Bram nodded and said that he needed to pay off the previous two as well as the one that he had just received. He should figure out how to control his lead foot or risk losing his new job at writing the Mataian constitution and figure out how to live remotely from his wife.

Ray said he would take care of his problem immediately and become a casual driver.

Bram thanked him and said that Erica Wilson would be in touch with him to arrange his transition into the Fold program.

After Ray signed off, Bram looked at Olivia and said that her problem was family oriented, and it was about her two children.

He commented that he had acted just as they were now acting and that it was a growing up phase thing. He wanted to let her know about it so they could figure out how to change the actions that put them at risk.

Olivia had her hands on the table, and they were trembling. She asked if they were into drugs.

Bram said that they were not into drugs, but they and their friends were into drinking too much at the parties they were throwing. This was the issue that they had to address.

He asked where the two were thinking about majoring at in college and what career they were interested in.

Olivia said that she had asked them and had been disappointed that neither had expressed a passion for any particular field and they were more or less at a loss to what they wanted to do.

Bram commented that he had talked with them during the weekend Fold vacation, and it seemed they were very smart.

Olivia replied that both of them got very good grades and were in the top five percent of their class.

Bram asked if perhaps they could get them more seriously focused in an area that would be fruitful for the Fold effort.

Eric spoke up and said that Dennison had expressed his interest in the FBI or in law enforcement. He could be on the team that designed the support and aid force on Mataia.

Zoe said that she had spent time with Angela and had learned that she wanted to design clothes. She might be enticed by setting up a fashion design shop on Mataia that at first imported luxury brands from Earth.

Bram smiled and looked at Olivia and said that it seemed they had two volunteers to engage her children and give them a vision of the future that might help get them to stop their heavy drinking at parties.

Olivia said she would love the help but how would they connect them in a natural way?

Zoe suggested that they use the fact of her new job would require them to move to a new location as a way to get them to come out to Dallas for a visit. While they are visiting, they could stay in the new home that you would be living in. They could meet a couple of the older members kids in the Fold community who are getting ready to go to college. They could be touring the work projects that are underway.

And then Zoe laughed and said that they could go fishing with Bram and be in some really live action.

Olivia laughed and said that it sounded like a good plan, but she wanted them to wear Kevlar vests when they went fishing.

Bram said that he would plan several fishing trips before they went out to make sure his fishing trips had entered a peaceful time frame.

He then declared the day over and that they would all go home and enjoy whatever dinner Bob and Thomas had prepared.

As they walked out, Linda stopped Bram and told him that Lacy had called her up and said that she thanked him for figuring out how to get lead foot Ray to slow down. He had called her and had said that he had paid all his speeding tickets and had ordered a throttle limiter that would prevent him from going more than five miles over the speed limit.

Bram laughed and asked Linda to tell Lacy that he hoped that it would work.

Olivia said hello to Pat as they walked to the van waiting for them. She thanked Bram for inviting her to join them for dinner. She asked what was on the menu.

Bram smiled and said that unless Zoe and Eric knew then it would be a surprise to all of them. Bob and Thomas were doing the cooking, and they always picked a recipe that they wanted to try out and rounded out the main course with salad and some vegetables.

Olivia said that she thought that was a great way to end the day.

Bram agreed and said that all of them, himself included had developed a broad set of meals they liked to prepare. He admitted that he probably had the narrowest set of meals that he periodically prepared, and he mostly did breakfasts and lunches. His meals were weekend ones where he had enough time to cook.

Pat said that Bram had improved over time, but Zoe and Eric were the ones that seemed to come up with the most interesting menu's and that she was just ahead of Bram in meal recipe preparation but not by much.

Zoe said that it was an unfair comparison. She and Eric got the opportunity to search out and cook recipes every other day. They had also gotten recipe help from the Stetson catering group who sent over recipes they thought would be of interest. All she and Eric had to do was to cut down on the ingredient amounts because the recipes were generally for a large number of people. She laughed and said that properly reducing the spicing often led to hilarious results.

Bram agreed that what the two put on the table had to be treated with a good amount of respect. He remembered two times when the spices were overwhelming and one time that he had to ask for the soy sauce and hot pepper. But some of their good meals could rival those of Chef D'Carluca.

Their van drove into the basement. Bram said that he was going to stop a moment in the office and then come up for dinner.

Pat escorted Olivia up the stairs.

Zoe sensed that Bram planned to share something that was on his mind. She and Eric did a thorough sweep of the office. There were no listening or other devices.

They signaled for Bram to enter. His Marine guards waved and backed the van out of the basement.

Ripples in Time

Bram walked in and sat at the front edge of his desk. He asked how the four of them were taking the move to Mataia and if there was something that he could do to make the transition smooth for them.

Eric replied first and said that he and Zoe had discussed this in length with each other and they had also engaged with Bob and Thomas.

They all agreed that they wanted to take the transition slowly. They would continue to maintain their current protection cycle until they got notice that the assignment was ending. This would allow them to use their FBI contacts to vet people and to check out suspects until the very end.

Zoe added that after that time they would use their knowledge about the system and the help of Linh and Duong to tap into the various systems when they needed to get the information to vet someone.

Bram said that he agreed with waiting until they got the notice that the bodyguard assignment was over.

He said that he would like to be informed when the more clandestine effort was needed. He was sure that they could pull off such efforts, but he wanted to make sure that when such an effort was needed that all the resources would be aligned to the effort.

Zoe nodded and said that the four had discussed exactly the point that Bram had just made.

Bram thanked them and said that they should complement Bob and Thomas for their great support for the expanding work of the Fold program.

Zoe said that there were two complexities that had surfaced during their discussions on the transition to Mataia.

She said that both Bob's and Thomas's remote love affairs had reached a new level, and they were wondering how to handle them.

Bram asked what the barriers to making their romances work might be.

Zoe replied that both of them wanted to have weekends off so they could pursue their romances. They were wondering if they might be able to use two of the smaller Fold vehicles so they could spend weekends with their girlfriends.

Bram replied that they should contact Melisa and arrange for that to happen. They should also ask to stay in the facility where the Fold would deliver them.

He asked where the girl friends live and learned that one had a position as a Bank branch manager in Philadelphia and the other ran a small leather goods boutique in San Diego.

Bram asked if Zoe had vetted the two.

Zoe replied that both Bob and Thomas had asked her to do that early in their romances.

Bram said that he gave them a green light and wished them well. He then pointed to the door and said that it was time to see what was for dinner.

<u>Chapter 3: Erasure</u>

The next day in the office, Bram was explaining to Isaac and Ada that there were several critical things to do in parallel. He asked them whether he was going to figure out how to contain the Fold knowledge on Mataia and if the team would be able to learn how to manage that knowledge.

Both of them seemed to nod in the affirmative to each question.

Zoe smiled and commented that she was beginning to believe the mice really understood the questions that Bram asked them.

She gave the two a small crumb of cookie and asked them if she should focus on erasing the Fold knowledge from Earth and if she should erase the political knowledge first. She gave a small laugh when the two seemed to nod in agreement to each question.

Bram asked if the move to Mataia should be done slowly and be paced at the speed of the Fold knowledge erasure.

He received a supportive nod.

He then asked if the boulder in the desert should be Folded to Mataia and again got a positive nod.

His final question was if any other animals should get Folded to Mataia any time soon and got a negative shake from both of them.

Then he asked if their parents should be included in the Fold to Mataia and got a positive nod.

Bram looked over to Zoe and Eric and asked if they had any more questions to ask of their two extremely intelligent mice.

They both held out their hands like paws and shook their heads back and forth negatively.

Bram laughed and then returned Isaac and Ada to their bookshelf home and sat down at his desk.

He commented that he needed to spend the next several days figuring out how to set up the Fold fences to keep the knowledge contained. He needed the knowledge to become a secret that only the Fold team knew. He added that he had to hide the equation details and how the equations worked from everyone including the team. He shared that he would record the essential equation details in the stored record but not share it with any living person. He commented that Marcus, Mallica and Zuri were the only three that had a current in-depth understanding, but they did not have access to all the changes he had made.

He asked Zoe and Eric what they thought of the approach he was taking.

Ripples in Time

They both agreed with what he was considering. They shared that they had discussed the topic of how to contain the knowledge and agreed that somehow limiting who knew the details was the only approach they could think of.

Bram had shared this approach with Pat and had gotten similar feedback.

He had also shared it with Elizabeth to test and evaluate whether it was ethical for him to set himself up as the only person who controlled such knowledge.

She had responded that the only thing he would need to control was his own desire to change the future history of the Earth. She then added that her statement also applied to the past history of the Earth.

In their discussion she brought up the fact that Mataia and Swoosh should be included in the concern of meddling by anyone in current time.

He smiled and asked whether having empowered the Mataians one thousand years in the future qualified as meddling.

Elizbeth smiled and said that it did, and she was sure that he had not created a ripple in time but most likely had created a tsunami going out into the future.

Bram nodded in agreement and asked Elizabeth to lead a team in establishing the guiding principles of how the Fold knowledge should be handled. He said that he already knew the temptations and had already created several ripples in time by eliminating the people who had attacked the team on Mataia and the additional two people that he Folded into the laser protective screen. He was sure that he would create more ripples, but he wanted to be guided by what the team thought would keep such ripples small and contained in a manageable way.

Linda interrupted his thinking to let him know that the meeting in the Viewing room would begin in ten minutes.

He thanked her and turned his focus to the topic of setting up the Fold Erasure Strategy.

He, in discussion with, Erica had agreed on a two-step approach to developing the strategy. He, Mallica, Marcus, and her would work together to outline the strategy. Then they would hold another meeting with the entire team and finalize the strategy.

This was the first meeting of the four of them and he had asked Erica to lead the meeting.

Once they had their strategy agreed to, they would all participate in the creation of an action plan with the entire team. Each action in the plan would have a team leader, clear measurable objectives and the timing that was to be achieved for that objective.

Ripples in Time

He was the last to enter and he noted that a cup of coffee and a bottle of sparkling water was set at his table. He looked at the clock and noticed that he was a few minutes late. He took his seat.

Erica stood and stated that they were most likely attending the first of several meetings. They were to establish the move of the Fold knowledge and the people supporting the Fold program to Mataia. She stated that they should consider the strategy they came up with as a draft strategy open for additional input from the entire team. She shared that she hoped they could get their draft to be ninety percent complete, but they should be open to modifications and improvements.

She suggested that part of their effort should also be to develop a draft execution plan based on the strategy they came up with.

Zoe asked whether she and Eric could participate in this current meeting.

Erica nodded and said that Zoe was leading the effort to erase the Fold knowledge from all the computer systems in the world and certainly should have input.

Bram spoke up and said that the transition to Mataia was something new to all of them and doing it in a fashion that preserved the camaraderie that they had established was of great importance to him. He shared that they would most probably miss some items, but he was also sure that they would be small and manageable problems.

Erica led the team through three days of strategy development. She suggested a one-day break and said that they would then spend about the same amount of time developing the draft execution plan before assembling the entire team.

Bram commented that they were making great strides, and he would work with Linda to set up several days with the rest of the team. He suggested they include Linh and Duong in the development of the detailed execution plans because he was sure that the digital world would be on the critical execution path.

Zoe reinforced Bram's suggestion by sharing that the two were on three of the current execution teams and they had recruited an additional group of IT specialists to help them with all the systems and computer languages involved.

Bram reiterated that there would be three areas they should think about as they develop their execution plans.

One area was to erase the Fold knowledge from the Earth.

The second area was to establish the Mataian, government, society, and environment.

The third was the physical transition to Mataia that included erasing the current physical Fold community from Dallas and perhaps their work center as well.

Mallica added that the timing of each was going to be critical. Every move needed to be thought out carefully so that the disappearance of the Fold program and the disappearance of its physical existence went unnoticed.

Ripples in Time

Marcus commented that perhaps they should ask Thomas who was already getting into monitoring the future of the Earth to periodically check on the gradual disappearance of Fold as a way to ensure that mistakes were not propagating into the future.

Bram said he was not against it, but they should review how they would monitor that situation to make sure that the monitoring did not end up being intrusive and noticed.

The draft strategy work and the draft execution plan were completed in two weeks. This was much longer than they all thought it would take but they had spent the quality time required to make their initial work as good as they could.

Erica worked with Linda and had her set up the meeting with the entire team for the week after they had completed the draft work.

She suggested that they use the auditorium where they would be able to use the huddle rooms for small teamwork when they broke up into work groups.

Linda said she would set up the refreshments at the back of the stage and have lunch catered in.

Bram had created a rendering of what he thought the community grounds that were currently in use for the Fold program should appear to a visitor in the near future or in about ten years. His rendering had the orchard refreshed but the old barn gone.

The current housing area was shown as a maple and oak mixed forest with a green area that had a small lake on the downhill area where the current swimming pool was located and featured a soccer-baseball field combination about where his house was currently located.

Erica commented that it looked great but where was the old barn and where was the apartment building? She understood that they were already in the process of Folding the houses out, but she had not thought about the larger structures.

Bram suggested that the location of where to Fold the structures other than the houses needed to be evaluated. The Fold location could be to either planet. Where to locate them on that planet was also a question.

Erica nodded and said she was demonstrating why the strategy, and a detailed execution plan was going to be critical.

Bram nodded in agreement and added that determining when to tackle the physical environment was going to be critical. He added that the transition speed when they did tackle the change of the Fold property was going to be another key consideration. They had to do it in a way that did not cause widespread interest or make the news.

Ripples in Time

Zoe brought that erasing the rather widespread Fold knowledge was going to be the bottleneck of the execution plan. She shared that she had already run into difficulties dealing with the technical side of eliminating the information. She highlighted that Linh and Duong had learned that almost every major computer system had multiple backup programs that needed to be addressed and set up so they would load a backup copy that had Fold erased from it. These backups needed to all be erased at the same time so they would not put the erasure effort into a do loop.

She then highlighted that eliminating the knowledge of people would most likely be more difficult. It would be great if all of them could end up on Mataia, but she knew a few that she personally thought should not be part of that migration.

Bram said that taking her input into the evaluation of the time required to make the transition was going to be critical and perhaps it would be a timeline that would actually be more manageable.

He added that selecting the people with meaningful knowledge would be difficult and the team would need to develop ethical guidelines for not only evaluating and convincing them to make the move to Mataia but also in how to deal with those who had no interest in doing so.

Erica thanked Zoe for speaking up and agreed that on the one hand she had surfaced some key barriers, and she had also provided a sense that the timeline was going to be longer than anyone had expected.

Bram asked Mallica what was on her mind.

Mallica replied that she felt that no matter how successful Zoe was in the effort to erase Fold from the Earth someone was going to remember, and they would write an expose.

She suggested the team instead become good Fold photographers. They should call what Zoe was currently doing the Fold aperture. She was reducing the amount of light and dimming the picture. They should set up the picture shutter speed to provide the least amount of Fold light possible. And finally, they should ensure they had a very low Fold exposure sensitivity so that what was exposed would be of little value.

She said that the Fold exposure should share very disappointing information to satisfy the person or persons digging for the Fold information so they would end their searching.

She suggested that the team write the expose. Tell the story the way they would want it to be told and then plan on the exposure event sometime in the future.

Bram smiled and said that maybe he had left her out in the desert too long and the desert heat had affected her. She had caught his disease of looking into the future and figuring out how to manipulate it.

He thanked her for the reality that she had just exposed and asked if she was willing to be the leader of the team that wrote the expose.

Mallica replied that she needed a master spinner of storytelling fiction and asked whether he would agree to participate in the fabrication of a good fairy tale.

Bram chuckled and agreed that the whole Fold effort seemed like a fairy tale fabrication, but he pointed out that they had all experienced its awesome power. They had seen the miracle of seeing a wheelchair bound young lady be transformed into one that could dance the tango and cha-cha-cha.

He commented that once they were all on Mataia they should figure out how that awesome power could be put to use in the positive fashion they all desired.

Ron Mueller

Chapter 4: Eastern Breeze

The final strategies for each segment, of what turned out to be a very detailed transition strategy, took several weeks. Bram complemented the team on creating a great set of strategies but even more important he complemented them on having turned the strategies into very detailed and measurable action plans.

He pointed out that the critical path to the transition was the area of eliminating the Fold exposure and information from all systems on Earth, that Zoe was leading.

He thanked Pat and Amy for joining Zoe's team while they waited to start implementing the transformation of the plant and animal life on Mataia. The critical path layout clearly highlighted that the Mataia transformation effort was going to take the longest and its timing was affected by the need to evaluate the resulting impact of transplanting first the sea life and then with land plant and animal life transfers.

Each evaluation period would take several years to complete. This meant that it was the most flexible and of course the longest action plan.

Pat and Amy said that they were setting up their transplant team in a fashion that would allow each area to run almost by itself. They said being on Zoe's team would fill in their days in a meaningful way.

Bram then reviewed Mallica' and Gerry's detailed action plan that dealt with the current and the far future of the Swoshian society. He reviewed what they were doing during each time frame. They pointed out that they were learning from the Swoshians in current time and then they were making sure that the future had not lost any of the critical elements that made the Swoshians such a great race.

Bram asked what they expected to learn from the Swoshians in current time and was pleased to learn that the two were focused on how Mataia should handle the way that food, medicine, and education would be provided to the Mataian society at no cost.

Mallica pointed out that the Swoshians had no need for money.

Gerry shared the fact that medical care was often required but it was administered as a normal part of the society.

They both commented that what they really liked was that education was considered a lifelong pleasure that was a part of daily life.

They both suggested that the people that would be the first Mataians be required to learn about the key elements of the Swooshian culture. They added that Chef D'Carluca had asked to be a part of their team. He had said he was fascinated with how they handled their food distribution and wanted to make sure that Mataia applied their methods. He wanted to organize on land what the Swoshians did in the sea.

The continuing and substantial analytical needs during the transition to Mataia and also associated with any exploration turned out to be another area that became very clear. Remi had led the development of a very clear and detailed plan and had worked with Lori to estimate the number of additional technicians that would be needed.

Once he had made his contribution, he stepped off the analysis team and joined forces with Luke Stetson to develop the plans that would establish a new manufacturing organization that would begin their efforts on Mataia with the development and production of the Fold transport bubbles. He would lead the development side of the effort and Luke would be in charge of the logistics and manufacturing side.

Luke pointed out that the manufacturing side would focus on small volume manufacturing so it could easily and continuously add the items that should be manufactured locally versus being brought in from Earth.

He added that he anticipated that Mataia would for generations to come be importing many items from Earth. He added that multiple logistical Folding locations need to be established on Earth and kept secret. This they felt was going to be a major challenge.

They had suggested that the current Fold hangar and all the work areas should be Folded to Mataia. It would become the Development and Manufacturing center.

Bram suggested that they would need to begin small and use the current hangar on Mataia and then when it came time to Fold the current Dallas based hangar, they could position it at the location that made the most sense.

Einstein City Planning and expansion was another area to be a surprise for Bram. Pat and Amy were the key leaders but Matt had requested to be part of that effort and made the suggestion that they needed to embrace the far future and begin with that end in mind and should plan the cities of the future so they would be located in the geographically right places. He suggested that the City Planning team become the Mataian City Location and Planning team. Bram complimented Matt on his expansive vision and jokingly said that he was glad that he had kept him from being swept off the ferry during their Norwegian adventure. Bram suggested that they cheat on the locations, visit Marial, and learn where the cities were located and if they were all successful.

Ripples in Time

Erica had listened as Bram reviewed and complimented each of the teams. She then pointed at him and said that she was going to complain about the fact that he had used all of them to do the dirty work of giving input to hiding the greatest secret in the world. She asked if he had enough information to figure out how to hide the Fold secret and close the lid on the Fold Box.

Bram put his Strategy and the action plan that he had developed into action. His strategy was simple. Work alone in isolation and make Fold invisible but easily accessible. His action plan was to put the Fold information on a journey that only he would know about. When he was doing his work there would be no bodyguards present.

He thanked everyone for having contributed their ideas and said that he would use many of them, but they would never know how he had used their input.

Pat had listened to Bram as he went over the various ideas on how to make the Fold information inaccessible. She knew that something that Marcus had suggested had crystallized an idea for Bram. She had been very curious about what Marcus had suggested and reviewed the video of the brainstorming session to see if she could tell how Bram had reacted to Marcus's suggestion.

She could not tell by any facial expression, but she realized that Marcus had only made one suggestion about sending the Fold Box on a long-distance journey in both the negative Fold and the positive Fold RCID's.

From that input she knew that the Fold information would be traveling a multimillion-year journey as it made its way methodically node to node, skipping between the RCID's in both the positive and the negative Fold realms. She had no clue how that would be set up, but she was sure Bram would accomplish that goal.

Bram had been watching Pat and knew that she had most likely figured out the general concept that he would implement. He smiled as he thought about her ability to figure out some of the most complicated problems. She had used that capability to save him when he had foolishly and ignorantly gone into the negative Fold realm trying to figure out what it was. He decided that she would be the one person with whom he would review his final solution.

Lacy had left the stage and was up at the other end of the auditorium. It was clear to everyone on the stage that something strange was happening.

Bram asked everyone to continue wrapping up, but they should be ready to do what might be asked by Lacy for them to do.

The call had Lacy talking to herself. Her team had uncovered the fact that the North Koreans had a submarine on the way to the west coast and their intension was to eliminate the Dallas Fold site.

She remained at the other end of the stadium but waved to Bram indicating that the stage get cleared.

Bram knew that something very troublesome was occurring. He asked Linda to clear the auditorium and then get ready to do whatever Lacy told them to do.

He got off the stage and walked slowly toward Lacy. He watched her give some sort of command and telling whoever was at the other end to do it immediately.

He then knew she was talking to the General and telling him get the attack bubbles into position. She told the General that she had no idea where to send the attack bubbles, but they needed to intercept the sub out at sea and eliminate it.

He knew exactly what he had to do. He was going to break the rule that he had expressed concern about using the negative Fold arena to alter history.

He waited until Lacy was ready to share what the problem was. He listened as she explained that her network had picked up chatter that North Korea had somehow learned about the Fold effort and had its one missile launching sub on its way to eliminate the Dallas site.

He then told her to take the necessary actions in the current time, but he was going to Fold back in time and eliminate the threat. He asked her how much time he had.

Lacy replied that she had no clue but figured that he had less than an hour in real time.

He then asked where the sub was located when it was not at sea.

Lacey called into her team and in a few moments was able to give him the location.

Bram called Marcus, Remi and the General.

He asked Marcus to get the coordinates in the past for the submarine.

He asked Remi for a Fold vessel to be ready to be used under water and have an exit chamber on it.

He asked the General for a diver that would be able to place an explosive to a hull of a sub that was under water.

Marcus replied that he would have it in a few moments and would meet him at the Fold vessel.

Remi asked if a bubble attached to the outside of the lager Fold vessel to serve as an exit would be acceptable.

Bram said that what Remi was proposing would be acceptable.

The General called back and let him know that he had two Marine divers with the required skill on the way.

Bram thanked him and let Lacy know that he was on the way back in time to eliminate the threat, but she should continue doing what she needed to do in current time.

Lacy nodded and turned up her fist with the thumb up.

Bram waved his small army of protectors on and led the way to the hangar.

Pat joined him just outside of the auditorium and took his hand as they continued to walk. She commented that he seemed to have become the Fold marauder. She asked who was going with him.

The entire protection team shouted that they were going along.

Bram hoped that Remi had prepared the twelve-person Fold craft because he figured he had no time to argue with his protection team.

Remi had just finished showing the two Marine divers how to use the bubble attached to the twelve-person Fold vessel.

He looked up as Bram approached and asked if his protection team was going.

Bram nodded. He watched as Marcus exited the Fold vessel and the two Marines practiced going in and out.

Castor asked the two Marines if they were ready and got a "yes Sergeant Major." He turned to Bram and asked if he was ready to go.

Bram turned to Marcus and asked if he was ready to go.

Marcus nodded and said that he and Remi would be standing by and communicating with him in the past negative Fold realm and providing him any seek and find help that he might need. He said that he had found the moment that the sub was leaving port. He added that the Fold vessel that Bram was taking had six scout bubbles that could go underwater.

He would provide continuous coordinates and depth for the sub. Bram would need to select the location that made the most sense to incapacitate the sub.

Marcus asked if the crew would survive.

Bram thanked Marcus. He understood how hard it was for Marcus to think about the crew losing their lives.

His reply to his last question was that the leaders of the crew would get every opportunity to save themselves. They would have to choose to surface or die. He said that the sub would be sunk at sea, but the crew would have the opportunity to get off.

Marcus thanked Bram and said that he would sleep much better knowing that no matter what the outcome the decision was going to be made by those most affected.

Bram got into the Fold vessel and Folded to the time and coordinates that Marcus had provided. He took in the port below and then Folded under water out at sea. He reviewed the pictures he had taken and verified that the sub seemed to just be casting off.

He sent up a scout bubble that skipped in millisecond skips in time alongside of the sub at the water line. This made the bubble virtually invisible but allowed Bram to follow the sub. When the sub submerged, he set the bubbled down on the hull.

He then asked Marcus to locate the tracking bubble out in the middle of Pacific.

A few moments later Marcus replied with the coordinates for the sub in the Middle of the pacific.

Bram noted that it was roughly a day and a half into the future and made the Fold to where the sub was located.

He placed the Fold transport on top of the sub's forward deck and asked the two Marines to go out and place the explosives on the forward planes at the point the planes attached to the hull of the sub.

He then watched as the two worked together to first set up their safety lines and then move the two boxes of explosives into place. He knew he was watching two extremely talented divers as they handled the swift water flowing past them while carefully moving their explosives into position.

It took them only ten minutest to have their explosives in place.

They returned and got back into the bubble. They simply said, "It's all yours," and sat down.

Bram thanked them. He then activated his radio transmitter set on the subs interior communication frequency and announced that the sub was going to be sunk. The bombs had been set on the forward control planes and would be detonated in ten minutes.

The choice of whether the crew would live, or die was up to the captain of the ship.

He waited until he got a reply. It was in clear English which relieved him because he was not sure if his English to North Korean translation was accurate.

The person replying asked how Bram could possibly sink his sub when there were no vessels within radar range.

Bram replied that it was very possible since he was sitting on the Sub's front deck and had just placed the explosives on the forward planes.

Bram then said that the conversation was over and that he would wait until the sub surfaced to blow the planes off and sink the sub. This would give the Captain a chance to radio for rescue and save his crew.

There was a momentary silence. Then the Captain came back on and said that he was bringing the sub up.

Bram waited until the water was breaking over the bubble and then Folded to a high point in the sky.

He wished the Captain and crew well and told them that they had ten minutes to abandon the sub.

He watched as part of the subs crew was getting into large life rafts, but he noted that some divers had been sent over the side.

He sent two observation bubbles down two where the divers were and used them to hit them on the side of their heads and then knock their goggles off.

He watched the two shouting up to their Captain.

He decided to hit the Captain on the side of the head with one of the observation bubbles. He knew that it would be a significant blow.

Ripples in Time

The Captain looked around trying to figure out what had happened. He shook his head and shouted to the two divers who swam to one of the rafts that were now joining together.

When the Captain stepped off the sub, Bram triggered the explosives and watched as most of the forward section of the sub pulverized and fell into the sea.

He then watched as the rest of the sub seemed to follow in slow motion but within a minute it was gone.

Castor complimented the two Marine divers for having done a great job.

Bram added that they were invited for Sunday breakfast so that he could show the video of them in action and then the sub sinking.

He added that he was going to do several Folds over their current location so they could make sure the crew got rescued.

Donna began cheering when they watched a US Navy destroyer racing at top speed and zeroing in to rescue the subs crew.

Bram called back to Marcus and asked him to find the news reel that highlighted the rescue of the North Korean crew.

Marcus replied that Bram's action had a surprising impact on what was transpiring off the coast of Oregon.

He explained that the US Navy had intercepted an unknown submarine and was about to drop depth charges when the sub disappeared. He commented that the Navy said that they did not know where the sub had gone but it was no longer in US water and could not be located.

Bram asked Marcus to tell the General to tell his Admiral friend that the sub that had threatened the US coast was sunk out in the middle of the Pacific.

Zoe looked around at those in the Fold vehicle and commented that she would never get use to how time and the actions taken during each moment of time could be so easily manipulated. She said that it was enough to give her nightmares.

Bram added that it was the stuff of science fiction, magic, stardust mixed with the horrors that might be perpetrated by those without scruples.

Chapter 5: Erasure Failure

The General had a band to greet them on their return. He shared that their actions had adverted a major political confrontation between North Korea and the US. He went on to say that their timing had been unbelievably well-timed and then he added that they had presented the Navy brass with a mystery of how a sub declared by the North Koreans to have been lost at sea could possibly have been spotted off the coast of Oregon. He laughed and said his Admiral friend, Dennis in San Diego had called and asked what kind of shenanigans the Fold team was up to.

He complimented his two divers for job done well done.

He laughed when they replied that it was the only way they had figured out to get an invite to a breakfast at Bram's house.

He gave them a salute and suggested they ask for the Pat Nielson breakfast special.

Marcus spoke up and thanked Bram for having made sure the sailors on the sub got rescued. He added that he had followed the reporting about the US Navy rescue and had found out that the rescue had been blacked out in the subsequent time period. He wondered if actions that might cause too big of a ripple in time were self-limiting. He had feared a time tsunami, but the ripple was hard to find.

Bram replied that Marcus should quit identifying investigations that they would have to follow up on. He, however, put it on his list of things to look into. He was curious how big the Time ripples he had so far created happened to be.

Pat walked across the hangar with the two Marine divers and got their names and ranks. She had a reason for doing so. She was planning to put their names on their pancakes for their Sunday morning breakfast. She had talked with these Marines before.   She made it a point of being personal and friendly with all the people involved the Fold effort.

Lacy came running across the hangar and gave Bram a hug. She had tears in her eyes.

She said that she had her team out with their observation bubbles right at the sub when the lids to the sub's rocket launchers opened and a missile began to rise slowly out of one of the tubes. Then the sub and missile disappeared. Her observation bubble was left looking at a spot where, for one moment, it seemed the sub was going to succeed and then it was gone.

Ripples in Time

Bram hugged her back and said that she should bring her footage of what she had just described and share it at breakfast on Sunday. He said she would be showing everyone the second miracle that the Fold capability had delivered.

Lacy nodded and said that she gave the credit for those miracles to the person she could give a hug to and get reinspired to continue what she was doing.

Pat gave Lacy a hug and said that she agreed with her perspective, and it was his personal humility for his immense capability and brilliant mind that made her not only love him but made her use all her capability in supporting him.

Bram shook his head and said that it was Friday, and it was time to call it a day. He was looking for a quiet evening sitting with his favorite couch buddy and focusing his mind on the warmth she radiated. He took Pat's hand and led the way to the van that would take them home.

The shiver that had run down his back when Lacy had shared what had happened once again made him realize how close he had come to losing his soul mate. He wanted to make sure that such a close call would not happen again. He had to accelerate Zoe's erasure of the Fold knowledge from the current time frame. He also wanted to accelerate the move of the Fold effort to Mataia where he had much better defenses in place and where the Earth attackers could not attack him or the people around him.

General Tilton asked his marines to walk with him. He complimented them and said that they had made him proud. He asked Donna to describe what she had been able to observe from inside the Fold bubble.

She sensed the General wanted an evaluation of the two Marines and replied that she was impressed with the speed with which her two Marine brothers had executed the placement of the explosives.

Castor spoke up and added that not only were they fast but when Bram triggered the explosion the entire front end of the sub was vaporized, and the sub went down like a rock.

The General chuckled and shared the fact that his admiral friend had already called him to ask how the Fold program could possibly make a sub that was being intercepted by a US destroyer that approaching it at full speed simply disappear.

He thanked all of them for providing him with crowing rights over his admiral friend's Navy.

Linda and Marcus had been walking behind the Admiral and the four Marines around him and they had heard the entire exchange.

Marcus simply asked the Marine divers where they had been when they sunk the sub.

One of them answered they had been in the middle of the Pacific.

The General said it would be hard to tell his friend, the Admiral, that the sub had never made it across the ocean.

The General stopped and looked at Marcus and asked him how that was even possible.

Marcus smiled and said that he should make sure to be at the Sunday breakfast when his two Marine divers were going to be in the spotlight.

The General looked at Matt, his aid, and said that now he should understand why retirement was looking so attractive.

Marcus smiled and commented that he understood that the General was looking at being involved in setting up the Mataian self-help organization that would ensure that crowds remained in control. It didn't sound much like retirement to him.

The General nodded and said what frighten him most was that he would actually have to work again the way he had done as a young man.

Linda said goodnight and said she would see them all at the Sunday morning breakfast. She said that she was just as intrigued how it had all happened. She added that the Fold capability twisted her mind into a pretzel.

She had no idea how Bram and Marcus had pulled off saving all of their lives, but she was extremely happy that they had.

Zoe had waited until after Breakfast on Saturday to ask Bram how the North Korean's attempt to eliminate the Dallas, Fold site would affect her effort to eliminate the Fold information from all sources on the Earth. She was bothered by the fact that information about Fold had somehow reached one of the most radical regimes in the world.

Bram replied that he felt that her efforts were critical and that they would have to make sure that the Fold elimination virus that her team was putting in place needed to be able to get into all the various computer systems in the world. He asked if she would mind having him work with her team to review their current trojan horse virus and see if he could add any ideas of how to make it more potent.

Zoe smiled and replied that she couldn't wish for more than that. She added that Linh and Duong had recruited at least six additional IT personnel to help in searching for Fold information and in placing the Fold information erase virus, but the task was immense.

Bram agreed with her on the size of the task. He pointed out that once her team had done their first cycle of elimination, they would need to improve their search engine and repeatedly keep checking all the various networks. He commented that the information might hibernate in someone's personal computer or thumb drive and then resurface sometime in the future. He suggested she add an alarm feature that would alarm and notify her any time Fold information resurfaced.

Pat had listened to the discussion and thought it was time to put work behind them. She suggested that they all go to the recreation center to relax. They could all play some pool and ping-pong, and someone might even be able to play snooker with Bram.

Bram said he was up for it but wanted to finish putting his Sunday morning presentation together. He said that he had all the video footage taken during the trip, and he had received the footage that Lacy's observation bubbles had captured of the sub off the Oregon coast. He commented that it was a fascinating twist of distance and time. He chuckled and said that it would twist everyone's mind.

Pat nodded and said that she was going to prepare the pancake dough for Sunday's breakfast. She then added that the names of the two Marines were Gary Tatum and Art Baratta, and they were both Marine Corporals.

Bram thanked Pat for letting him know. He then said that he expected the General to promote both of them to Sergeant on Sunday.

Pat said that gave her an idea for their pancakes.

Bram knew that the two were going to get a unique surprise. He suggested including both Castor and Donna who were sure to get promoted as well and thought they would both get promoted to Master Sergeants.

Pat asked how Bram would be so sure of what the General would do.

Bram smiled and said that was the last thing that he had asked the General to do before leaving the work center to come home and he had gotten his agreement.

Pat looked over to Zoe and told her that it was her job to get Bram to the recreation center for lunch and walked out of the office and went up to the kitchen.

Bram saw that Zoe and Eric were both sitting down with a bottle of water and were engaged in a discussion. He focused on getting the video ready for the next day.

He was surprised when Zoe stood before him and asked if he was ready for a game of ping-pong.

Her timing was perfect he had just finished his video. He closed his laptop and stood up and told her to lead the way.

Mallica had been talking with Pat at the recreation center when she saw Bram walk in. She had been worried about the situation on Swoosh and had asked Pat for her advice about sharing it with Bram when he came to the rec center.

Pat had suggested that Mallica approach him with a beer and a brat and share what she was concerned about.

She took Pat's advice and met Bram with the beer, and brat.

Bram thanked her and sat down at one of the tables. He knew something was concerning Mallica enough to cause her to approach him in the way she had done.

Mallica waited until Bram took a sip of his beer before sharing her concern.

She then shared the fact that the shrimp-like creatures that was the main meal for the Swooshians were dying at an alarming rate. If they could not figure out how to reverse the trend the Swooshians faced starvation.

Bram took a long sip of his beer and remained silent for a moment as he thought about the problem.

He then smiled and said that she must have missed his exchange with Ohaan the fifth when they had visited Swoosh. He suggested that she go back to that exchange and realize that she had solved the problem.

Then he suggested that they send a care package of each type of shrimp on Earth and see how they flourished on Swoosh. Then they could select the ones that did well and that were palatable to the Swooshians. They could send a continuous stream of the selected shrimp to Swoosh until the Swooshians were able to grow their own supply.

Mallica smiled and thanked him for confirming but also broadening her initial idea. She had already decided on sending some shrimp for them to try growing. She liked the idea of sending a sample of each type of shrimp to see which ones did well. She would then let the Swooshians decide how many varieties they wanted.

She asked if that is what she had done to solve the Swooshian food problem.

Bram said that he was not going to answer and asked Mallica whether she was up for a game of pool.

She laughed and replied that one critical win was satisfactory and now she could face the loss at the pool table bravely.

She commented that she was now eager to review the interchange that had gone on during their visit to Swoosh because she realized that the Swooshians had survived at least one thousand years into the future.

Bram added that it was nice to know that you had succeeded even before you had done the work.

Mallica nodded and accepted that she had just lost another game of pool to Bram.

Chapter 6: Fold Erasure

Bram was prepared and anticipating another interesting and captivating Sunday morning breakfast.

He was going to orchestrate a time Fold story that was sure to twist everyone's minds. He knew that it had twisted his mind, and he was still thinking through how two separate events could be happening to a missile launching submarine at the same moment of time. It highlighted the complexities of playing with the flow of time.

He was now certain that fooling with time was fooling with everyone's lifeline, and he had no clue how that ripple in time would affect an individual.

At the same time, he was in the middle of the Pacific sinking the submarine, it was off the coast of Oregon ready to launch missiles to destroy the Dallas site. Lacy had her observation Fold bubbles and had the submarine in sight but was in shock because she was watching the missile leaving its tube and beginning to rise and then there was nothing.

He again wondered how that could be.

Pat had made special pancakes for all the Marines that had accompanied him on the Fold to sink the sub. She had made one pancake for each that had their name and their new Marine Corps rank. The Names were elegantly written in red Edwardian Script. She had made the pancakes and frozen them so they could be warmed to be added on the top of a pancake stack that would be served.

Zoe had worked with her and added the Marine corps insignia. The insignia was a twisted rope golden circle, then a black background that had the words in gold, United States at the top of the black circle and Marine Corps at the bottom of the circle. Four golden stars were on each side between the two. Then the Eagle, The Globe and the Anchor were set on the red center that had two thin gold lines enclosing it.

Bram commented on the amazing beauty of the Marine corps insignia. He said that he doubted the pancakes would be eaten. He was sure all of the Marines in question would ask for it to be frozen.

He took a picture of each Pancake and added the pictures to his presentations. He was sure that they would be a highlight to his presentation.

He joked with Zoe that she had earned four nose tweaks for doing such great artwork on the pancakes.

Zoe replied that she instead wanted him to help her tweak the noses of their adversaries and help her eradicate the Fold information from all the systems on Earth.

Bram replied that he would spend all the time she asked from him. She was leading one of the most critical tasks that would allow him to guide the Fold program to a continuing and successful effort.

Zoe was pulled back to her role of protecting him when the doorbell rang. Bob and Thomas were the two that answered the door, but Zoe and Eric were the ones that stood between Bram and the entrance area.

Bram as always, was amazed at the willingness with which his bodyguards always stepped in toward the potential threat.

He was delighted that once the door opened a steady stream of arrivals came in.

Bram noted that the newlyweds, Lacy, Ray, Linda, and Rafael all came in together.

He was impressed by the fact that the General, Castor, Donna, Gary, and Art were all wearing their formal parade uniforms as they came in. Each gave him a salute before sitting down at the table.

He was pleased that Melisa was one of the persons that was attending.

Pat purposely saved serving their Marine Corps guests until last. Then she announced that on this Sunday morning the Marines got special treatment.

She then led out, Amy, Zoe, Eric, Bob, and Thomas who each carried out a plate of pancakes. The special decorated pancake was on top, and she had worked with Marcus to have a camera bubble hovering at the top of the room so she could show the plates as they were placed in front of each of the Marine guests.

The Generals top pancake had a large Marine Corp symbol that covered most of it. Then each of the other Marines were served their plates and every one of them commented that there must be a mistake because it addressed them at the next rank up.

The General stood up and thanked Pat for having provided him the moment. He then turned and asked Donna and Castor to stand. He congratulated them on their very good work and their willingness to put their bodies at risk every day. He then gave them their new insignia and a metal. He saluted them and then asked Corporals Gary Tatum and Art Baratta to stand. He complemented them on the exemplary work they had done in sinking the missile launching sub and presented them with their Sergeants insignia and the same metal he had given to the other two.

He saluted them and said that they had made him proud. He then said it was time to enjoy breakfast.

When he sat down, he looked at his pancake and asked if he could save it.

Ripples in Time

Pat replied that yes, he could but as she showed each of the pancakes on the big screen, she said that the picture that was worth a thousand words had been taken but the picture worth ten times that would happen when it showed each of them eating those pancakes.

Donna and Castor uttered a loud "Hurrah" and poured their maple syrup over the pancakes and took their first bite.

Everyone at the table repeated, "Hurrah" and began to wolf down the pancakes.

Melisa said that she could get the insignia sewed on and that by noon they could have their pictures taken with their new ranks on their uniform. She made a couple of calls, and a few moments later there was a knock on the door. The "community seamstress," one of the wives of a Fold employee had come over to get the Marine jackets.

Once breakfast was over, Bram turned on the video. The lead in was a full version of the Marine Battle Hymn and then it faded into the background and the view of a missile launching submarine came on the screen. It left the harbor and then it slowly sank below the surface.

The view then switched to an underwater view of the sub that lasted for a few moments before the Fold craft appeared on the sub. It was in front of the subs conning tower. The flow of the water was emphasized by the stream passing across the front of the Fold vessel. The bubble attached to the side of the Fold vessel held the two fully dressed divers and the two boxes of explosives.

When the first diver exited, it became clear that he was fighting the flow of water as he hooked his safety line to the front of the bubble. The two divers pulled out the first box of explosives and carefully maneuvered it to the point where they were just in front of the port diving plane. One of the divers lowered himself and stood on the diving planes leading edge. He was leaning forward as he fought the flow of water. The second diver slowly lowered the box down to him. Once the box was in place, the diver flipped two wings out from the edges of the box, and they snapped onto the hull.

Bram stopped the video and asked "Sergeants Tatum and Baratta" if they had anything to add to what had been shown.

Gary Tatum commented that he had been the one to go down on the port fin and that "Sergeant Baratta" was the person to go down on the starboard fin. He then commented that their training had included simulating how to sink a sub, but the real thing was a lot tougher to do than the practice.

He admitted that when they got back to land, they had all sat around drinking beer talking about what everyone had seen on the screen. Now that he was seeing it for himself, he was ready to take part in drinking another round of beers to celebrate their survival.

Bram praised both of them and added that when he watched them from the safety of the Fold bubble, he felt lightheaded. He said that he could feel the water trying to rip each of them from the sub exterior.

He then turned on the video and watched the second box of explosives being place.

Then the scene changed to a picture of the same sub as the cover of one of the missile tubes slowly opened. Then the scene was of a US Navy destroyer plowing through the sea and a crew preparing to launch depth charges. It flashed back to a missile slowly rising.

Then the scene switched back to the sub with the bombs on the diving plane. They all listened as Bram explained to the submarine captain that his submarine was going to be sunk and that he had ten minutes to get his crew off the sub and into their survival rafts. The scene then took in the set of rafts as they moved away from the sub and suddenly the explosion roared, and the front of the sub disappeared. The remainder of the sub seemed to quietly back itself down into the ocean.

The screen then split, and two US Navy ships were shown. The background music softly played Anchors Aweigh. One ship was approaching the rafts holding the sub crew. The other ship was clearly in a search and destroy pattern looking for a submarine that had vanished. An underwater view of nothing closed the scene.

The music switched to the Marine Battle hymn. Bram commented that how both ships could have existed at the same time was a Fold mystery that he could not explain. He added that Lacy had captured the part of the video that took place off the Oregon coast and asked her to add a few words.

Lacy was shaking her head in disbelief. She said that the video clearly showed what she had seen but it could not convey the unbelievable fear that had gone through her when the missile tube opened, and a missile began to rise. She shared that she had awakened for three nights screaming, NO! NO! NO! and wept in Raymond's arms. She said that she had attended several sessions with Dr. Windal and was finally over most of that trauma.

Bram shook his head and apologized that by being the target of people trying to kill him, the entire community was at risk. He added that he was using all of his resources to reduce that risk.

He then said that erasing all the Fold information from Earth was the only way that he knew to address the risk. Zoe was leading that effort, and he was joining her to see how to accelerate the erasure.

Ripples in Time

General Tilson stood up and thanked Bram for having provided him a reason to retire from the Marine Corp and to make the transition to Mataia. He asked how he could help expedite the Fold information erasure.

Bram smiled and said that the General should delay his official retirement until the final Fold to Mataia was planned. He was welcome to be part of the Erasure team but his presence as the Marine Officer in charge of the Fold facilities was critical and he was needed in that role until the last moment.

The General nodded and said that he understood besides, he had to synchronize his retirement with his long time Admiral friend that would be going to Mataia with him. Meanwhile he would use the video to tease his friend on the fact that the Navy had provided much entertainment in their cluelessness.

Bram shook his head and said that he was not going to be involved in that exchange.

Pat stood and suggested that they end breakfast, take a break and they could all go to the recreation center in the afternoon and end the day relaxing and discussing what they had seen at breakfast.

Bram thanked everyone and said he was heading for his office.

Half the table emptied as he and his bodyguards left. Zoe and Eric led the way, and they all went down into the basement. Zoe and Eric checked the office and cleared it for Bram to enter.

Bram asked Zoe if she wanted to spend a little time to noodle how to proceed at a faster pace of erasure.

Zoe nodded her head and said that living their sub sinking experience again really made her want to work twenty-four seven until the erasure was done and she could move on to contributing new substance to the Fold effort in a positive concrete way.

Bram displayed his Excel spreadsheet on the large screen and typed in, "Rapid Earth Fold Resource Erasure Strategy Hammer, (REFRESH). There were seven columns with each of the words in one column.

He then said that they had to make a list of actions or ideas under each column.

He gave an example for rapid multiple people, parallel actions.

Then he did the same for every column. When he got to Hammer, he listed Zoe, Eric, Duong, and Linh.

He then made a bad joke about how refreshing getting the task of erasing would be.

Zoe laughed and said she was going to go back to tweaking his nose.

Bram smiled and replied that he was glad that his bad jokes were at least understood and that the point he was trying to make was that utilizing all their resources they could get the initial erasure task implemented in less than a month and the longer-term validation put in place to operate on an automatic routine that would last for a lifetime but would only take a few hours each year to maintain.

Zoe came over and gave Bram a hug and said that she could now go down to the recreation center and be able to relax and enjoy herself. She felt like a weigh had been lifted off her chest.

Bram said that she should never do what depressed her and to always look at how to make what you had to do as enjoyable as possible.

Zoe replied that she normally did just what he was suggesting but she had already been warned about tweaking his nose and erasing stuff from computer systems had turned out not to be fun. She went on to say that figuring out how to automate that work to the point that it would only take a few hours a year sounded like fun, and she had two folks on the team who could make it happen.

Bram suggested they take one run through the seven columns and then hustle down to the recreation center and enjoy the rest of the day as Pat had suggested.

Ron Mueller

74

Chapter 7: Past History

Bram played a couple of games of pool and one game of ping-pong. Then he overheard Lacy, Linda, Amy, and Pat talking about how they should approach studying past history.

The twenty-thousand-year boundary eliminated many of the topics that were of interest to all of them, but they had come to the realization that there was more than five million years of human history that would take their entire lives to study and share. They were talking about the twenty-five major segments that they had decided would guide their efforts. They were sure that they needed to make their team large enough to have all twenty-five segments investigated at the same time. Even after that split it was still clear to them that their work would take them a lifetime.

Bram asked about the specific time frame split.

Pat took out her phone and displayed a list of time frames that took them back five million years. She pointed out that was the time when the ancestors of humans were just making their appearance.

She added that they were following a part of a timeline that was published online that had highlighted events that occurred at various periods. Their small team had decided to focus on all twenty-five periods because it would provide a tremendous amount of information to the Mataian society. She then said that their team of three should grow to be at least two hundred and fifty individuals on twenty-five teams.

She then added that there were several other ways to look at the history of the Earth,

The formation periods where the oceans and the crust of the Earth developed.

The tectonic plate movements and watching mountains grow.

The weather cycle and pole position and pole shift.

Understanding of the creatures of the past and the associate evolution processes

She asked if he got the gist that her team could put triple the number of people she had mentioned to work for a lifetime.

She smiled and said that they also thought a supercomputer should be made available to them.

Bram gave out slow, low whistle. He said that he was impressed with their approach and was pleased that they were looking to populate the effort with a substantial number of people. That last fact alone made her request for a supercomputer reasonable. He suggested the team also determine where the team would work and that perhaps they needed a large work center of their own.

Pat thanked Bram and said she was going to talk to Erica about a supercomputer and that she and the team would think through about a separate Earth History Center. She then said that the team had recommended that initially they work from home and once every twenty-five days they would meet in the large meeting room in the Mataian Work Center and work together. She said that each team could also schedule work sessions on their own that would be based on their need to do so.

If they decided to populate more efforts the team might need to rethink how they managed all the people.

Bram said he like what they were doing and to have Erica clear the people that they selected to work with them. The people they selected should be brought on board to the move to Mataia and be willing to do so.

Amy spoke up and said that she had asked the question of Erica about the number of people moving to Mataia and she said that currently there were three thousand folks working at the Fold compound.

They had ten times that many people involved in some support capacity. Erica said that it would take about fifty thousand folks to have Einstein City functioning on its own.

Bram walked over to where Erica was sitting with Gerry and sat down. He lifted his glass of beer and complimented her on the good work she was doing to get Einstein City up and running. He asked her if they were financially well enough off to make the move.

Erica smiled and replied that he knew they were financially well off because he was the one funneling money into their bank accounts. She said that he was doing well and that the finances would not be an issue. She pointed out that finding enough people that met his criteria would be the challenge.

Bram asked if they should speed up the timeline in getting people to begin living on Mataia.

She suggested that all the current Fold personnel and their families begin spending fifty percent or more of their time on Mataia. She would work with the current facilities maintenance folks to do the same. This would ensure that everyone had time to adjust to a slightly different set of homes and facilities.

Bram lifted his beer and said that she should make it happen. He added that Pat, Amy, and their team would be asking her for a supercomputer, and he was in support of their request.

Gerry commented that he really enjoyed being on Mataia and that he had Folded a small sailboat to Mataia and had enjoyed the relative calm sea off the coast of Einstein City. When he did so he immediately realized that there should be a rule against any use of engines out on the Mataian seas. He had already written down a set of rules and he wondered how they would be enforced.

Bram smiled and said that his Admiral sponsor was planning to retire to Mataia. Gerry should get in contact with him and set up a rules of the sea team.

Gerry shook his head and asked how Bram knew about the Admiral's retirement location.

Bram smiled and said not to worry about the tight relationship that he had with his supporter. The information he had was via a certain General who was planning to retire to Mataia and was going to help set up the Mataian organization to maintain social calm and distribute help when needed.

Gerry nodded and gave a small laugh. He said that the Admiral had shared with him that he and the General planned to retire to the same location. He, however, had not told him about the location. He asked how a Marine Corps General had gotten the role of setting up an organization with the goal of maintaining social calm and distributing help.

Bram replied that he had asked him to do it.

Gerry again shook his head and asked why Bram thought that a Marine General would be able to set up an organization that would establish such a warm social order.

Bram smiled and replied because he demonstrated that he could be lifelong friends with a Navy Admiral.

Gerry laughed and said that it was a logic he had not thought about, but he was sure Bram had somehow connected everything together and that it would work.

Bram asked if having a visual tour of the last five million years of human history would be of interest for a Sunday morning breakfast.

This time both Gerry and Erica asked how he had gone from talking about the retirement of an Admiral and a General to a tour of human history.

Bram thought for a moment and then replied that he had an earlier discussion with the General about announcing his retirement at the next breakfast. He then talked with Amy and Pat about their plans for their study of Earth' past. Then as he was talking to the two of them the idea of sharing retirement announcements and updating folks on what the history team was doing merged.

He then asked if they should invite the Admiral to come up and announce the location where he planned to live after retirement.

Gerry replied that he would love to invite the General for the Sunday breakfast. Gerry asked why breakfast had become the meal when Bram made all his spectacular announcements.

Bram smiled and said that breakfast allowed it to be a simple meal that had some great food, and it did not need catering.

He thanked them for letting him talk business with them.

He headed to where Marcus, Remi and Marcus's kids were sitting.

He got hugs from both of the kids and then asked what they had been doing all week. He listened as they talked about their time in school and the fact that they were both on a basketball team at the school.

Ripples in Time

Pat had been sipping on her ginger ale watching Bram making his rounds. It was clear to her that he was following some thread in his mind, and she would later listen to him as they sat together, and he shared what he was thinking.

Zuri's comment about Bram's nonlinear mind came to her and she smiled. Nonlinear, inventive, and always with people's wellbeing at the forefront.

She wondered what he was thinking as he talked with Marcus' kids.

She knew that since their trip one thousand years into the future and meeting Marial their distant granddaughter he had become much more interested in speeding up the move to Mataia.

Bram noticed Pat watching him and smiled. He decided that his information fishing trip should end, and he would see if she would play a game of ping pong with him.

Linda was sitting with Rafael at a table next to where Pat was sitting. She commented to Rafael that she had just watched Bram load up on ideas that would lead to additional work for her and for everyone on the team.

Rafael replied that Bram had demonstrated to him that he was capable of almost anything, but he was sure giving Linda more work was not his direct intent. She was just caught in his friendly fire and not involved in what he now knew about Bram's deadly fire with both bullets and Fold executions.

Linda nodded and said that he had made sure she got out of the way on the last interaction with the antagonist in the future. Bram had never mentioned what had happened to that antagonist but had asked her to get him put on Dr. Windal's schedule. She wished she could get a look into Dr. Windal's mind. She had to know more about each of the team issues and problems than anyone.

Bram stopped at Linda's table and asked her to contact Elizabeth and set up a meeting to discuss the School on Mataia.

Linda smiled and said that she would be pleased to do so and to schedule all the other work he had just now been rounding up.

Bram lifted his now empty mug and replied that he was sure she would be the one organizing everything. He lifted his empty mug and said he would fill the mug, and he was sure she would fill his schedule.

He then wished both of them a good afternoon and went to sit with Pat, Amy, and Jose.

Amy asked whether he had been flying his helicopter close to the ground so he could see all the plants and animals.

Bram smiled and said that he was not that talented and instead was more like a bumble bee that bounced from flower to flower hoping to find an open bloom with some nectar in it.

Pat asked to see all the pollen pellets clinging to his hind legs. She said that she doubted they would be pellets but would be more likely to be pollen baskets or giant corbiculae.

Bram replied that he was just being social. He had not gone out intentionally seeking anything in particular, but he always listened to the ideas people had.

He then asked if he could get a brief overview of each to the twenty-five time periods that they had defined.

Pat gave a little moan and said that would cost him a glass of Moscato and then she would share what she had.

Amy asked if he would bring back two glasses so she could join in.

Bram asked Jose what he would like.

Jose stood up and said that he would go to the bar with him.

On the way Jose asked how soon he should be planning to have bubble production established on Mataia.

Bram did not hesitate to say that he could start immediately to move production of whatever he could to Mataia and to continue to add to the things that got produced on Mataia. The only thing that should be kept in mind was that there should be no short cuts that would pollute Mataia. The practice would be to continue to import all goods that they could not be produce cleanly.

Jose smiled and replied that he sounded a lot like Amy and Pat on making sure he didn't bring pollution along with the manufacturing effort. He said that it would be a challenge that he was going to make sure he accomplished.

Bram said he should hear it from every person that would live on Mataia.

Pat and Amy thanked Bram for the wine. Pat asked if she and Amy were next in his gathering of pollen.

Bram smiled and took a sip of his wine. He nodded and asked if they would share how they were approaching the study of the history of Earth.

Amy replied that the team that they were leading had decided that their current interest was on the history of humankind and that other teams should be formed for the other periods and other topics. They had chosen to focus on the last five million years and had up to this point chosen to accept the splits of time that they had found that was currently in use.

She said that she was going to share the information that they had gleaned from the online information and later they would develop a more detailed investigative plan to work from.

The **first period** was 5.5 to 4.5 million of years in the past. It was when the very first erect beings were believed to have been living. In this time period Mammoths, polar bears and brown bears were present. We figure that these animals indicate that many other smaller animals were also present but that will be left for some other team to study.

The **second period** is from 4.5 to 3.5 million of years in the past. It is the time of Australopithecus a bipedal great ape. It is known that zebras were present so again there had to be a variety of other animals.

The **third period** is from 3.5 to 2.8 million of years ago. Our distant relatives had developed stone tools. It was also the time that those that were to be called human lost their fur. Cats, condors, raccoons, armadillos, opossums, the giant sloth, and hummingbirds are known to have been in existence and moving around in North America. This is the time when Lucy existed in what is now Ethiopia. She has been credited to be the mother of everyone else. We don't believe this a true fact but finding her energized an entire generation of anthropologists.

The **fourth period** is from 2.8 to 2.2 million of years ago. Megalodon becomes extinct. More tools were found in Africa, China, and India. It is the start of an ice age.

The **fifth period** is from 2.2 to 1.8 million of years ago. It is when homo erectus is said to first appear.

The **sixth period** is from 1.8 to 1.4 million of years ago. One of the first up right beings, Australopithecine goes extinct. Homo erectus begins to migrate out of Africa and is found in Europe and a true hand ax exists.

The **seventh period** is from 1.4 to 1.1 million of years ago. One line of early humans dies out and another evolves. We figure this time period had as much activity as most of them but there has been less evidence found for this time period. We plan to be through in looking at this time period and bring our knowledge of the time up to the same level as all the other time periods.

The **eighth period** is from1.1 million to 900 thousand of years ago. Humans cross the seas to Indonesia. Cooking fires are thought to have existed. Human stone tools and footprints are found in England.

The **ninth period** is from 900 to 700 thousand of years ago. Early humans are found in northern China. There is evidence of use the of fire. Branches of the human species are found in the Philippines, Indonesia, Sub Sahara Africa.

The **tenth period** 700 to 550 thousand of years ago. Homo Antecessor and Heidelbergensis are in existence. Indication that cannibalism was occurring.

The **eleventh period** 550 to 450 thousand of years ago. Spear stone points found in Africa. Etchings on a seashell in Java. The oldest known spear is found in England. Homo Heidelbergensis exists across Germany, France, and Greece.

The **twelfth period** 450 to 350 thousand of years ago. It is the early first appearance of the Neanderthal. First believed homicide case is found. Hominin footprints in Spain.

The **thirteenth period** 350 to 280 thousand of years ago. Middle stone age tools and long distant trading is documented. Evidence of fire used to pretreat stone for making blades.

The **fourteenth period** 280 to 220 thousand of years ago. Woman bearing traits between Homo Erectus, and Homo Sapiens is found in Korea. Evidence of deliberate entombing of the dead is found. Stone tools are found in Mexico.

The **fifteenth period** 220 to 180 thousand of years ago. Homo Sapiens in Greece and Palestine.

The **sixteenth period** 180 to 140 thousand of years ago. Neanderthals build circular piles of stalagmites. They wear clothes by this time. Sea fish and other marine food enters the diet. Mitochondrial Eve from whom all living humans are said to descent. Amy pointed out that this was of particular interest for them to investigate.

The **seventeen period** 140 to 110 thousand of years ago. Crete artifacts indicate that seafaring had begun. Evidence of humans in Victoria, Australia. Spear point made from whale tooth is documented. Numerous indications of improvement to tools and the higher use of symbols and paint to decorate items and walls.

<h1 style="text-align:center">Ripples in Time</h1>

The **eighteenth period** 110 to 90 thousand of years ago. Homo Erectus goes out of existence. Shells with holes found indicating that they were used to make jewelry. Evidence of Paint being made in a cave on the Southern Cape coastline.

The **nineteenth period** 90 to 70 thousand of years ago. Homo Sapiens in Arabia. Shell beads are found in Morocco. Evidence of use of insecticide and glue in Sibudu cave in South Africa. Arrowhead like projectile points possibly poisoned arrows discovered.

The **twentieth period** 70 to 55 thousand of years ago. Start of one-thousand-year ice age most likely due to super volcano eruption. Evidence of aboriginal Australian culture and humans at Australian Northern territory. The Cave art in Spain is discovered. Neanderthals build circular post structure near Poitiers France and also reenter Britain.

The **twenty first period** 55 to 45 thousand of years ago. Denisovans use sewing needle and thread. Remains of string found in France. Depiction of warty pigs in cave drawing.

The **twenty-second period** 45 to 35 thousand of years ago. Homo Sapiens in Bulgaria. First painted story. Needles and sewing documented. Tools made from animal bones, hematite, and other stones. It appears that shoes are being worn as indicated by foot bones. Tuna is being eaten which indicates deep sea fishing. Dyed Flax fibers found in Georgia eastern Europe. Neanderthal disappears.

The **twenty third period** 35 to 28 thousand years ago. Ostrich egg beads being traded over a long distance. Surgical Amputation in Borneo. Humanoids are in Ireland. Oats are ground into floor. Evidence of human presence in Japan. Stone mortar and pestle used to grind fern and cattail. Aboriginal Australians make first settlements at Sydney, Perth and Melbourne and they apparently do first cremations. Rock paintings in India. First known ceramic documented. First ovens found.

The **twenty fourth** period 28 to 22 thousand years ago. Twisted rope, harpoons, boomerang, and saws are being used. Woven cloth makes an appearance. Ivory sculpture indicates art continues to be made. Natural fiber used to make baby carriers, clothes, bags, baskets, and nets. Carving of a face found. Huts are being built of rocks and Mammoth bones. First apparent permanent settlement. Cave Bear thought to be extinct. Humans living in Alaska, and Yukon.

The **twenty fifth period** 22 to 18 thousand years ago. Early humans known to live in Canberra, Australia. Tally stick indicates understanding of how to use the primary number sequence. Human footprints at White Sand Natural Park in New Mexico. Stone tools use evidence at Toca da Tira Peia, Brazil. The making of traditional Inuit clothing. The remains of mud huts at Ohalo, by the Sea of Galilee. Artifacts found on Cactus Hill at Virginia, USA.

Pat asked if everyone was still awake and said that there would be a quiz on what they had just been taught.

She went on to say that Bram should not worry about employing all the personnel at the site. He had just listened to Amy share a brief focus on the human history. Their team had commented that the heavens, the solar system, Earth's land mass, the creatures in the ocean, land, and skies all needed to be studied and documented.

She suggested that what Bram needed was a team to identify and launch teams to do all the learning and studying.

Bram nodded and said he would take her up on the suggestion. He then said the important question was should he get another glass of wine or some other drink.

Chapter 8: Future History

Bram looked across the rec center and spotted Bob and Thomas sitting with Zoe and Eric. He figured he might as well finish his round of querying folks about what they were up to. He was interested in how Bob was approaching the effort of studying Future history. He had high interest in learning how seeing things in the future compared to looking at history in the past. His highest interest was how his actions would play out in the near future and how he could learn to change, modify, or improve how he made decisions on the work he was doing or contemplating. He wondered how choosing one priority over another would affect the near future.

Marcus had been making progress in identifying the various nodes on the rhombicosidodecahedron (RCID). He had made the discovery that the RCID expanded to match initial distance the Fold vessel was sent out but luckily the first early nodes on the RCID remained the same and they learned that the new nodes once defined by their color spectrum remained the same.

The two of them had come to the conclusion that the RCID that was generated from their current Earth launch point was actually one entity that achieved its size by the distance chosen at the very beginning.

They had discussed the strategy of space exploration by setting the initial distance to the maximum and then jumping to a desired location by choosing the node that was closest to the point of interest and then going to the next desired Fold using the specific color spectrum of that node. They speculated that they could send out numerous exploratory Fold bubbles and explore a huge portion of the Universe. They agreed that for Earth they would stick with the Milky Way Galaxy. However, they speculated that to find other intelligent beings they would need to send several search bubbles out on a RCID that encompassed more of the universe and encompassed Galaxies that were many light years away.

Then when they got to Mataia they would need to set up a new interface between the positive and the negative Fold realms and establish the RCID that had its focal point near Mataia. This meant they would have another view of the Universe and would most likely be looking at a totally different set of Galaxies. They both believed that having two RCID focal points doubled their chances of finding other intelligent beings.

Bram was also interested in guiding Bob in his forward look to see how the action that he and Marcus took affected the future.

Ripples in Time

By having visited the future he had learned that with none of the initial actions he was planning but not yet taken had not provided the forward flow Fold of benefits to the future. He had been very successful in locking the knowledge up but the condition out one thousand years was not as advanced as he hoped it would be.

The other concern he had was that a change during his lifetime would have a negative impact on Marial's time in the Mataian year 1000.

One of the tasks he would ask Bob to perform was to check the future after every action that he took in the present.

Once he understood the ripples in time he was creating, he desired to control them so remained a reasonable size that the future could comfortably surf.

He was pulled back to the present when Zoe asked if he was going to join their world or was, he going to stay in his mind and ignore them?

Bram shook his head and apologized and explained that he had envision how Bob and Thomas were going to contribute to the transition of the negative and positive Fold interface being moved to a Mataian focal point.

Bob took a sip of his beer and asked Thomas if he had any clue what Bram was talking about.

Thomas shook his head and said he must have been asleep when Bram explained that concept.

Bram asked what they knew about studying the future.

Both of them said that they had been Folding bubbles to the future and slowly learning to control how to get to the time they were interested in. They both complemented Marcus on being willing to help them set the controls so that they got their viewing bubbles close to the time they were targeting. They had learned how to time skip their observation bubbles to avoid being discovered.

Bram said that it was time to accelerate their learning.

Bob asked whether both he and Thomas would be able to close on their long-term, long-distance love affairs before they devoted their hearts to their future Fold History studies and learned how to navigate that from their new Mataian home world.

Bram smiled and lifted the glass of beer that Zoe had brought him and said that he was glad to hear that they were getting serious about their life and asked when he would be getting an invitation.

Zoe spoke up and said that both Bob and Thomas wanted a Rushing River wedding, and they wanted to ask the most famous river preacher to reside.

Bram laughed and said that as long as he did not have to stand in the river, he would be honored to perform the wedding. He asked when he should be planning to perform the weddings.

Bob said that he was going to propose on the coming weekend and had already scheduled his Fold to his hometown of Philadelphia.

Ripples in Time

Thomas said that he was doing the same thing at the same time, and he was proposing to the girl next door. However, his next door lived a good two miles away and they had gone to a one room schoolhouse that was located almost exactly halfway between their two farms and later they had ridden the same school bus to a consolidate junior high and high school that was about five miles away.

He shared the fact than neither his parents nor hers had been financially in a position to handle the cost of college, so they had both attended a small community college and each of them went to separate Universities. He had worked his way through the University of Iowa, and she had done the same at the University of Illinois.

They had continued to reunite at Thanksgiving and Christmas, but they had also dated other people.

They had reconnected when they graduated. Thomas said that he had been hired by the FBI and she had gone to work as a finance manager with a large manufacturing company. He said that he had refreshed that connection by using the Fold weekend vacations to do so.

Bob asked if Bram had found where to press Thomas's talk button and that he had never been around him when he talked so much.

Bram asked Bob how he had reached the marital stage point.

Bob said that he had met his future wife at the agency. She was an office manager that managed a team of secretaries or that were now called support personnel. Like Thomas he had used the Fold weekend vacations to develop closer ties.

Bram smiled and said that it seemed that the two of them had changed roles for the afternoon, but he was very pleased that the weekend Fold vacations had made it possible for them to reach the "I do" decision point.

He asked them to make sure all their intended guest got FBI clearances.

He asked Thomas whether his wife to be family might be interested in farming on Mataia. He then suggested that if so both his father and his wife's father should be linked to Amy and Pat who were in charge of the Mataian transformation.

He suggested that they call and arrange a good time for the wedding with Mike and Marry at the Rushing River.

Zoe said that she would be glad to handle those arrangement when she and Eric went fishing on the following weekend.

Bram said that he planned to engage a couple of other folks and then he would signal them when it was time to head for the house.

He put down his full beer glass and told Zoe that she should have given him the same iced tea with lemon that she was drinking.

She smiled and said that she was just trying to put a new curve into his non-linear mind.

He smiled and said that she would need to be better at figuring out how to affect his spiraling nonlinear mind.

He then headed to where Remi was sitting.

He engaged him and asked if he was having a secret affair that he wanted to share.

Remi laughed and asked how many beers Bram had consumed.

Bram replied that it had nothing to do with beer, but he had recently learned that Linda had arranged a date for him. He had also heard that Melisa had done the same and that Jina had done something similar.

He commented that indeed Remi seemed to have become the center of their attention. Remi said that he appreciated them introducing him to some very nice women. He had enjoyed the outings. He smiled and said that he had found the person of interest on the other side of the fence in the apple orchard. He had watcher her picking apples and had used an observation bubble to get a closer view. Then he had a gate installed in the fence and went out and asked her if she would pick an apple for him. He said that her smile and the apple she gave him had convinced him that he wanted to know her better.

He had asked Zoe to check her out to ensure she had a clear background before he got more involved and was pleased that she could get a secret clearance.

Bram congratulated Remi in finding his apple in the apple orchard.

He then asked Remi his thoughts of how they could leverage Future history to make sure that the Fold effort would continue to make improvements on the human condition.

Remi thought for a minute and responded that there would be two views of future history. The Mataian centered rhombicosidodecahedron would view the universe from a different perspective than the rhombicosidodecahedron that was Earth centered. They would be able to see the past and the future from two different perspective. He suggested that once they began to understand those two different perspectives they might desire to establish another rhombicosidodecahedron that was Swoshian centered. He wondered what they would learn from the past and the Future of Mataia and Swoosh. What they would learn from the Earth centered rhombicosidodecahedron was already presenting the Fold organization with a challenge that would absorb most of the current available resources.

He then added that on Mataia they could use forward history to evaluate decisions made in current time and might allow making changes in current time to adjust what was happening in the near future. He commented that he had no idea how being able to quickly evaluate the choices made in current time and then adjusting them by what was learned would turn out.

Bram commented that for a simple lab scientist Remi had developed into a Fold whisperer. He asked if he wanted to be a Fold change guide and advisor.

Ripples in Time

Remi replied that the changes that Bram was planning to make to protect the people around him looked to him like an experiment. He went on to say that every experiment he conducted began with defining how the experiment would be verified and the technique of verification. The verification for both experiment success and its failure always resulted in new learning. The new learning often led to additional improvements or modifications.

He commented that doing it at Bram speed would be challenging but it would also be invigorating. He had engaged Marcus and Mallica to improve his understanding of the Fold theory. He hoped that he could be the lead in verifying the actions that Bram took managing Fold.

Bram asked what resources Remi would need to do what he had so eloquently described.

Remi replied that he would love to have a small group of evaluators and suggested Marcus, Mallica, Pat, and Amy. He said that having one senior IT and four Lab technicians to support the actual gathering and evaluation of future data would make things run smoothly.

Having someone other than himself looking forward evaluating his actions solved one of his concerns. Having someone like Remi doing it reassured him that changes would be thoroughly evaluated. Having the evaluation pass through a team consisting of Marcus, Mallica, Pat and Amy reassured him that true open thinkers were using their judgement.

He thought of Elizabeth and decided to add her name to the list. He valued her viewpoint on social matters.

He asked Remi about having Elizabeth join the change evaluation team.

Remi replied that he would love to have her on the team.

Bram asked that Remi get the Evaluation team launched immediately.

He shared that the Fold information was being erased from the records on Earth and would be transferred to three super computers on Mataia. At the moment only one supercomputer was available, but Erica was working on getting the other two installed.

He suggested that Remi work with Pat and Amy to arrange the work area where the Fold Evaluation Team would meet and do their work. He should immediately establish the team and get organize because they were a month late already.

Remi laughed and commented that he was going to ask Pat for a ditty on how fast her partner moved and the fact that there was a trail of supporters that could not catch up. He then thanked Bram for giving him an opportunity that he was sure would keep him engaged and growing for the rest of his life.

Bram smiled and said that he thought the ditty would be available a few moments after he asked Pat. He commented that what Remi was calling a growth opportunity was critically important to him and would most likely remain critically important for the foreseeable future.

Chapter 9: Sealed

Pat's warmth seemed to flow into him as the two of them sat on their two-person recliner. He was thinking about how to contain the Flow information and ensure that it was used for good. He thought about Zoe's comment that he had opened up something much worse than Pandora's box. He thought about the Greek mythology that told of how Zeus had punished Prometheus for stealing fire from the heavens and giving it to the common people of Earth. The punishment was that the wife to Prometheus's brother Epimetheus, overcome with curiosity, opened a jar left to her husband. When she opened the jar she released the curses of sickness, death, and many other evils into the world. That incident became known as, Pandora opening the box of good and evil.

A shiver ran down his back when he recalled Zoe commenting that the Fold container held a much worse set of curses. Those were not exactly her words, but he was feeling the dramatic impact, both positive and negative that it had so far released.

He thought about the two marriages that he had made and the two-Fold wives he had embraced.

When the veil of his positive Fold wife was lifted, he was greeted with warm radiance and beauty and knew that he had a lifetime of warmth and comfort ahead.

When the vail of the negative Fold wife was lifted he knew that he had a tumultuous life ahead. It would not be boring. It would be challenging. It would require his constant attention.

He shook his head as he envisioned the Ying and Yang of two very different powers that he had unleashed.

Then it struct him that he had a polygamous mind that had many more mental wives than just two.

His thoughts were interrupted, and Zoe surprised him by asking if he was thinking about the Fold Box and how to get all the Fold curses back in it.

He wondered what made her ask.

Zoe commented that she had been talking with Thomas and Remi and had put two and two together.

He complemented her on her keen sleuthing and replied that she had hit the nail on the head.

Zoe said that she had been thinking about it as well and had concluded that erasing the information on Earth was a huge accomplishment that seemed to accomplish much of what he was concerned about. His management of that capability on Mataia was now the challenge and agreeing to set up Remi's Fold Evaluation team was a monumental step forward.

She said that she wanted to rephrase her comment about the Fold Box. Fold should not be in the box, and they should not be gods. Self-determination within the net of "treat others as you wish to be treated" should be nourished by the actions taken using the Fold methodology.

Pat had quietly listened to the exchange. Once there was a break, she spoke up and suggested that Zoe should consider taking her place on Remi's team. She and Amy were duplicates in how they currently thought about Fold whereas Zoe would add a truly different perspective. She pointed out that she and Amy talked every day so she would be able know if there was something that she wanted to be involved in.

Zoe thought for a moment and then thanked Pat and asked Bram if he agreed to the two of them changing seats.

Bram said that he supported the move. He smiled and said that Pat got an earful of his thoughts and ideas every day and probably should get a break of having to evaluate his Fold actions. He just needed her to save him from himself from time to time.

Pat got up and poured herself another cup of tea. She looked over to Eric and asked what he thought of the discussion.

He said that he agreed with all of it, and he was saving himself to discuss where in the three-Fold rhombicosidodecahedron (RCID)s to send the Fold scouts and what they would be looking for.

Pat returned to her seat and asked when had a third RCID been decided on.

Bram replied that he had discussed this with both Bob and Thomas. He did not recall who had suggested establishing the third RCID, but they had agreed that one with a Swooshian focal point should be considered. That would provide the ability to triangulate a huge portion of the Universe giving them a new way to measure special distances, the speeds of galaxy movement and other objects, and the overall size of the Universe.

Pat commented that the current set of people employed in the Fold project was not going to be enough to be involved in the Fold effort and to be involved in populating and maintaining Einstein City. He needed to accelerate getting people to Mataia and in bringing new people on board so they could be vetted.

Bram agreed and would make sure to give Erica a heads up on accelerating the Fold program hiring and the Fold movement of people to Mataia.

He asked whether she and Amy were ready to handle the influx.

Pat commented that they had set up the production of houses on Earth so that once a month six new houses were Folded to and set up on Mataia. They had also worked with Remi and with Marcus to set up Fold stations that would allow a person to Fold to anywhere in the city or to other parts of the Fold housing area. They had decided to keep all Fold locations outdoors so that buildings could be modified and not affect the Fold stations.

Bram said that even with the regular weekly update meetings happening, he was learning about the Fold stations as they talked.

Pat smiled and said that all the teams he was setting up were all trying to match his pace. However, he had set up so many teams that the week-to-week sharing sessions would always surface another surprise. She had come to the conclusion that it would be great since they would not have boring meetings, and the Fold effort would continue to be fun.

Bram gave her a hug and looked over to Zoe and Eric and commented that his four bodyguards were stepping up and surrounding him with their help. He went on to say that from the General on down, every Marine were eager to make the move to Mataia. Instead of the hesitancy that he thought he would face, he was faced with not moving fast enough with the transition to Mataia.

He said that Erica had recruited several of the Marine support staff to help in managing the transition and had said that she was still shorthanded.

He looked at Zoe and asked how her bottleneck at removing the Fold data from Earth was coming.

Zoe shook her head and said she was not talking until the next day when they met to do the review. She asked who was ready for a late snack of grapes and strawberries before going up for a long hot shower and getting a good night's sleep.

Pat took the lead and said that she loved the idea of a snack but wanted to add a scoop of vanilla ice cream to go with the strawberries,

Bram shook his head and said that he would just refresh his tea and watch. He added that a late snack would only fuel his wandering mind, and he would spend the night flying through either the negative or positive Fold universe and wake up exhausted.

Pat and Zoe sat and quietly talked to each other and chuckled. They were secretly penning a ditty for the following morning.

Bram knew that the two were up to something, but he was more focused on the three RCID's and what the objectives he should consider for each and did not try to figure out what they were up to.

As usual, the next morning Pat was one of the first down to the kitchen. It was not long before Zoe joined her. The two sat down with their coffee and wrote down the ditty that they had created.

> Bram is fast, but so are we.
> We have time to drink our tea.
> He creates so many teams.
> Then complains of work in reams.
> He gets himself so far behind.
> That at night he's an easy find.
> Lap top up he's working hard.
> Struggling to be the Fold's true bard.
> Writer of equations, founder of nations
> But has worries and trepidations.
> Worries about what's in the box.
> Not to worry it's not a fox.
> Bram is fast, but so are we.
> We have time to drink our tea.

When Bram came into the kitchen, Zoe went out to where she knew Donna and Castor would be and handed them the ditty.

The two of them nodded as they read it and said they would start as soon as they started the jog.

Bram was oblivious to everyone around him. He was deep into how to manage the three RCID's but then the ditty registered, and he had to smile. He knew what Pat and Zoe had been up to. He smiled and joined in on chanting the ditty as they jogged. It was clear to him that everyone on the Jog had been waiting for him to join because the volume of the group then increased dramatically.

He smiled as all the Marines on duty joined in and the entire compound reverberated with the ditty.

Linda smiled and asked if he wanted some tea before they set up the next two-week work plan.

Bram smiled because she never made him any tea or coffee so he knew she had heard the ditty and was pulling his leg.

He shook his head and said he had to get his lap top up.

Linda smiled and said he had his fifteen minutes of peace and then she would be in.

Bram walked over to the bookshelf and opened the small door and held his hand open so Isaac and Ada could get onto it. He then carried them over to his desk and they got out of his hand. He put down a few crumbs of a sugar cookie and then proceeded to tell them about the desire to utilize and manage three RCID nodes.

He looked over to Zoe and Eric and asked them to pay attention. He then asked Isaac and Ada if he should utilize all three RCID nodes in both the positive and negative Fold realms.

Isaac and Ada both seemed to shake their heads in the affirmative.

He then asked them if there should be three teams assigned and each team handle each Fold realm.

The two mice once again nodded in agreement.

He then asked if he should be an active member on the teams.

The two mice seemed to shake their heads and indicate a no.

He then asked if the teams should evaluate the effect of his decisions.

The two mice shook their heads in the affirmative.

He thanked the mice and was going to put them back when Zoe stopped him as she put down an oatmeal cookie crumb.

Zoe said that their sage advice and direction deserved an extra treat. She then put down her hand and the two mice got on board, and she carried them back to the bookshelf and let them get off and scurry into their abode.

Bram congratulated her on being accepted by the mice.

Linda walked in and said it was time for the two-week work plan.

Bram dutifully followed Linda's planning process. He called it Linda's, but they had worked together and polished the planning process to the point that they got it done in less than a half hour.

This morning, he was going to meet with the team that would be involved in managing the three RCID systems. The Earth system had been exercised for the past several months and they had learned a ton from having use it. It provided the framework for the other two.

The two new RCID's were going to be very different from the Earth centered RCID. They were dealing with two planets that they had very little knowledge about. In fact, Bram put what they knew about the planets close to a zero.

The very first thing they had to do was to establish the node points for each one.

Zoe led the way into the Viewing Room.

Bram looked around the room and thanked everyone for being there. He highlighted three objectives.

One was to charter the three RCID Fold teams. Another was to agree on the Strategy and Objectives for each RCID Fold. And the third objective was to charter and kickoff the Fold Change Evaluation Team.

They would lay out each team's draft work plan and then have each team separately develop the schedule they would follow. Before leaving the meeting each team would have their next steps identified and scheduled.

Each of the those in the room asked a series of clarifying questions that took more time than Bram had expected.

He was conscious that he had been thinking in a very detailed way about the four efforts. He recognized the fact that he would need to be involved with all of the teams early on so that they would be on the right path and not be wandering around.

He asked each team to work with Linda to schedule his time so that he could attend at least their first three meetings. He promised that he would then get out of their way. He was pleased that all the participants seemed to be pleased that he was going to spend time with them.

Zoe, Remi, Bob, and Thomas, all thanked him for being willing to help them launch their projects. They unanimously agreed that they were overwhelmed as they thought about the span of each of their projects. It was, they all agreed, a lifetime span.

Bram nodded and agreed that managing the Fold effort would be a lifetime endeavor for all of them.

Pat stood up and invited anyone interested to the Mataian Transformation team review that would take place in the Viewing Room at nine the following morning. The team would review its strategy and current execution plan. The team was interested in getting input as well as starting the education process for everyone that would be moving to Mataia.

Bram thanked her for reminding all of them and asked that those planning to attend should let Linda know.

Chapter 10: Mataian Transformation

That evening as Pat leaned against Bram quietly reading, she wondered if the conservative approach that she and Amy were taking in the biological transformation of Mataia should be done more quickly. The two of them had spent quite some time interacting with specialist on Earth. They had concluded that it would not happen in their lifetime. Now she was wondering if they had been too conservative. She closed her book and put her hand on Bram's chest and asked if he had a moment that he could listen to her doubts about how she and Amy were approaching the Mataian transformation.

The request brought Bram immediately into the present. Pat normally quietly read and periodically got up to refresh her drink, but she seldom disturbed him. He said that of course he could listen.

Pat shared the basic Mataia transformation timeline and asked if it was too slow.

Bram said he had no clue. He was sure that Pat and Amy would be close to the required timing. Pat was the methodical, thorough person that would insist on thorough results testing while Amy had the tenacity and the aggressive approach that had made her a top helicopter pilot able to skim the desert floor and scare the devil out of him. He figured the two would reach a balance that would most likely be close to what it would take.

He decided to reinforce the current timing and suggest that they use Bob on their team to verify the progress of their plan was close to what they had predicted and if not, they could make adjustments. The forward look would allow them to modify the timing that they had agreed to.

Pat nodded and said that she would make sure that they engaged Bob and had him move slowly forward along the timeline. She asked how they could make corrections if things were not working out.

Bram shook his head and said that she, Amy, and their team would need to work through each specific issue and determine what the appropriate action would be. He added that he had no clue what they would face but he was quite willing to get involved when they determined he might be able to help.

Pat patted him on the chest and thanked him. She got up and asked if he wanted anything to drink or eat.

Ripples in Time

Bram asked for a bottle of sparkling water. He watched Pat as she walked over to the snack bar. He realized if the most confident person he knew was having doubts about her upcoming role on Mataia then most likely every person would be having similar doubts. He realized he had sensed some of the doubt surfacing in almost all the team members. He looked over to Zoe and realized that she was watching him. He realized that she had shared a similar doubt about the erasure of the Fold information on Earth.

He decided to say something out loud that applied to all of them.

He said that he had his own doubts about how things would turn out and he was sure he would make numerous mistakes. However, they should all use their thousand-year trip to the future and remember what they had found. The learning for him was that they might be able to do better but everyone in the future had survived.

They should also spend more time to evaluate what they had learned and see if they could think of actions, they should take in their current time to make things better in the future.

Zoe nodded and added that as she thought about the condition of the Earth, she would like to adjust her erasure plans to include some sort of education and development that would make what they found on Earth at the thousand-year point more appealing and an Earth that had become kinder.

Bram nodded and replied that he agreed with her, and she and her team should take on the challenge to have Earth as ready as Mataia was at the thousand-year point.

Zoe shook her head and said she would set her goal at the height that he suggested but would be very pleased if on their next excursion to the one-thousand-year mark her team had hit fifty per cent of their goal.

Pat had been listening and added that she now felt better knowing that she was among a group of folks that had similar doubts but were charging ahead.

Bram asked Eric about his reaction to the discussion. Eric said that he was on a challenging assignment working with Marcus, but it had less of a social or environmental impact. He would be willing to work with any of the teams if he could be of help, but he was less affected emotionally than the leaders that would be molding the social and environmental changes that they were in charge of.

Bram suggested they put on a Straus soundtrack and relax so they could get a good night's sleep.

He listened to the music and in his mind, he worked on a ditty that he would ask Castor and Donna to chant as they went in to work.

Doubters, Doubters, a team of many Doubters.
If I challenge their feelings, they will call me a jerk,
Doubters, Doubters, a team of many Doubters.
Planning social, sea and mountain transformations.
Doubters, Doubters, setting up the Mataian population.
What could possibly go wrong,
What could they possibly know?
About how to make the Future Flow
Doubters, Doubters guiding change,
Change aimed at making them all grow.
Doubters, Doubters will work hard to make it so.
I am a doubter, you are a doubter, we all make it go.
Doubters, Doubters, embrace each other we will make it so.

The next morning, he was the one that handed the ditty note to Donna.

Pat and Zoe caught on immediately, laughed, and then chanted the ditty with enthusiasm.

When they went through the compound and the other Marines joined in, Pat felt like a weight had lifted from her mind.

Later as they got ready to enter the Visual Meeting Room Pat gave Bram a hug and thanked him for the ditty.

Bram was pleased that he had a positive effect on her and now that he was clear about the issue, he would ask Linda to set up a meeting to address the issue of doubt. He would ask Dr. Windal to attend and give them all her view of what doubt represented.

Pat and Amy more or less enthralled all those listening to their strategy and plans of transforming Mataia. There was great interaction. Everyone seemed enthusiastic about what the Transformation team was planning. There was great interest in the timing as well as the order of the transformation.

Amy's explanation about a truly bottom-up approach where she said that they were going from the bottom of the ocean and working themselves up to the sky gave everyone in the room the gist of how the transformation would proceed.

Both Amy and Pat repeatedly responded to various questions that required lengthy explanations that they were not prepared to go to that level of detail, but they would keep everyone informed on a weekly basis about the details.

As the session drew to a close, Bram stood up and thanked Amy and Pat for being the first to share their Strategies, Work plans at a high level and the general flow of the Mataian transformation.

He then shared that he had asked Linda to set up a session where they would discuss the issue of doubt and concern about the actions, they would each be leading or be involved with. He said that he would share many of his own concerns and get Dr. Wendall's take on how to handle his doubts.

That afternoon Linda informed Bram that his couch session with Dr. Wendall was the following day at one.

Bram was surprised at how quickly Dr. Windal was able to respond. He asked Linda to arrange to have Dr. Windal's chair and the chair she used with her patients located in the middle of the viewing room. He said that he would think about his top doubts and share those with her.

Linda let him know that Dr. Windal was really excited about hearing of your doubts. She shared that you had never discussed your doubts with her and now you were going to do so in public.

Bram put a call into Dr. Windal and asked if she had time to discuss the session they would do in public. He could not miss the eagerness as she let him know she was available and would love to discuss the session with him.

She said she would immediately walk over to his office and hung up.

Bram looked at the phone in his hand and as he placed it on the desk, he saw the grin on Zoe's face. He asked her what the grin was about.

She said that after he volunteered to share his doubts, the fact that he had doubts spread like wildfire. Linda had been rejecting plea after plea from people wanting to be in the session.

Bram shook his head. He thought for a moment and then called Linda and asked to record his session with Dr. Windal.

Linda brought Dr. Windal in and before she left, she let Bram know his request to record the session would be met.

Bram asked Dr. Windal if she wanted some refreshments. He was using the same entrance question that she always used with him.

He was pleased that she immediately caught on and asked if he was taking on her role.

He shook his head and then said that he would like to walk through the analysis that she was going to lead on the following afternoon.

Dr. Windal asked if it was to be a real analysis or a staged one.

Bram shared that it would be a little of staging and a lot of real analysis. He shared that it would be recorded and be made available to everyone in the Fold program.

Dr. Windal looked around the office and muttered a quiet "Wow."

Bram said that he would share some real doubts and concerns. What he wanted was for the session to be an educational one that highlighted how doubt could be a catalyst that could lead to doing great work. He also wanted to distinguish between Identity Doubt, where a person doubted their abilities, character or personality, and Idea Doubt when there was some doubt about an idea that was going to be implemented.

He *emphasized* that he wanted the team to focus on how to handle Idea doubt. He wanted to emphasize how doubt makes one explore, listen, and reinvent what was done. He added that it also led a person to risk more.

He wanted to highlight that handling doubt was a tough ask. He said that everyone should embrace doubt and make themselves capable of handling the uncertainty of the future.

Ripples in Time

He wanted doubt to be what inspired everyone to work harder and hone their skills to increase their self-confidence. Though it does take time, you can overcome your doubts.

And when one feels doubt no matter what, they should take a smaller step.

Dr. Windal looked to where Zoe and Eric were sitting and asked if he was going to share the doubts now that he would with her on the following day and was, he fine doing it with two other people in the room?

Bram nodded and said he was fine. He made the point that his bodyguards had saved him multiple times. He then said that he was going to use an example in the past and his top two in the current time.

She asked if she could record his doubts so she could think on how to weave in the educational points he had highlighted. She added that she was supper excited about what he planned to do. The session would apply to everyone including herself.

Bram agreed to her recording their meeting.

He said that his first doubt would be out in the desert and the ritual he went through at five in the morning. He walked out to a large boulder thought to have been pushed there by the ice age glacier. He would sit on top of it in the dark waiting for the sun to rise.

Once the sun's rays reached the boulder a little mouse that I named Einstein came up and sat beside me. He earned the name because he would answer questions that relieved my doubts. He provided the release of many of my concerns, and he was always right.

Bram clarified that doubts at the time was whether his idea of merging the various theories developed by several genius minds that he felt were superior to his.

He stopped and walked over to the bookshelf and brought out Isaac and Ida. He put them on the desk and introduced them to her. He said that these two were the offspring of Einstein. They were now the ones that listened to his doubts.

Dr. Windal asked if she could touch them and after his nod, she stroked each one and asked where they had received their degrees in psychology.

Bram smiled and said that one did not need to be a psychologist to help someone get over doubt. It could be a pet, it could be a friend, it could be a mental self-exercise, and it could be a talk to a psychologist. He then smiled and said that he would ask the two if they had a degree from the Desert College of Phycology.

Dr. Windal said that she didn't need to see the degrees. She agreed that managing doubt really depended on each individual. She then asked what the second doubt he was going to share.

Ripples in Time

It was a doubt about what Zoe was doing in erasing the Fold technology from the records and systems on Earth. This was as big as his first doubt, and it was happening in the present.

Zoe got up and walked over to the desk. She petted the two mice and then walked around the desk and gave Bram a hug. She looked over at Dr. Windal and said that knowing that Bram had doubts about the Fold information erasure, already helped her deal with hers.

Dr. Windal smiled and said that she was beginning to understand why her clientele seemed to be from outside the circle closest to Bram.

Dr. Windal shook her head and said that the erasure of the Fold information was the first she had heard about it. It surprised her and she said that she was going to have to process that to be ready by the following day.

She then said she had some trepidation about asking about his third doubt.

Bram stood up and walked to the window and looked out. He then turned and said that the third doubt was about his ability to manage, control and leverage the Fold technology out into the future. He had already experienced messing that up several times. He was not sure and had many doubts about his and the team's ability to take the actions in current time that would be most beneficial in the future.

The room went silent. Dr. Windal bent toward the desk and stroked the two mice. Zoe gave her a cookie crump and said she

119

should give it to the mice and then ask them the question that was in her mind.

Dr. Windal smiled and asked the mice if she was capable of running the analysis session in the way Bram had envisioned.

Zoe pointed to both Isaac and Ada bobbing their heads up and down.

Dr. Windal laughed and said that the two had just erased her doubt about their capabilities. She said that she had come over expecting a dry discussion and had never dreamt of a session where mice were analysts and Bram would share such significant doubts.

She said that she felt that she had just been called up to from the farm team to be on the professional first team.

Bram commented that she had always been on the professional team and that it was her time to hit a homerun. He would pitch the doubts, and she would hit each of them out of the park and they would all win the game.

Dr. Windal stood up and said she was going to spend what little time she had practicing in the batting cage, so that she would have a chance to hit the homeruns.

Bram watched her leave. He picked up Isaac and Ada and carried them back to their home.

Zoe asked him why he was exposing himself to the broader team to so much of what he was doing.

Bram said that only the folks in the room would be hearing the doubts and countermeasures for the doubts. The video would be used selectively with other key individuals. He felt that it would be a useful tool to bring other folks along the journey and make them more relaxed about what they were being asked to do.

He then said that he felt they should accelerate the move to Mataia. He needed to have his inner team move almost immediately and they should have no doubts about their transition to a very different way of life.

He added that it would be a good time to prepare the FBI for the departure of his four bodyguards. He wanted to orchestrate the situation so that their bosses closed down his protective duty. He thought maybe someone like Jeffrey, or ex-senator Newton from Maine could effectively plant the suggestion back at FBI headquarters. Once that happened, he wanted them to be more or less full time on Mataia.

Zoe looked at Eric and asked if he was ready. He smiled and said that he loved the house on Mataia. He laughed and added that he would only be cooking meals for the two of them.

Linda gave Bram his ten-minute warning that it was time to go home.

Ron Mueller

Chapter 11: Doubt Analysis

Pat lay against Bram and took in his easy breathing as they sat on their dual recliners. She was nervous for him, but he seemed perfectly calm. She had never expected him to talk openly about having doubts. He was the bedrock of the Fold program. He had made all the Fold breakthroughs. The entire team had made improvements and additional breakthroughs, but they were all built on his initial work.

She asked him what had made him decide to expose some of his doubts.

He smiled and said she was why he was doing it. She had inspired him. She had openly admitted to having doubts about the effort to transform the Mataian world. He recognized that he had always had doubts about some of his actions, but he had simply plowed ahead. She had saved him from himself by rescuing him from the negative Fold realm. He wanted to save the team from the stress that doubt caried with it.

Zoe spoke up and said that the meeting with Dr. Wilkins when he shared the doubts that he was about to make public about the correctness of erasing all Fold information from Earth immediately lifted the stress that she had unconsciously built up as she did that work. She had almost jumped with joy when he had mentioned his own doubt.

Bram smiled and said that he never realized that on a daily basis he had used Einstein and now Isaac and Ada to release the stress generated by doubt. He said that it was a mystery how a small mouse first found and befriended him and had helped him get over the stress of what seemed like a hopeless circular effort in absurdity. His relationship with Einstein had slowly evolved and now he realized that it had a calming effect.

He had never thought about how the ditties they chanted as they jogged into work helped address the doubt about what he was doing.

He shared that the first Fold of the two wheels had taken him up into the Mount Everest of doubt and he had almost given up doing any farther development on Fold.

Then all the attacks began to put up mountains of doubt about his ability to guide the Fold effort and not lose the people around him.

He then gave Pat a hug and said that doubt was his friend in that it made him think through each of his actions multiple times and his work through multiple failures until he felt that he could deliver a successful, safe product.

Pat gave Bram a hug and said that he might have doubts, but she could not think of anyone that had more fight and bravery. He had inspired all of them with his willingness to run in towards the battle and gun fire, while the rest of them either froze or ran the other way. She said that she agreed with Orlando when he claimed that Bram was a Marine in heart and action.

Bram thanked both Pat and Zoe for erasing any doubt that he had about holding the session with Dr. Windal with everyone watching.

He asked Eric to turn up the volume so he could close his eyes and listen to Nat King Cole.

Eric got up and turned up the volume. He then quietly said that being around Bram seemed to have a magic effect on him. He always got energized. He commented how lucky they had been to have been selected by the FBI leadership to guard him.

Zoe commented that all four of them were assigned to the duty because the FBI leaders did not want to send in their best to protect someone so far down on the food chain.

Bram smiled but remained silent. He thought about the fact that he had almost refused to accept the four bodyguards and now they were an integral part of the Fold effort and would take on some very important roles in the very near future. Roles, that he thought would put them several steps higher and in more influential roles than their bosses held.

He had just received a message from Jeffrey that President Natorly that had supported them through both of his terms had contacted him and asked if there was a role to play in the Fold organization. The president had commented that he wanted more than the three candy kisses that had convinced him that the Fold effort would change the world.

Bram had immediately envisioned the president working with ex-senator Newton to establish the Mataian government. He also knew that the more people that knew about the Fold capability and moved to Matai, the easier it would be to erase the Fold knowledge from Earth.

The next morning on their jog in Donna and Castor took up a ditty.

> Doubt is good, Doubt is fine.
> Well, managed it tastes like wine.
> No one is free, we all have doubts,
> Is a good fight where we win most bouts.
> We redo when we lose, redo, redo till we win.
> We work hard to give it the right spin.
> Hard work, good thinking, and a pinch of luck
> Keeps the effort from running amuck.
> Doubt is good, Doubt is fine.
> Well, managed it tastes like wine.
> Bram is going to share his doubts.
> Bram has doubts what about?
> No, he cannot, No, he cannot, have any doubts
> Oh! My but yes, he does.
> He makes our doubts into sweet wine.

This time Bram couldn't figure out who had written the ditty, but he enjoyed it and sang along as they jogged into work. He asked later and found out that Zoe, Eric, and Pat had collaborated on it.

Linda teased him by greeting him and letting him know that she had no doubt that he would do fine.

Bram smiled and replied that he had no doubt that that they would all shout when they found out what he was about.

He then asked if she had enough and that they should both just head for the Viewing Room and get the sessions started.

Linda nodded and said that she had worked with the film crew. They had set up two cameras so they could switch between viewing him from the front and then viewing Dr. Windal from the front. They had let her know that the front view would always be on the person speaking.

Bram nodded and got a bottle of water from the back of the room and then sat down on the chair across from Dr. Windal.

He could tell that she was very nervous. He smiled and asked if she had a good night's sleep and if she had any doubt about the good outcome of the inquisition he was about to face.

Dr. Windal smiled and thanked him for getting her on the road to overcoming her doubts about doing a therapy session in public and having it filmed so it could be shown to others.

She then caught the rhythm and began with a lengthy period where she highlighted the various forms of doubt and then focused it to the purpose of the session. The session would focus on idea or decision doubt. She defined idea doubt as doubt about the goodness of an idea. The reason for that doubt was often due to the lack of clarity of what the meaning of good actually might mean. She then went on to and pointed out the fact that idea doubt often lead into a series of decision doubts as the idea was transformed into actual actions.

She then made the point that within decision doubt there was the doubt before the decision that often delayed a decision. Then there was the doubt after the decision that caused extra verification work to prove that it was at least an acceptable decision.

She said that she had heard that Bram's decision making both before and after was the rapid fire of a machine gun. She smiled and went on to say that his idea and decision-making train had no delays, no stops, just forward movement.

She then asked Bram to share one of his doubts.

Bram hesitated for a moment and then shared that many of his doubts were experienced in the desert where he had worked to develop his Fold equation. He took his doubts out early in the morning to a large boulder where a friendly and wise mouse who he named Einstein would join him at sunrise.

Ripples in Time

He would ask Einstein questions that surrounded the doubt that he carried out to the rock each morning. Einstein would listen and shake his head in the positive to show agreement and in the negative when he did not agree. He earned his name Einstein by providing guidance to the creation of a successful Fold equation. He helped me overcome my doubt that I would ever be successful, and each day gave me the inspiration to try again. I tried again and again for the better part of a year.

Dr. Windal shook her head and said that having a mouse be a psychologist was a first for her, but Einstein had indeed played that role. Bram had spilled out his doubts and Einstein helped him keep on going by relieving the tension and pressure of the doubt.

Bram nodded and said that he had never thought of Einstein as a psychologist, but he had thought of him as a friend. So, can friends act in the place of a psychologist he asked?

Dr. Windal replied that friends that listen to an idea and how one was dealing with implementing that idea without judging but with encouragement helped to reduce doubt.

Bram looked around the room and thanked all his friends for helping him overcome his doubts.

Dr. Windal asked him to share his second doubt.

He said that his second doubt was whether having Zoe erase the Fold information from all the systems on Earth was an appropriate action. This doubt was as big as his first doubt, and it was a doubt that was happening in the present.

Zoe interrupted and said that knowing that Bram had doubts helped her deal positively with her doubts.

Dr. Windal nodded and commented that Idea doubt was often overcome by knowing others had similar doubts. The caution when that occurred was to keep the work going forward and not stop because of mutual doubt about an idea. Improvement to the idea should be pursued but then action taken. The result of the action should be evaluated.

She asked Bram to detail some of the doubt he had with erasing the information for the record of Earth.

Bram replied that he had weighed the danger of having the Fold capability spread around the Earth and had concluded that it would turn the Earth into chaos. His doubt was about the rightness of acting like a judge that denied bail to an accused person because they seemed to him to be a flight risk when there was no real reason to believe so.

Dr. Windal noted that the world seemed to be constantly ricocheting from one major man-made catastrophe to another. It had seen two major world wars, and a continuous run of battles from Vietnam, Korea, Iraq, to Afghanistan. She asked the question if Fold could possibly add more chaos than was already happening.

Bram asked Zoe if she had an opinion about the level of chaos that Fold might unleash.

Ripples in Time

Zoe nodded and replied that everyone knew the story of Pandora's Box and the pestilence and disease she unleashed when she opened up a box her husband was safe keeping for the gods. She looked around and then said that the Fold box that Bram had opened had unleashed a power into the world ten time worse than anything that came out of Pandora's box. The Bram Fold box could end both history as they knew it and any future that they might be imaging. There was no fixed event in time. It was all fluid and malleable. There was no event in the future that was fixed. Time might not exist and only distance might mean anything. She finished that Fold was non-linear and mind twisting.

Giving this power to the various totalitarian governments invited them to create a chaos that would have no end.

Bram agreed that his doubt was trumped by the risk of the chaos the Fold knowledge would mean.

Dr. Windal commented that she was out of her league. She was not equipped to give guidance on a topic that was so deep, so random and seemingly so nonlinear. It was becoming clear to her that progress was not progressing smoothly from one stage to the next in a logical way. It seemed capable of making sudden changes and to develop in multiple directions at the same time.

Bram nodded and made the point that it was impossible to operate in the Fold environment with only linear thinking. He made the point that until Fold had become a reality there were only five non-linear relationships in mathematics: Quadratic, Cubic, Exponential, Logarithmic and Cosine relationships.

The Fold realm had introduced the sixth nonlinear relationship: the rhombicosidodecahedron (RCID) relationship. This Fold RCID relationship had the most complex existence possible because it varied in size as a factor of distance. Time was a variable and it flowed with distance.

Dr. Windal shook her head and said that she had heard what Bram had said and could verify it was shared in English, but she had understood maybe five percent.

She then said she was afraid to ask for his third doubt, but she would do so.

Bram said that the third doubt was about his ability to manage, control and leverage the Fold technology out into the future. He had already experience messing that up several times. He was not sure the actions they had carried out were appropriate given what they had all learned since then. He had many doubts about his and the team's ability to take the actions in current time that would be most beneficial to those in the future.

Dr. Windal smiled and asked if there was any one in the room without Idea Doubt.

Ripples in Time

Pat and Amy stood up and replied that they were continually reviewing their Mataian transformation and discussing the steps they were taking. It was their way of addressing the doubts they had. They did not want to mimic Earth's current situation but wanted to slowly bring Mataia into a natural balance as Earth might have been some time in the past. Their doubts were about the order of establishing a supportive environment and still keep Mataia pristine.

Mallica and Gerry stood up and commented that their doubts was on the ability to evaluate the conditions on Swoosh and take the corrective actions soon enough to ensure the Swoshians environment reached a balance that might be different from their previous world but ensured their survival. They had faced one such event when the krill from the original Swoshian world began a rapid die off. They introduced a variety of Earth krill and shrimp with some doubt that it would work.

Mallica said that Bram had relieved them of their current doubt by reminding them that the leader one thousand years in the future had thanked them for having saved the Swooshians by introducing the best krill mix in the Swooshian world. They said that knowing that their actions would all be on the positive side had almost eliminated their doubts about their current work.

Dr. Windal looked around and nodded her head. She commented that she was impressed with how they managed their doubts and now understood much better why so few of them came to her office. She laughed and said that she did not have two smart mice to help her eliminate doubt and stress and such close friends to also help.

Bram replied that her work was essential for the team. The current group sessions and for the individual sessions were paying off. He valued her skill with providing the support those sessions required. He thanked her for her willingness to hold the session with him in front of everyone.

He then addressed the team and thanked them for speaking up and sharing their examples. He would continue to ask them to help him resolve his doubts and they now knew about his other two confidents that resided with him in his office. He then looked over to where his FBI bodyguards were sitting and added that he was not talking about them but about Ada and Isaac.

He waited until the clapping died down and then said that it was time to go and celebrate the lunch which Linda had scheduled for them and Chef D'Carluca had prepared.

<u>Chapter 12: Mataian Move</u>

Bram stroked Ada and Isaac as they nibbled on the crumbs and as he listened to Erica update him on the moves to Mataia. He had asked her team to accelerate the moves, and she was following up with an update and had indicated that to accelerate she would need additional help.

Erica was describing how she had organized the moves and who she was working with. She let him know that Pat and Amy were the ones that were determining the locations for the additional homes on Mataia. She shared the fact that she was pleased to learn that the two were working with a city planning group on Earth and with the crew that would maintain the infrastructure on Mataia. This reassured her that the additional homes would have the same treatment that all previous homes had experienced.

The interior home decor was being provided by a very happy team which commented that they were enjoying the best business year ever. It was the same team that had worked with her on the initial homes.

She finished by saying that at the current rate they were transitioning everything seemed synchronized.

She then shared that Melissa was determine the location where the current homes in the Fold community that were to stay on Earth would be Folded to and working with Marcus and the same city planning group that was working with Amy and Pat. She added that the sequence of moving people to Mataia was determined by who lived on the edge of the current Earth Fold community. She was trying to keep the elimination of the Fold community shielded from the public until the last moment. They had left all the empty homes around the very edge in the community. The next layer of homes was being folded to the locations determined by Melisa. The moves of the homes were followed by landscaping where the home had been.

She brought up the fact that she was working with Luke Stetson and Remi to move the bubble manufacturing to the current hangar on Mataia. The bottle neck was in arranging the manufacturing material logistics and coordinating that with the movement of the people working in the manufacturing.

She commented that the people able to work from home had a lower priority to the new homes than the priority of the people that had hands on type of work. She praised all those involved for understanding and accepting how she was determining the Fold move priorities.

She then shared that General Tilman, and the Marines were in this second priority group that were not needed in the same capacity on Mataia. He had his in-house personnel management team working with all the other teams to determine where to place all three hundred Marines that wanted to remain as a part of the Fold effort. A great deal of time was spent on matching a Marine's discharge date, their interests and qualifications and the help various teams had identified that they needed. She complimented the General and his staff for communicating their detailed plans and listing the key skills of their Marines. This was a great help to the Fold teams that were all looking for additional people.

She then brought up the fact that Elizabeth had asked about recruiting and including a set of medical specialists in a move to Mataia.

Bram responded that they should consider clearing Dr. Windal but recruiting additional medical specialists should wait until later.

He suggested that the initial focus should be to set up a suitably sized hospital and then begin the recruiting and the vetting of specific medical personnel. Until Mataia had a local facility, she should arrange to have a medical bubble available to transport anyone needing immediate medical attention back to Earth.

Erica asked if Bram was willing to discuss this directly with Elizabeth and Dr. Windal and felt relief when he agreed. She agreed one hundred percent with him, but she sensed that Elizabeth was expecting the go ahead and did not want to be the one who pricked the bubble.

She then brought up the Stetson family. She highlighted that they wanted to maintain their presence in both worlds.

Bram responded that it was fine with him and asked her to clarify the issue.

Erica commented that she had no issue with their request, but she was just verifying with him that such an arrangement would be acceptable. She pointed out that this might increase the number of Folds between Mataia and the Earth.

Bram said that they should worry about that when they were running short on Fold bubbles or were having difficulty achieving the goal of maintaining a zero increase in the weight of Mataia.

He pointed out that the Mataian Transformation team had a goal of zero additional weight add to what Mataia began with. He said at the moment he had no clue how they were proposing to achieve that goal. He asked Erica if she wanted to attend the meeting, he was having with that team to better understand how they proposed achieving such a feat.

Erica asked when and where was the meeting being held.

Bram replied it was in the viewing room that afternoon.

Ripples in Time

Pat and Amy had brainstormed how they could protect the environment from all the people that would be living on Mataia. They and the other team members had set a goal that the move of people to Mataia would be managed in a fashion that there would be zero pollution and zero added weight to the planet.

One of the team members asked how would they achieve that goal when they moved whales to Mataia.

No one had an immediate answer.

Pat suggested that they stay away from speculation and focus on the actual problems they currently faced. Each additional home weighted in on the average of at five hundred fifty tons. She pointed out that it meant the building of a house, the infrastructure to support the house and the people themselves.

The new hospital would weigh in almost one hundred times more than that. She went on to list the fire station and additional manufacturing and suddenly it became a monumental issue.

Amy suggested that they use Mataian material to make each house. She suggested they develop the home building capability as soon as possible so that the additional homes could be constructed on Mataia from Mataian materials.

The team quickly pointed out that the material gathering infrastructure to achieve such capability was not available on Mataia.

Pat then suggested that they use one of the other dry worlds as a way to achieve their zero-weight gain goal. They would Fold the excess soil from the construction of homes and buildings to that world.

This was immediately agreed to. A sub team was set up to oversee the way the material was transferred to the chosen dry world. The goal was to enrich that world and not condemn it to be just a dumping site. They had all agreed that they were cheating and pushing their problem to another planet.

The next improvement that the team suggested was that all the human waste would be processed and then sent to Earth to enrich the garden products that were to be produced on several Mexican farms that were being established.

One of the team members highlighted that once again they did not have the facilities on Mataia to do waste processing. She pointed out that the waste could be sent to Earth and the water that was Mataian could be sent back.

Amy suggested that they should see if the water should be sent back or if that additional weight loss would cover the gain in other areas. She suggested that a couple of members work on that problem and let the rest of the team know what they had determined.

Ripples in Time

The team arrived at the goal that each home would be energy independent. Each home would generate all the power it needed. This was feasible but it required redesign of the current way homes were built but could be immediately applied to all new homes and the existing ones would be slowly retrofitted.

The team then extended this concept to all buildings and processes that would operate on Mataia. This eliminated all power and sewer systems.

Then the challenge was extended to making each home free of any water piping. The suggestion was that each home have a large Fold water bubble that would sit on the top of the home and would provide the water and the water pressure for distribution through the house. Empty Fold water bubbles would automatically Fold to the refill site. Full Fold water bubbles would arrive at each house when the empty water bubble Folded away.

They then decided that the kitchen would be totally electrically operated. They discussed the option of delivering preordered meals via meal Fold bubbles. They agreed that Fold in food service would be part of the service that would be available.

Pat led the team through a planning exercise that identified that learning how to terra form the third dry planet was the bottleneck. It was clear that it represented the solution to keeping the weight of Mataia what it had been when they first discovered it. However, they did not want to ruin another planet.

She was pleased that the team had made a group of significant decisions. She was also pleased that the choices they had made would make it possible for them to meet Bram's request to speed up the move of the Fold personnel to Mataia.

The only thing they needed was to expand the team to handle the additional workload.

Bram entered the meeting room right on time. He immediately sensed that the team had made progress that they were eager to share.

He sat down.

Amy took the center of the floor and said that Bram could move as fast as he desired. She said that the team had leaped across the barriers facing them and were zooming along at ground level height and they had blasted their way through to a solution that met the needs for speed and for environmental maintenance.

Bram smiled and asked if she had been at the controls.

Pat joined Amy and slowly point around to the members of the transformation team and said that each and every one of them deserved recognition for identifying both barriers and the solutions to overcome the barriers.

She then shared the way they would maintain the pristine environment of Mataia and at the same time continue to expand Einstein City.

Amy then said that there would be no electrical, water, or gas lines as part of the Mataian infrastructure.

"Each house and building on Mataia will be totally independent," Pat added.

Amy added that any imbalance of weight would be handled by moving any increase in weight to the third dry world. She went on to say that the team to manage the third dry world transformation was identified and needed staffing.

Pat then shared that the handling of waste from each home would be folded to Earth where it would be processed and used on the food raising farms. She said that eventually this capability needed to reside on Mataia but until that was feasible the initial approach would be implemented.

Bram commented that he was impressed with the speed and the depth of their approach. He was eager to see them implement their plan.

Erica said she agreed with Bram, and she was prepared to respond to their requests for the resources and qualified people they needed.

Bram asked that as soon as possible he would like to view the third dry world. He suggested using a camera Fold bubble to do a tour of the third world. He asked if Pat was going to have a naming contest and give the third planet a name.

Pat smiled and replied that they had already had the contest. Before revealing the name, she wanted to know how bad Bram wanted to know the name by the size of the prize he was willing to award.

Bram responded that he would award the same prize that had been awarded for the naming of Mataia.

Pat shook her head and said that inflation should be factored in, that the prize should be at least twenty percent higher.

Bram chuckled and looked around and commented that the team had picked the right person to bargain with him. He raised his hands and said he was in agreement with the increase in the size of the prize.

Pat smiled and said that the winning name was Terimund which was a smore name smashed together from two Portuguese words.

Bram said he liked the name and complimented the team in naming a planet. He asked whether the plans included doing more than moving excess weight from Mataia to Terimund.

Pat replied they had not discussed this in any detail since they knew so little about the Terimund. She added that they would first do a thorough analysis of Terimund's environment.

Bram said that he was interested in knowing if Terimund should be considered as another world that they might populate.

Pat and Amy both nodded and then agreed that they would follow through with a thorough evaluation of Terimund but that would require them to properly staff that team. At the time they did not have the people to properly set up that effort.

Bram commented that they should be able to rapidly get the people they needed because the General had his staff processing the Marines wanting to be part of the Fold effort on Mataia.

Erica said that she would be glad to facilitate getting the people they needed.

Bram smiled and said that he had no doubts about the Mataian Transformation team achieving their goals.

Amy returned the smile and slowly moved her arm to bring in the whole team and said that she had been super impressed at how well and how fast the team had developed their challenging but doable plan.

She thanked Bram for having reviewed their plans.

Pat then stood up and said that it was time to name the winners of the prize. She shared that one person was from Mexico and the other from Portugal and that the two had collaborated on the name. She handed them a large cardboard check for Fifteen Thousand dollars. She then added that she and Amy were gifting them with a hundred dollar each to spend however they wished.

Amy then declared the meeting over.

Bram walked around and chatted with each of the team members. He then cornered Pat and Amy and congratulated them on setting him up.

Amy smiled and asked what made him think such a thing.

Bram chuckled and pointed to the large cardboard check that they came in with that had already been made out and signed for fifteen thousand dollars. All they had to do was orchestrate his agreement. He added that they had done it very well.

Amy nodded and said that it was all Pat's doing.

Bram gave them both a hug and said that he had enjoyed their pranking him.

Chapter 13: Mataian Living

The move of people to Mataia became a constant but slow stream. Bram was impressed by the homes being built for the new arrivals. Pat and Amy managed to build new homes that were totally self-sufficient. From where he was now spending every night, going to the main work center was an easy jog in and going to the Fold work center in the hangar was a longer jog but one that he chose to do most of the time. He had a bubble at his disposal to go anywhere he desired but chose to move around on foot whenever possible. He monitored the number of people that had moved to Mataia, but he stayed away from the actual details.

Zoe had relented on how intense his protection needed to be but insisted that during work hours he would always have two bodyguards. She insisted that he have the full contingent of bodyguards when working on Earth.

Most people that had moved to Mataia were living there full time and were very pleased with their experience. He and several of the team members worked on Earth part time. He was maintaining his Earth presence until the time all of Fold information would disappear.

This would be a hat trick timed to coincide with the work that Zoe was doing to erase Fold information. And the fading memories of those outside of the Fold family. A third consideration was to erase the Fold site without making local or national news.

Pat had set up a contest to see who could guess the date closest to when the three consecutive actions would happen. She shared the history of what a hat trick meant and named the contest, New Hat for Mataia. The prize was a hat that had Mataian Hat Trick Winner written across the front and had a five thousand dollar check inside. The contest allowed everyone to select the date, but Pat made the point that the contest was set up so there would be only one winner.

Erica had continued working with Melisa to move houses out of the Earth Fold site and had let him know that it was time to think about closing down the Earth Fold facility.

He asked if everything was coordinated with all the folks managing the move.

Erica said that she was working with the General to finalize the movement of the Marines that had been assigned to the Fold site.

When Bram called the General, he learned that all of the Marines had been processed and when Bram gave the word, they were all free to Fold to Mataia. He said he was pleased that all of the Marines that had been at the Fold site had been eager to make the move

He thanked Bram for letting him know that visits and vacations to Earth would be available because this had been the one concern of some of the Marines. Visiting their families and continuing the personal relationships they had with friends and sweethearts was the one thing that had been a barrier.

He had contacted Melisa and learned how taking the Fold weekend vacations were managed and had let his Marines know.

He praised Pat and Amy for providing the video tour of Mataia and showing the homes that were available to choose from. When he and the Marine guards and the support personnel took a tour, they had all raised their hands when he asked who wanted to move to Mataia. He added that it was the best opportunity for every one of his Marines. He included himself in the comment and added that it allowed him to remain relevant.

Bram thanked the General for the information and asked him to work with Erica to coordinate the moves and to work with the project team leaders to get the ex-Marines on the teams that fit their interests.

Marcus, Mallica and Remi had been working on establishing the hangar Fold Work Center. They had recruited several of the IT folks that worked for Linh and Duong to set up the three new super computers. One supercomputer was designated to be used only by Bram.

Another supercomputer would be used by the teams studying the histories of Mataia, Earth, Swoosh, and the additional dry planet.

Another supercomputer would be used for those studying the past for managing the Transformation of Mataia.

Bram had let the team studying forward history know that they should expect to welcome another team studying the future of Terimund. He then introduced Castor as the Leader for that team. He said that Castor had resigned from the Marines after a heroic career and would move permanently when the final move to Mataia occurred. He then asked Castor to say a few words.

Castor stood up and quietly said that he would not accept the role.

The room fell silent. Then with a broad smile he went on to say, "Unless Bram agrees to preside over my marriage at the Rushing River Inn."

A cheer went up in the room and everyone clapped.

Bram gave Castor a handshake and said that he would be honored to preside. He then asked if they knew who that lucky woman happened to be.

Castor replied that it was a long-ago high school sweetheart that he had left when he became a Marine. He had reconnected with her when he went on one of the weekend Fold vacations to Green Bay, Wisconsin and the two of them had accidently run into each other. She was still single and the two of them reignited their romance. He had Zoe have the FBI clear her as soon he got back from that first reconnect. He had then been seeing her every weekend possible.

Bram smiled and commented that he did not know that Melisa had established a Fold location in Green Bay, but he was pleased that she had and that for whatever reason Castor would go to Green Bay he was pleased with the outcome.

Castor shook his head and replied that you go to Green Bay to watch a great football team play. He laughed and asked Bram if he had ever gone to a football game before.

Bram shook his head and replied that he had never gone to any sports game and had never watched one all the way through.

The room started a chant of, "Bram has got to see a game, Bram has got to see a game."

Bram put up his hand and asked when the next game was going to be on television. He would ask Melisa to set up the event when the recreation center was Folded to Mataia.

Donna stood up and asked if it could be a double wedding. She said that she had just accepted the proposal of the most handsome Marine attached to the Fold effort and would love to have Bram preside over her wedding as well.

Bram smiled and commented that the move to Mataia was triggering a spate of weddings. He asked who that handsome and lucky Marine might be.

Donna smiled and said that he was the one Bram had saved from being washed into the sea and saved for her.

Bram looked over to where Matt was sitting with the General and commented that his choice of soulmates repaid the debt for being saved but he did not want to hear any future complaints about his romance.

Matt replied that it had been hard to hide their romance. It had started right after he got recruited to be the General's Aid. It was not an allowed romance within the ranks, but he discovered that they could not be apart and had kept it under wraps until Donna's announcement in this meeting.

The General smiled and said that Matt was fired and then congratulated him on selecting among the best for his, "beautiful Marine."

Bram was pleased that his close friends were all finding happiness. It was clear that the Fold technology rivaled the internet technology and maybe surpassed it in the sense that it opened a person-to-person interface versus a virtual one.

Pat brought up the issue of waste management. She said that it had become the bottleneck to finalizing the move to Mataia. She said that the clean waste, the soil from digging basements for the homes was on track and easily managed since it was being folded to Terimund. She said that they were currently keeping all the soil in one location so that it could be handled by the oncoming Terimund Future team that Castor would be leading. She revealed that setting up the waste processing that would be used on the farms was the bottleneck.

Ripples in Time

The purchase of the farms in Mexico, Canada, Argentina, and Vietnam were getting executed and set up in a timely manner by Melisa who was doing a superb job. The issue was in setting up waste processing facilities. It turned out that close investigation of the required permitting in each of the countries required too much exposure as to where the waste originated.

She said that they had found a sugar mill on the Island of Maui that already had a waste processing license that Melisa was in the process of purchasing. Once the purchase was complete, they would not only own a sugar processing plant but a large amount of land to grow sugar cane.

They could easily put the Fold terminal there and improve the waste processing system that already existed. The waste would not need any additional Folding since it could be used in the sugar cane fields.

Bram said that sounded like a good solution but suggested they look far enough forward so that the balance being used on the Island matched the quantity of materials they were taking from it. If there was an excess of material going in, then they should consider Folding the excess to the farm locations in an even dispersal manner.

Olivia, Jeffrey, and ex-President Samuel Natorly were sitting together in the corner of the room. Jeffrey stood up and said that the three of them had finished drafting the proposed Mataian Constitution and were prepared to review it and have improvement work sessions.

The clapping in the room was loud and continued for some time.

Bram raise his hand to quiet everyone. He pointed out that the clapping indicated how important having a constitution was to everyone. He asked that they work with Linda to set up a constitution finalization event.

The General asked to work with the Constitution Team before the event to make sure the work that he was leading in setting up a crowd management and relief organization would be addressed as part of the constitution.

He thought it might influence the wording that they might have used in the constitution. He added that he thought that the leadership traits of the Marine Corp, Bearing, Courage, Decisiveness, Dependability, Endurance, Enthusiasm, Initiative, Integrity, Judgment, Justice, Knowledge, Loyalty, Tact, and Unselfishness should also be used during the constitution finalization event. He suggested that bearing should be considered when thinking about how the wording in the constitution would affect the future.

Unselfishness could be thought about in how the constitution described shared responsibility. Dependability should be thought about when considering all the various scenarios that would be faced in the future. Constitutional endurance should be considered when choosing the wording that was used. Justice for everyone should be a fundamental consideration. Integrity should be the goal that the constitution espoused.

Olivia replied that she was sure her two partners on the team would love to sit down with the General and see how his concepts could be woven into the work they had done.

The General put up his hand and said that General should be dropped, and Les or Lester used to address him. He went on to say he would set up a time with them to share his thinking.

Bram smiled and commented that "Lester" was sure to influence the constitution team. He said that his only input was that the constitution should state that people should treat others as they wished to be treated.

Lacy had enjoyed the discussion that had seemed to flow naturally from one key topic to the next. She asked if Mataia would be doing any search for additional intelligent beings. This was an area that greatly interested her, and it was an area that so far, she had heard little about.

Bram replied that she had touched on one of his continuing interests but that current events had prevented him from pursuing it. He suggested that Lacy set up a team to search for intelligent life and set up a Fold beacon system that sent out a query looking for that intelligence.

Lacy nodded and said she accepted the challenge.

Bram asked if there was any other information or actions that needed to be taken.

Zuri, who was currently in England, commented that she had been busy writing lyrics for an album she was planning to record called Mataian Melodies. She said that she was planning to reside on Mataia to complete her album, would enjoy getting suggestions from anyone and would like help to merge her songs with the right melodies.

She said that the meetings discussion had added several lyrics to her list, and she was eager to engage everyone that was interested.

She shared that she would receive her diploma at the end of the current semester and would then be ready to Fold to Mataia.

Everyone in the room clapped.

He dabbed the tears he had in his eyes. Bram knew that the Fold miracle, genius child, had been transformed not only in body but she was leveraging her mind and fulfilling the opportunities that had opened before her. He complimented her on her graduation and on pulling Orlando along with her.

He later found out that Zuri had graduated number one in her class and that Orlando had graduated number five. He made a point of having that shared with everyone.

Chapter 14 Leveraging Fold

Bram was pleased with the way the transition was proceeding. Everyone seemed willing to adjust to a different way of life from what they had experienced on Earth. Their homes were not only comfortable and somewhat on the luxurious end of the spectrum, but they were arranged so that each neighborhood had a central green area that included a tennis court, and swimming pool. He noted that Amy and Pat were laying out a series of communities that supported an outdoor lifestyle.

He was surprised when Pat let him know that their home would be moved to a location that was almost exactly between the main office building and the hangar where the Fold Work Center was located. It would also be improved. She said that the move was in conjunction with having each housing area having the same arrangement. She said the area that they were currently living at would be redone to have the same layout as all the other areas.

She went on to share that their home would have some modifications made that would make it totally self-sufficient and it would eliminate all the early work that they had done when they were thinking about underground services. She and Amy were leveraging the Fold technology.

She likened the novel approach to the green thinking on Earth that was focused on taking everything back to its natural low energy footprint. On Mataia it was not making unnecessary footprints.

Bram asked how far it was to the waterfront. Pat smiled and assured him that she had that in mind when she arranged the move. The view from their living room window would have the beach in front of them and the mountains out to each side. She was having the living room enlarged and new windows put on each side. In the back of the room would be an open dining area with the kitchen behind it. She said that it would really be a great enhancement.

Bram asked about the other homes and learned that those living in each of them were doing similar upgrades and were excited about the new location.

Bram let Pat know that he liked what she was doing.

The first meeting of the week was with Marcus and Remi. Marcus shared that he had hired one of the female Marine guards to take care of the kids. He was pleased with how she got along with the Marcus Jr. and Mylan.

He said he was also pleased with the new educational facility and how quickly Elizabeth had gotten the school up and running. He was also pleased with the large campus that surrounded the school. It seemed to be a park big enough for several schools.

Bram let Marcus know that Elizabeth had shared her vision of establishing several sites for continued learning. She wanted to place the sites around Mataia so that students could get away from parents and learn to be on their own.

He suggested that she should pick the location and have the schools established. Once she had that done she could see how to staff the schools and universities. He had let her know that he was very supportive of making the Mataian society a very well-educated society.

Remi asked if Elizabeth's vision included schools of medicine.

Bram nodded and said that Dr. Sewal was working closely with her and was the one focused on establishing the medical practices and facilities on Mataia. He had agreed to get that done before recruiting other doctors and physician. He said that this was the approach he and the two of them had reached. It was a slower approach than the two of them had at first argued for, but it was one that he felt kept the horse before the cart and it allowed time to vet the people that Dr. Sewal had in mind.

Linda called into the office and let Bram know that Mallica and Gerry were standing at her desk and wanted to share an idea that they wanted his opinion on.

Bram asked Remi and Marcus if they wanted to hear what the two were thinking about doing or if they would rather go about their workday.

Marcus said that he would go to work on setting up the coordinates of all the building moves that Pat and Amy were throwing his way. He added that Elizabeth had started doing the same with school buildings she was having Folded in from Earth.

Remi said that his effort was having a slow start, and he was interested in what Mallica and Gerry were up to.

Bram let Linda know to send the two in.

Mallica headed to the service bar and grabbed two bottles of water and handed one to Gerry.

She then asked Gerry to share the idea that he had.

Gerry corrected her and said it was their idea. He then said that he wanted to provide the Swoshians underwater robots that they could command to build things for them. He described a robot that could extrude plastic shapes, or one that could assemble a structure or maybe one that could herd the krill. He said that he was not sure what the exact robot mix should be, but he suggested they work with the Swoshians to see what they wanted to do.

Bram smiled and reminded them that their work and apparently his supporting decision had been on exhibit on their Swooshian visit one thousand years into the future. It was the communication tower that rose a good thousand feet into the air above Swoosh's ocean surface.

Additionally, they should have spotted the various Swooshian Fold bubbles that were recording the Fold bubble they were in. He said that the recording Fold Bubbles had a distinct Swooshing shape that looked much like a sea lionfish with a center camera where the mouth would be located and lights where the eyes would be. He said that he had the scenes captured and stored on the recordings he had for that trip. They should look at the scenes. He admitted that at the time he had not seen what he was describing but he had reviewed the video multiple times since their return.

Both Mallica and Gerry said they would love a copy of what had been captured on that trip.

Bram looked down at his computer and a moment later said that the information was sent to them. He suggested that they move slowly and make sure the Swooshians were leading the way because the capability they were proposing would be a significant step up in what the Swooshians would be able to do. It could throw off the balanced way of living that they had enjoyed for centuries.

Mallica said that they would make sure to ask the Swooshians to thoroughly think through each change idea.

Bram smiled and congratulated them on their upcoming good work.

Gerry shook his head and said that he would never get use to how knowing the future affected what he was choosing to do in the present.

Bram voiced his support to the fact that he did not think there was a way to get used to it.

Linda called in and asked if she could come in and work with him to lay out his two-week calendar.

Remi got up and said that now it was time for him to get to work on his own stuff and that he had no desire to listen to Linda load Bram up for the next two weeks.

That statement made Bram think about the calendar and how time was being kept on Mataia. He knew that a day was slightly longer than on Earth and the year was about the same. However, he needed to have the Mataian time and calendar reviewed and made Mataian.

Linda began by saying that almost every team was asking for his review. She wondered if there was a better way to handle his time.

Bram nodded and said that he would like to get Erica back into the project management role and let her review the progress of various teams and filter what he should be involved in.

He empathized with the lack of confidence that the teams were experiencing. He suggested that each team also set up a regular session with Dr. Windal to share their doubts and concerns. He did not think the work would get easier, but the team members needed to develop a way to check their progress that reinforced what they were doing or thinking about doing.

Linda asked him how she should handle the requests coming to her.

Bram suggested that they agree to a request filtering approach using at least the four kinds of filtering.

A request that had a clear objective and goal that needed his input.

She would ask:

- When the project was ending.
- For the meeting objective.
- For the critical time element associated with it.
- If the request could be delayed for a short period.
- If an open time on his two-week agenda fit their need.
- If the review was on an effort about to be done.

Linda said that what he was suggesting was very similar to her approach. She liked the fact that he had clarified what she would say to the requester based on their needs.

Bram reinforced his confidence that she could handle all the requests. He added that he wanted to shield himself from too many of the important but smaller details that he hoped the team leaders would handle. He had learned that encouraging the leaders to make the decisions in most situations was the best choice. They were closer to the action.

Linda said that she had adjusted the next set of meetings based on the new criteria and would get them on his calendar when she got back to her desk.

Bram suggested she do that after lunch and the two of them should go to the cafeteria in the Main Work Center and enjoy lunch with Pat, Amy, and any of the rest of the team that might be there.

Linda said that she would love to do that. She confessed that she had not gone there for lunch since she had moved to Mataia because the staff that Chef D'Carluca had put in the Fold Work Center cafeteria put a mean menu out almost every day. She wondered if the Main Cafeteria fared any better.

Bram confessed that his experience was the other way around, he ate very often in the Main Cafeteria because Pat worked out of the Main Mataia Work center. He would have to ask the two to alternate lunch sites so he could enjoy both cafeterias. He went on to say that he enjoyed his breakfasts at the Fold Work Center Cafeteria and knew all the kitchen personnel. A few of them had been Marine guards at the compound on Earth.

Linda commented that it was a little strange to be working with and around all the Marines now turned Mataian civilians. She said that they seemed so young and made her feel a little old.

Bram chuckled and simply replied that he was a member of the old age club.

When they arrived at the Main Cafeteria Pat and Amy were sitting and discussing the latest home placements and central park completions.

Ripples in Time

Pat commented that Bram had been surprised at their action to relocate the initial homes that they had put in place first. She had convinced him that making all the homes similar in capability was important in the long run. He had supported the move and then had complimented the two of them for making the homes self-sufficient.

Amy asked how he liked the new location, view, and the closeness to the ocean.

Pat replied that the location and the proximity of the ocean had drawn praise from Bram. He said that now his jog into work was just right, his closeness to the ocean was just right and his house was just right. He had joked that all was as right as right could be.

Bram took in the discussion going on between Pat and Amy and figured it was about his attitude to the house move that they had made.

He went through the line and selected a slice of baked ham, a mixed salad and a tall lemonade and carried it to the table.

Pat asked if he had forgotten the mashed potatoes.

Bram shook his head and said that the morning jogs into work had warned him to get in better shape.

Amy teased him by saying she had noticed how slow he was pacing himself.

Bram replied that he had not seen any helicopters passing over head.

Amy replied that she missed her red helo. She enjoyed zooming around in a Fold bubble, but it was hard to generate the thrill of skimming the surface of the ground and hearing the purr of her helo.

Bram said that she had just reminded him of sitting on the boulder with Einstein and that he was going to visit him after lunch and see how the boulder fit on Mouse Island out in the Mataian sea.

Pat asked if she and Amy might go along.

Bram said that he would love their company. He said that after lunch he was going to round up Ada and Isaac and take them along.

Amy asked how he liked the tunnel arrangement her team had added for the two mice that ran completely around the eves of the building and the home they had in the bookshelf in his office.

Bram complemented her on providing the two mice with a spacious home. It was clear to him that the two spent a great deal of time roaming around their tunnel.

He said that the favorite feature for him was the air blast cleaning system that kept the tunnels clean. He complemented Amy on the pigging system that also periodically did a thorough scrubbing of the tunnel system.

Pat and Amy returned to his office with him and once he had Isaac and Ada in hand, he led the way to the transport area. Pat grabbed a cookie to take with them and then they all got into the bubble and Folded to a spot high over Mouse Island. The island was about ten miles in circumference but was more egg shaped than round. It was in fact a desert island.

Pat commented that the island represented an action that went against the protocol they were following everywhere else. Since the island was far away from all of the rest of Mataia's mainland, they had folded everything that had been around the boulder when it was on Earth to the island. It was in fact a small piece of the Earth on Mataia.

Bram smiled and said that he would ask Einstein what he thought about the move. He then Folded to the back of the boulder and they all climbed out and got on the rock.

He let Isaac and Ada loose and they scurried down into the crack on the boulder.

A few moments later Einstein came out on the rock and was followed by his mate followed by Isaac and Ada. One small additional mouse followed as well.

Pat broke off a piece of the cookie and put it on the boulder.

Einstein took a couple of sniffs then a small bite.

Bram asked whether Mataia was an acceptable home and smiled when Einstein seemed to indicate that it was.

He then asked if there was enough food on the island. This time Einstein shook his head to indicate that there was not enough food.

Bram looked around and wondered what might be missing. He noted that Amy and Pat seemed to be doing the same thing.

He asked how often it rained on the island, were there any birds or any flying insects that might not have made it. He suggested to Amy and Pat that in the short term they put a self-filling feeder near the boulder and make sure there was both fresh water and food available. In the long term as they repopulated the Mataian environment they could study the desert more and determine what might have been missed and then determine if the missing elements could be Folded to the island.

Pat and Amy looked at each other and said that the one place they had thought they had nailed by Folding what they thought was the entire environment was showing them the complexity they faced in populating Mataia with the plant and animal life from Earth.

They both agreed that they were glad that they came along with Bram to visit Einstein.

Einstein pushed the little mouse into Bram's hand when he lowered it for Isaac and Ada.

Bram smiled and told Einstein that he would be eating better by the end of the day and that his new little one would flourish in Ada's and Isaac's kingdom. He let Einstein know that on the next visit to Ada's and Isaac's home he would get a tour of the Mataian mouse kingdom.

Chapter 15 Alien Discovery

The next morning, Bram was having a conversation with Zoe about her work when suddenly Linda came in and simply said "incoming, I couldn't stop her. Zoe drew the gun she still carried and stepped between him and the door.

Bram was surprised!

Lacy was surprised. She stopped and raised her hands in the air. She was breathing hard as she stood very still.

Zoe put her gun into the holster and asked what was so important that she would rush unannounced into the office.

Lacy then said that she had intercepted an alien message. She said that she had received an entire string that resembled the message that they had received from the Swoshians.

Bram smiled as he remembered Zuri's challenge about whether the Swooshian message was fresh or ancient.

He asked whether it was a fresh or an ancient message.

Lacy's eyes opened and asked how she could tell.

Bram asked whether it was a Fold message.

Lacy shook her head and said she was not sure. The message had come to her exploratory bubble, and it had relayed the message to her monitoring computer, but she was not sure whether it had passed through it.

Bram asked if she was able to use his computer and locate the bubble that had received the message.

Lacy said that she could. She spent a few moments and then had the bubble's coordinate.

Bram asked if she had a second bubble that could be used.

Bram called Marcus and asked for his help to send a bubble back a few hours in time so that he could determine if a message that Lacy had intercepted was a Fold message and fresh or not a Fold message and an ancient message.

Once Marcus received the exact time that the message was received and the coordinates for the bubble that had received it, he verified that it was the same a few hours earlier. He then set up the second bubble's coordinates so that it would be directly behind the bubble that had received the message.

The second bubble was in place when the message arrived, but it did not receive it.

Bram shook his head and said he was disappointed but remained hopeful that those sending the message might still be alive and exist. Decoding the message was now the important next step.

He saw the disappointment set in on Lacy's face.

He said that he had hoped it was fresh, but it was not. He went on to point out that it might be millions and even billions of years old.

He complimented Lacy on having intercepted the message and let her know that it was a great achievement even if it was old. He asked her to work with Marcus and determine the source of the message so they could know its origins and how long ago the message had been sent.

He said he would ask Mallica to work with her to set up a team to decipher the message. It was an ancient message but nonetheless it was very important for them to decipher it.

Lacy began to apologize about having rushed in unannounced and then immediately stopped. She realized that Bram had praised her for her efforts and that he never looked for an apology. She switched what she had started to say and instead complimented Zoe for the action that she had taken to protect Bram.

Zoe smiled and complimented Lacy on her quick thinking.

Bram said that he was going to the cafeteria for a snack and take a moment to think through the rest of his day. He asked if they wanted to join him.

Zoe quickly said she was in.

Lacy asked whether they could noodle on how to move forward on the translating the message.

Bram said that was exactly what he had in mind. He put in a call to Marcus and Mallica and invited them.

On the way out he asked Linda to join them.

The cafeteria was empty, but the line staff was immediately asking what they might provide.

Bram asked for a cup of strawberries, a stick of mozzarella cheese and half of an avocado.

Zoe asked for a banana with chunky peanut butter.

Linda asked for fresh apple slices that had cream cheese on them.

Lacy shook her head and commented that she needed to come with them more often for snacks. She said that she would copy Bram's request so that the other half of the avocado would not lay around and turn black.

Mallica and Marcus walked in shortly after and joined them.

Mallica congratulated Lacy on her messaged intercept.

Bram went right to the point and asked Mallica to reassemble the team that had deciphered the Swooshian message and work with Lacy to set up a deciphering meeting.

He went on to say that even though this was an old message he wanted the deciphering to be a priority for everyone involved. He asked Linda to set up a series of meetings and to make sure he was included

He asked Marcus to work with Lacy to locate the source of the message and then to send some observation bubbles to examine the source, but he did not want the source to know they were being observed.

The snack break had taken a little longer than expected and the cafeteria line was being set up for lunch when they left.

Bram asked Linda to work with Lacy to share the find with the rest of the Folks on Mataia. He wanted a positive uplifting message that would capture the interest of everyone.

Bram went into the office and opened up the small door leading to Isaac's, Ada's, and Einstein Jr.'s kingdom. A few moments after he opened the door the three came out and climbed into his hand. He had installed a call system that was at a frequency that only the mice could hear to get them to come out of their vast tunnel system.

He carried them to his desk and put them down on the glass.

Zoe brought over some cookie crumbs and put them down by the mice and let them know that it was time to answer some key questions.

Bram looked down on the new picture the was beneath the glass. It no longer was the spiral of the Milky Way galaxy, but it was the Spiral galaxy in which Mataia was located. The stars in the background were not as familiar as those that he had come to know from his time on Earth, but they were astounding and beautiful.

He smiled at Zoe's comments and then asked the mice the first question.

Was deciphering the Alien message as important as he was making it?

All three mice seemed to answer at the same time and shake their heads in the affirmative.

Bram thanked them for their answer.

He then asked if having Mallica lead the deciphering team was the right choice?

Again, he got three affirmative head shakes.

He asked whether his decision to visit the source of the message was appropriate.

For a third time he got affirmative head shakes.

He then asked if he should ask Zoe to quit carrying her weapon?

This time all three mice shook their heads in the negative.

Zoe complimented the three for being such smart mice as she put her hand down and let them climb into it.

She carried them over to the little door where the three got out and scurried into the tunnel.

Bram asked how she knew that he was done asking questions.

Zoe said that it was obvious that he had moved on to non-critical questions.

Bram smiled and agreed.

He was now thinking about a dual path of dealing with the knowledge that another Alien race existed.

He wanted to know the message and he wanted to get a firsthand look at the origin of the message.

He called Marcus and asked how long he figured it would take to pinpoint the location of the message source.

Marcus replied that he might know as soon as the day after. He had bubbles that were rapidly making their way toward the source. They were leap frogging their way almost a light year at a time. It was clear to him that the alien location was a very long way away.

After talking with Marcus, he walked down to Remi's lab. He asked Remi to set up a bubble for twelve to go to the alien home when Marcus located it.

Remi asked if he was one of the twelve going.

Bram went down the list of people he was considering. There would be at least eight counting Remi. He replied that Remi was one of the top people on the list.

Remi asked how long they would be out on this Fold.

Bram replied that he expected that it would be a full work cycle.

Remi said that the upcoming Fold would let him evaluate his new model that had a bathroom facility at the back of the enclosure. He had designed it specifically for longer Fold times.

He added that he had installed new vibrating seats, and the floor of the aisle could be turned on to act like a tread mill. The seats were in the middle but were separated by a ten-inch space that had pull up tables and refrigerated and heated chambers to hold snacks and meals.

Bram complimented Remi and asked him where it had been built.

Remi replied in the Mataia production facility that was now running.

Bram said it was great to know that Mataia now had production capability.

Remi commented that perhaps he should qualify his statement to say that the assembly was done on Mataia, but the extrusion of the shell was still being done on Earth. They had yet to develop a pollution free extrusion process.

He pointed out that it would take a long time to begin producing extrusions on Mataia. The ban on digging and using minerals from Mataia was another limitation. He had talked with Pat and Amy and had been instructed to look on Terimund for the materials. They had warned him that even there they expected to maintain the environment as clean as possible.

Bram reinforced the position that Pat and Amy had communicated.

Remi replied that he also supported them and had no problem maintaining the current approach.

That evening as he and Pat sat together, he shared his plan of visiting the alien planet as soon as the day after tomorrow.

Pat voiced her surprise. She asked if he had already invited the folks that would go with him.

He said that he had not. He wanted her to go, and he would have Linda send out the invites to Amy, Mallica, Marcus, Remi, Zoe and Eric, and Lacy. He asked Pat if there were any additional folks of which she was thinking.

Pat thought for a moment and asked about Linh and Duong.

Bram said that he would decide on the final names when Marcus shared what he had found. He expected to have initial information about the Alien planet before they departed. That information would help him decide on the final list of passengers.

Linda greeted him the next morning and asked if his work agenda needed to be changed.

Bram let her know that he wanted to have a meeting with Mallica and Lacy. He said that he wanted to make sure that they understood how important understanding the message was.

He then wanted to meet with Linh, Duong, Wang, and Zhang and get them to be thinking about how they had contributed to breaking the Swooshian message and that he wanted them on the effort to decode the recent message from another alien civilization.

Finally, he wanted time to go see the new Fold vessel that Luke and Remi had designed and built.

Linda said that she would let him know when each meeting was to take place.

Bram walked into his office behind Zoe and Eric followed him in.

The primary change of his new office versus the one on Earth was that both Zoe and Eric had desks locate on each side of the entrance door. There was a wall that blocked direct entry and the person entering had to turn left, take a few steps before entering into the room.

Ripples in Time

Zoe occupied the desk to the left and Eric had a desk on the right side.

This morning as they entered, Zoe quickly made a search of the office before sitting down at her desk. She had mimicked Bram's idea of a glass top with a picture below it. She had chosen a picture of the Mataian valley where she and Eric had honeymooned.

Eric had done something similar, but he had a picture of Zoe and himself on the beach where they had honeymooned.

Bram was pleased with the layout of the office. It was spacious and well appointed. Most of his books had been replaced by objects that he had gathered in his Fold travels. Each object had its history written on a white card that Linda had written in calligraphy. The small door to the Mouse Kingdom was an elaborate little door that Remi had presented to him. The intricate carving on the door made it a masterpiece.

It seemed he had just gotten in looking at the work that Bob, who was looking into the near future and reporting on when Linda said she was ready to share his schedule changes.

He clicked on the calendar symbol and saw the times and location for the meetings.

Linda commented that the order was based on the availability of the people he was seeking to meet with.

The order was not important to him, and he said that the times were fine.

He noted that the first meeting was with Jungfeng Wang his Cantonese speaking person he wanted on Mallica's team.

He made a quick call to Mallica and shared his intension of speaking with at least one of her team members and asked if she wanted to participate.

Mallica said that indeed she did and would join him. She asked where the first meeting was to be.

Bram said that it was at the main Mataian Work Center in about ten minutes.

Mallica chuckled and thanked him for giving her plenty of time to get ready.

Bram replied that he had learned the time one minute before her.

The Fold over to the Main Work Center made the timing possible.

Mallica commented that the ability to almost instantaneously call a meeting to take place anywhere on Mataia or on Earth made a huge difference in the ability to hold an impromptu meeting like the one they were going to.

Zoe added that it allowed meetings to be scheduled at Bram speed.

Bram knocked on Jungfeng's door and entered when he heard the come-on in.

He shook hands with Jungfeng and asked how he and his family were doing.

Jungfeng asked everyone to help themselves to drinks while he got a couple of more chairs. Eric went with him, and they returned with four chairs.

He then replied that his family was doing well. He thanked Bram for being patient with him about the move to Mataia. The fact that he could Fold back to Earth to spend time with his family had been all he needed to know. He was in love with his work and could not think about working anywhere else. He shared that he was having his longtime girlfriend checked out by the FBI.

He looked over to Zoe and thanked her for making the check happen.

Zoe nodded and said that she was personally always enthused by helping someone with their love affairs.

Jungfeng shared that the current situation was that his potential bride was in China, and it was very hard to get her cleared. He had personally taken it on himself to hire a Chinese friend who was more or less a detective to run a check as well.

Bram let him know that he hoped she would be cleared so she could join him on Mataia.

Bram asked Mallica to explain why they were meeting.

Mallica did an excellent job in briefly describing the situation and how she and Lacy planned to proceed. She shared that they were going to use their Swooshian experience to guide them on this decryption process.

Jungfeng said that he was super excited about being part of her and Lacy's team. He was fascinated that they had been able to find another alien civilization so quickly.

Bram agreed and said that it was the ability to Fold the scout bubbles to multiple location that seemed to have accelerated that situation.

He then invited Jungfeng to join him on a trip to the Alien home world.

Jungfeng immediately gave an exuberant yes.

The meeting just before lunch with Haoyu Wang the Mandarin speaker was almost a duplicate to the meeting with Jungfeng.

Bram suggested they eat lunch at the Main Work Center cafeteria and say hello to Chef D'Carluca.

Pat and Amy joined them in the cafeteria.

They were not surprised when Chef D'Carluca came to their table and offered to serve whatever Bram desired.

Bram smiled and replied that he saw that the main course was spaghetti alla vongole which was one of his favorites. He said that a serving of the spaghetti and an espresso after would make a great lunch.

Chef D'Carluca smiled and asked everyone else what they wanted. After he had their orders, he walked briskly to the kitchen area where they could hear him giving his team instructions.

Bram brought Amy and Pat up to speed and let them know that a Fold out of the Alien planet was planned for the following day.

After a great lunch they all returned to the Fold Work Center where both Linh and Duong met them in his office.

They were excited to be part of the decoding effort and were thrilled when they were invited to be part of the group that was Folding to the Alien planet.

Bram went down the list of the people that he had currently in the Fold vessel and realized he was up to ten people. He had room for two more but was not sure who the two seats should hold.

Ron Mueller

184

Chapter 16: Alien Planet

The next morning as he was preparing to go down to the Fold launch area, he got a call from Lester, who he still thought of as The General who asked if there was room for, he and Admiral Becker on the Fold vessel.

Bram said the two were welcome, but he had just heard from Marcus that everyone would be asked to participate in managing the thirty small bubbles that would sweep across the planet and get a complete visual and environmental survey of the planet.

The General said that he and Dennis would do their part.

Bram said that the two had about ten minutes to hop on board and that they had the last two seats in the back.

Bram grabbed his laptop and said it was time to go to the launch area and led the way out.

Zoe led the way and Eric was right behind him.

When they arrived at the launch area, Marcus said that Pat was already on board and that Bram should go down the right-hand aisle and sit next to her. He then called out all those sitting on the left-hand seats and followed by calling out the names in order for the right-hand seats.

Once everyone was on board, he asked them to power up their laptops and download the aps that he had sent each of them.

He then told them that each of them would be managing three observation bubbles that would make many small Folds around the Alien planet making visual recordings and taking air samples. He let them know that the bubbles were very sophisticated and would capture images in multiple frequencies so they would have a very thorough understanding of the planet.

He said that their role would be to set the elevation coordinates that he called out. It would require typing in some numbers each time he decided that the bubbles should be at a lower or higher altitude.

He then said they were going to practice three times to make sure everyone had their role in hand and mastered.

A few minutes later he said they were ready, and Bram should Fold to the coordinate that had just been sent to him.

Bram pressed the button and said Fold.

They were several thousands of miles away from the planet. It at first seemed to have no life present. From their distance the planet presented itself as a black planet that had three oceans that looked grey.

After a few moments of observation Bram suggested they get a closer set of coordinates, and he asked Marcus to make the Fold.

Ripples in Time

The next view was a thirty-thousand-foot view of desolation. From this vantage it was clear that the land was suffering from a major devastation and was mostly black with random patches of green and brown areas. There appeared to be rivers, but they appeared as grey flowing water that entered a less grey sea. There were scattered clouds that displayed a range of colors.

Everyone was silent. Marcus spoke up and said that he was launching the video bubbles and gave the high coordinates with which they should begin.

Their vessel began to make a series of Folds that kept up with the bubbles. The devastation was total but when they arrived at the coast it appeared that there was some sort of life that was struggling to survive.

Marcus stopped the Fold progress and sent his three bubbles down to get a closer look.

What they saw was a rude awakening.

There was a group of what resembled walking cats cutting pieces from a grey skinned sea animal that looked somewhat like a spoon billed platypus. The group they were observing were having to fight off a flock of what appeared to be parrot-like birds that had huge claws.

Some sort of animal that looked somewhat like a ground hog but had more of a canine mouth was sitting patiently for the periodic chunk of meat that was thrown their way.

Marcus had the bubbles scan across the horizon, and it seemed that there was some sort of village up away from the sea.

Bram suggested they continue with the scan of the world and then they would address the situation of the beings they had just observed.

The rest of the day the conversations were minimal and subdued.

The General made the comment that the Earth was a candidate for the destruction they were witnessing.

No one replied.

They absorbed the eight hours silently.

Bram had seen some areas that looked like there might be ruins of those that had once populated the land.

They were all silent as they returned and got out in the Mataia Fold landing area.

Bram suggested they all call it a day and that he would host a breakfast in the cafeteria the following morning for all of them and they could talk about what they had seen.

He then went to his office. On the way in he asked Linda to work with Marcus to set up a meeting that everyone on Mataia was to attend. They should attend in person whenever possible and that the auditoriums, Recreation Center, and the cafeteria were all places where they should gather.

Linda said she would see that everything was coordinated. Then she asked how bad was, what they had found?

Bram shook his head and said that it was impossible to describe in words and the scenes they would all see would shock them.

Ripples in Time

Once they got home Pat asked what Bram was going to do about the situation.

He replied that he was not sure, but he was going to find out how something like it could possibly happen.

He then texted Marcus that he would like to focus on the survivors of whatever holocaust had occurred. He said that after they had absorbed the horrendous situation that they found the Alien life in, he wanted to Fold back in time to just before it had all happened.

Pat said that it probably happened by accident. She said that at least she hoped so.

Bram asked her to say more.

She replied that it most likely happened when someone accidentally spilled their coffee on the keyboard of the computer controlling a nuclear missile and it got launched. Then the oppositions responded, and the response triggered the remaining rockets to be launched.

Bram nodded and agreed about it being an accident, but he did not think it was a nuclear war because the environmental stuff he saw did not indicate radio activity. He wondered about whether some other weapon powerful enough to create the destruction that they had witnessed had been developed.

He thought the fact that the planet was slow to recover had to do with the type of weapon that was used. It seemed to have turned everything into a powder or dust.

Pat asked if he planned to go back in time and see how it had all happened.

Bram replied that, yes, he was planning to do so and to record how it had happened. He felt that understanding that might possibly help them understand the situation on Earth and maybe they could take some sort of action that would save it.

Pat asked how he would intervene on Earth.

He replied that the team would need to be creative in how it influenced the key players that might be able to have influence taking a step back from the brink.

He hoped the doomsday clock could be set back a few minutes every year as they moved into the future. He said that the objective of the team would be to identify the little things that would help Earth take those baby steps back from the brink.

Pat asked what will happen at if baby steps back didn't happen.

Bram asked if she had been with him on the thousand-year trip.

Pat nodded and said that they must have been good enough that the Earth did survive to that time. She said that she would be interested in seeing what could be done for the Alien survivors.

Bram suggested that they see if they could determine what the makeup of the animal that was being harvested was and make food similar to it. He said as they got better information, they might be able to provide a more nutritious mix of food.

Pat said that she and Amy would most likely step forward and lead such an effort.

Bram asked if they could handle another project.

Pat said that she would see what they might face once they reviewed the footage that Marcus was editing.

The next morning Bram stopped at Linda's desk and asked if she had heard from Marcus.

She said that he was the first person to talk to her.

Bram asked her to contact Marcus and see where he stood with organizing the material that they had collected.

Linda called him shortly after and said that Marcus was in the viewing room and asked if Bram could join him.

Bram walked over to the new viewing room that they had on Mataia. He liked the layout, which was more spacious than the one they had back on Earth.

He and Erica had agreed that their work building and hangar on Earth would remain in its current location until sometime in the future when they were sure Folding it to some other location would not be noticed.

He walked in and immediately knew that Marcus had been at it all night.

He asked how he might help.

Marcus commented that he had used all the power of the supercomputer and finally had one massive video file that showed all of the Alien planet.

He estimated that there might be about a million Aliens still living. It appeared that at least ninety percent of them lived along the coasts of three oceans that like on Earth were between the land from the upper part of the planet to the southern part.

He said that it would take a great deal of study to get to all the details. He asked what Bram wanted to highlight to the Mataian population.

Bram asked if there were any ruins anywhere on the planet.

Marcus said that surprisingly there were only a few. He was not sure what had caused the destruction, but it seemed that there were only a few locations that had any large structures. He wondered if their population had moved off the planet's surface.

Bram said that was a possibility. He asked to see the ruins before they began to make the video they would show.

He stopped the display at one of the more visible ruins. He asked Marcus what he was looking at.

Marcus said that he was not sure. It was nothing that he had seen before.

Bram said that he thought it was a space elevator anchor point. He pointed to the anchor point and the remains of what appeared to be a container that might have been a space elevator laying on the ground. There seemed to be a pile of rubble around the anchor point that Bram said could have been a building that had crumbled.

Marcus said that he could see it now.

Bram asked how many similar ruins Marcus had seen.

Marcus said that he had lost count but there were quite a few.

Bram said that they would need to send exploratory bubbles to take a closer look at the ruins. If most of the people were living in space on city platforms there should be a few platform wreckages somewhere on the planet.

Marcus said that it would be a large project to study the planet.

Bram agreed and said that at the moment he was not sure who that might be and who was available to be on that team.

Marcus suggested they focus on the video that Bram wanted to share with the Mataian crowd.

Bram said that he wanted to start with the solar system and point out the various planets in that system and then zero in on the fourth planet. He asked if there were any other habitable planets in the system.

Marcus said that he was not sure, but he could immediately send out ten observation bubbles to the other nine planets of that system.

Bram told him to do it, and he would get Mallica to help him put together the video.

Marcus left the Viewing Center and went to the lab.

Remi saw Marcus come in and said that he looked terrible.

Marcus replied that it had been a long night, and it had not ended yet.

He asked for help so that he could send out nine observation bubbles.

Remi said he would get each one ready, and that Marcus should give them their coordinates.

It only took them a half an hour before the bubbles went out.

They then decided to go to the viewing room together.

Bram and Mallica had worked smoothly and had pieced together what they thought would be a very interesting video. Bram had left gaps in the lead in where he figured he would highlight the other planets in the system.

Marcus said that in about fifteen minutes the observation bubbles would be returning and would have video of all the planets.

Bram asked that Marcus and Remi scan the third and fifth planed and look for the ruins of space anchors.

Almost immediately Marcus let out a whoop and said he had one on the fifth planet. He and Marcus scoured the fourth planet and a few minutes later they said they had an anchor.

Bram asked for the video and then he inserted it into the spots that he had saved for them.

Marcus asked if there was time for them to review the video.

Bram said there was, and he wanted them to add music to the video.

Mallica said she had a piece and was adding it as they talked.

Ripples in Time

Bram went slowly through the video and added his take on what had happened. He described three planets that were the home of the Aliens. These Aliens lived on giant platform cities anchored to the surface with huge cables attached to a ground anchor that must have reached down toward the core of the planet.

He pointed out that three planets in the system were in the habitable zone and each had a series of cities in the sky. There must have been a fierce battle among them, and all the cities were blasted out of the sky. He knew a few of the Aliens survived on the fourth planet. At this point he did not know if there were any aliens on the other two planets.

The video then went in closer, and it first displayed the space anchor and what could be a space elevator. It then went to the coast and showed the aliens harvesting meat from an apparently large sea animal that had washed up on the beach. The grey and black seemed to make the video a black and white one but it was in color. The color of the environment was a monotone grey that covered everything.

The video approached a collection of shelters that were about three football fields from the sea and showed a group of adult looking Aliens and few much smaller ones that seemed to be young aliens. It was clear from the video and the actions of the people eating what looked like blubber that they were very hungry.

Bram then observed the passing scenery on a tour of the coast they were on. He saw similar shelters some of which appeared to be abandoned. He pointed out that so far, they only had time to view the beach they were all looking at but there were thousands of miles to study.

He ended by saying that it would take a substantial amount of effort for a team that he would charter in the near future, but he first needed to review the current staffing assignments and then charter the team.

Chapter 17 Initial Plans

Before Bram walked into the main Mataian Work Center Auditorium. Linda let him know that there was almost one hundred percent attendance. The finding of another alien civilization was of great interest to everyone.

Bram thanked her and said that unlike the discovery of the Swooshian where they met a very intelligent society of other sentient beings, this alien connection was going to weigh heavy. It was an extremely sad situation.

Bram walked up to the stage where Lacy, Marcus, Mallica, and Remi were sitting. He had kept the group on stage small. He wanted those in attendance and the viewers to focus on the video.

He quickly introduced the four and thanked them for their arduous work to get the video ready so quickly.

He warned everyone that it was a sobering video.

The video screen went white then black and Vivaldi's concerto in A minor played for ten seconds before the first scenes of the Alien solar system came on.

Bram's voice was dubbed over the music that continued playing. He explained that there were three planets that seemed to have been populated. He explained that they had only visited the fourth planet. The picture zoomed in, and the dead dark grey surface of the land filled the large screen. The scene then went to a coastline where the incoming waves were not blue as on Mataia but a distasteful grey that spoke of some sort of pollutant similar to the ash from a wood fire. It was camara panned across the ocean that was almost the same color as the land.

The music and Bram's sobering flat voice had the viewers in the auditorium very quiet. The silence was deafening.

Bram raised his voice and said they were looking at, "the remains of an advanced alien civilization that had destroyed itself."

He was silent as the scene did a close up of the Aliens and the work, they were doing to harvest the fat and meat from the dead beached animal that looked somewhat like a huge platypus but with the skin of a shark.

Then the scene changed. The video panned out to show huts visible from the beach. It then zoomed in to the area around the huts and very hungry people roasting the meat over an open fire. It was clear how hungry they were by their gaunt appearance, and they were eating some of the fat directly.

Ripples in Time

Several of the smaller aliens that Bram said were probably children were being given food by those closest to the fire.

The video took a quick tour around the planet and focused in on several space anchors. Bram explained that the only structures that had been found on the planet were the anchors. He said he believed the Aliens had moved off the three planets and were living on platform cities in the sky.

He ended by saying that the war they had fought had reduced them to somewhere around a million people on the fourth planet. He stated that there might be additional survivors on the other two planets and the team that would be formed to study the alien worlds would first see if there were additional survivors.

He then announced that the study of the Alien planets, providing food for the survivors and potentially rejuvenating the planets would be the work of a team that he would form in the coming days.

He let the audience know that separately he was immediately setting up a small team to provide food for those they had discovered.

There was a polite clapping, but it was clear that those in the audience had been emotionally affected by what Bram had shared.

The next morning Linda said that she had received more than a dozen calls from people volunteering to feed the Aliens.

Bram went into the office and looked over the list. He selected two former Marines. One had been a cook, and one had been in logistics. He let Linda know to ask them to come in for a quick interview.

He had no sooner hung up when he received a call from General Tilson and Admiral Becker who were in the General's office at the Main Work Center.

They wanted to volunteer to lead the Alien project. They said that they were the most qualified two people to evaluate what had happened.

Having them volunteer was what Bram needed. He felt the two were underutilized and would do an excellent job in analyzing what had transpired. He would guide them in the use of negative Fold capability to actually see what had transpired. He knew that their military history would allow them to understand what and how such an apocalyptic event had happened.

He asked to meet with them to set up a team charter, agree on the strategy, and get a work plan established.

He let them know about the two former Marine personnel that he was putting in place to immediately feed the Aliens and asked them to consider the two for the Alien research team.

The General asked for their names. He commented that Bram had chosen two good people.

A short time later Linda announced the arrival of the two people that he was going to assign to feed the Aliens.

Bram welcomed them in. The two looked over at Eric and Zoe, then at him. He explained that the two were his bodyguards that refused to quit.

He then asked if they wanted anything to drink or to snack on. He asked each of them to share their background and what made them volunteer to take the lead in feeding the Aliens.

The female ex-Marine began by stating that she was Gwen Southerly who had been on a logistics assignment in the Marines. She shared that she was emotionally affected by seeing the aliens struggling to survive. She said she had grown up in a very poor family and had often, just before the day that her parents got paid, only ate peanut butter on day old bread. She had never been as hungry as the aliens she had seen but she knew how it had felt to her when she was young. She felt that her logistics experience in the Marines and her personal background should qualify her for the task of making sure the aliens got fed.

He thanked her for sharing her personal experience.

He asked the second volunteer to share his reason for volunteering.

"I am Will Faterly. I grew up in Wisconsin to a middle-class family. I had a great childhood and then in High School I was a first-string football player, and I wrestled as well. I joined the Marines, went to culinary school, and became a certified cook. I am currently working for Chef D'Carluca and taking the Chef's training classes he is giving. I am planning to become a chef in a couple of years.

I figure that feeding the aliens will give me a deeper perspective of what a Chef should be considering as he develops new dishes.

He finished by saying that his background uniquely qualified him to be on the team that fed the Aliens.

Bram thanked them both and let them know that they both had the job, and he was recommending them to be on the longer-term team that would study the Aliens.

He asked them if they had any questions.

Gwen asked if the leader for the Alien Study Team had been selected.

Bram smiled and said that there would be two people sharing the lead role. One would be General Tilman, and the other would-be Admiral Decker

Will let out a quiet whistle. He commented that he would have to work up his courage to work directly with the General.

Bram suggested that he approach the assignment as an equal. They were all on new ground and no one had any pre-knowledge.

He suggested they get with Marcus to understand how many care packages needed to be organized and positioned. He went on to say that they should also work with Marcus on sending the care packages to the coordinates that he provided. And that they should also work with Pat and Amy to determine what the care package should contain.

He asked the two to act proactively to know how much, how often, what kind of food and to where food should be folded. He said they should work within their team to see if there were survivors on the other two worlds that might need food as well.

Gwen looked at Will and said that they had their hands full.

Bram agreed and said they should spend their next couple of hours putting together a plan and then review it with Marcus, Pat, and Amy by late afternoon and have food going out by the end of the workday.

They both stood up and gave him a salute.

Bram smiled and loudly said, "Hurrah."

Once the two had left the office, Zoe commented that it seemed hard for the Marines to transition to a less structured life.

Bram said while he agreed with her, he felt that the instilled Marine discipline would serve them well.

Shortly after the two left, Linda called Bram to let him know that the General and the Admiral were both standing at her desk asking to meet with him.

Bram replied that he was not ready for a serious meeting with them, and he was planning to go to the cafeteria for a morning snack. They were welcome to do the same and then afterwards they could get into the serious work.

Linda replied that she would let them know.

Bram stood up and signaled Zoe and Eric to lead the way.

After returning to Bram's office, Lester, and Dennis, as the two asked to be called, shared their initial Charter, their strategy, and their plans.

Bram was pleased that the two had already taken a big step in organizing the Alien Study Team. He complimented them on the great start. He then suggested they determine when the war had occurred and if recent enough, they should seek any survivors that remembered the war. He also suggested that one of the initial actions was to locate all the survivors and make sure they had food. He asked them to remain as invisible as possible until they were ready to engage the survivors. Bram then asked them to lead the deciphering of the Alien message and to learn their language.

Lester smiled and commented that Bram had just doubled their work, and they would need to go through another cycle of integrated planning.

Bram nodded and responded that studying the aliens was a lifetime project. He was interested in how they had destroyed their civilization, but he was just as interested in guiding the survivors back to a state where they were growing and flourishing.

Dennis commented that he and the General had zoomed in too close to the battle events and needed to take a step back and look at the bigger and longer-term situation.

Ripples in Time

Bram volunteered to teach them how to use the ability in the Negative Fold area to go back in time and view the events that led up to the doomsday battle. Those learnings would be valuable for all of them, and it might affect how the team dealing with Earth should be influencing politics and impacting the economic side.

Lester thanked Bram for his input and said that the two of them would get back to him after they organized their team.

Bram asked the two to accept the two Marines, that he had just sent off to get the feeding of the Aliens organized.

The General said that Bram had select well and that they were on the Alien Analysis Team.

Bram suggested that they try for the following week to get a trip back in time to view the Alien civilization before it destroyed itself.

Dennis stood up and said he was pumped and ready to go and that the meeting had given him the same feeling as when he had graduated from the academy.

Bram smiled and said that he was constantly getting reenergized by the work going on around him. He commented that he had once worried about running out of challenging things to do but now he was worried he would never be able to accomplish all the things he could see needed doing.

The General let out a "Hurrah," and everyone in the room echoed it back.

After the two left the office. Zoe commented that everyone she talked to seemed to have the same viewpoint about the fact that the atmosphere on Mataia was a positive one of discovery, growth, and personal enjoyment in what they were doing.

Bram responded that it was great to hear that what he had hoped for was being experienced by those around him.

That evening as he and Pat were sitting with each other on their dual recliners, he asked her about her experience on Mataia.

She smiled and replied that it felt like a comfortable, safe place and that the people were into following the new Mataian Constitution that began with, "Treat others the way you wish to be treated."

She reminded him that they now knew those words had been put into the constitution in their time and that it was still in the constitution one thousand years in the future.

Bram nodded and agreed that it was great to know. He said that he was going to spend a significant amount of time with the General and Admiral to learn what happened to the Alien civilization.

He asked that she and Amy spend some time with that team and see if their terraforming knowledge might be applied to the three Alien planets. He hoped that with their knowledge and utilizing the negative Fold capability they would be able to re-establish the three planets.

He suggested they train team members in actually carrying out the re-establishment role because he saw it as a big and long-term effort.

Pat agreed and added that she and Amy had their hands full adding Earth life to Mataia. She said she wondered if they should also consider adding life from Swoosh and now from the Alien worlds.

Bram suggested they get done with their current effort before expanding it to looking at other life forms.

Pat said that she agreed that it was too early to expand their Mataia transforming work.

The next day Bram spent some time with Marcus and Eric to organize their involvement in the study of the Alien worlds. He wanted to get them ready for a significant amount of work in determining specific coordinates on and around the Alien world.

Marcus suggested they set up some algorithms that asked for the time, the location, and the altitude that someone wanted to put a specific bubble.

Bram thought that would be a good idea but pointed out that the two needed to consider training the users of the algorithms. There were no experts on any of the teams and the new team would most likely have the lowest capability as they began their efforts.

Eric spoke up and said that he would enjoy writing that algorithm and presenting it as an App that could be on a person's computer or phone. He wondered what other teams could use some Apps that might simplify what they were doing and improve overall efficiency and effectiveness.

Bram said that Eric had a good idea, but he should focus on the Alien team before doing any work for other teams.

Bram then asked Marcus to determine the coordinates for a series of Folds back in time to a coordinate that put a bubble close enough to the three planets to get pictures with good resolution of the surface of each of the three planets. He said that he wanted to be able to see the plant life, the cities anchored to the surface of each planet and if possible, views of the oceans. Later he wanted to send bubbles into the oceans to get a sense of what the sea life might be like.

Marcus volunteered that he had bubbles that would go back in time and collect samples and perhaps capture fish and animals for transport to the future.

Bram replied that the Alien Analysis Team would most likely take him up on that capability. He on the other hand wanted to take the General and the Admiral for a firsthand look at the earlier situation.

Marcus said he would have a series of coordinates available by the next day.

Bram thanked him and said he was off to meet with Mallica and her team trying to break the Alien code and learn the language.

He listened to Mallica bring him up to date about her team's effort.

After a few moments, he stopped her and said that they were missing a key piece that would significantly accelerate their effort.

He suggested that her team take a trip back in time and visit the alien planets and learn their alphabet and the language firsthand. Maybe they should find a school and send in some tiny observation bubbles into a classroom and learn the alphabet, the language and the form of writing that might be in use.

He pointed out that the information they surfaced needed to be shared with the new team that had been established and was being led by the General and the Admiral.

Mallica replied that things were, as always, moving at Bram speed. She said that she and the team would immediately accept his approach, and they would coordinate with the new team.

Bram thanked her and said that once again he needed to get home and relax so that he could keep up with all the good work that was being done by all the teams.

Ron Mueller

Chapter 18: The Way it Was

Marcus sent the miniature recording bubbles back in time to the coordinates of the three Alien planets.

Bram had decided to give everyone the opportunity to view the three Alien planets before the destruction. He had arranged with the IT folks to make the videos for the three planets show up on screen side by side and accessible on the computer as well as on the viewing screens that were in most offices.

The recording bubbles were being folded so they would go around the planet. Marcus had determined the height of the ground anchored cities and had set the recording bubbles so they would pass about a thousand feet above them.

Bram was impressed with the control precision and asked Marcus how he had been able to do so.

Marcus confessed that Eric had figured out how to get the supercomputer to be constantly adjusting the height as time passed. He said he was glad that Eric had chosen to work with him otherwise he would still be trying to figure out how to control the viewing bubbles.

Bram looked over at Eric and commented that he was too smart to be an FBI bodyguard.

Eric smiled and replied he was glad to have gotten the right bodyguarding assignment.

The three planets came into view on the screen and the Viewing Room went silent. Each of the planets had a different appearance as the bubbles approached.

The third planet seemed like one large desert with a few oasis-like spots distributed randomly around. It was what one would call a desert world.

The fourth planet had three dark blue oceans that split the land in almost three equal continents that ran from one pole to the other. The three continents were covered by lush forests and wide green valleys. Unlike Earth there were no large mountains but only some large hills.

The fifth planet was a cold planet that had two continents separated by what appeared to be frozen water.

All three planets had cities in the sky. The cities were all located towards the top sides of the planets. All the cities were covered by some sort of clear material that formed a bubble over the structures inside. It seemed that the Aliens built each of the cities to be the same size. There were only twelve cities on the third and fifth planet. On the fourth planet there were in excess of one hundred cities. It was clear that the Aliens were spreading their civilization out and utilizing the two planets that were nearest them.

Ripples in Time

Bram asked if they could get one of the recording Fold bubbles to go into one of the city enclosures.

Eric said he thought he could do it but wanted a moment to check the calculation of the coordinates he needed to use.

Then the center screen displayed the inside of one of the anchored cities. It displayed a city not unlike New York that was made up of many high-rise buildings. It was clear there were no vehicles, and that transportation was by moving walkways that moved at different rates. There were green areas evenly distributed around the city. The city had roughly a five-mile diameter. Eric commented that he had given the computer an estimate of how many beings would live on each floor of the high rise building and had gotten an estimate for the number of people in the city as thirty-five million. That meant that the initial estimate for the number of Aliens on the planet was roughly three and a half billion people.

Bram asked for a close up of a statue that caught his eye. The bubble went up to it and they were able to see that it was a statue of planets circling a star. The names of the planets were engrave on each of them.

They were not able to understand the names, but they got the lettering associated with the star and the planets in that system.

Bram looked over to Mallica and said that as soon as she learned the Alien alphabet he would like to know the names of the star and the planets in that system.

Mallica replied that she had already scheduled her visit to the Alien school and would very soon be able to give him what he was asking for.

Marcus said that the quick tour was over and that he would work with the Generals and the Admirals of the Alien Study team to schedule similar future update videos.

Bram smiled and thanked Marcus and went on to say that there was only one General and one Admiral leading a team to study the Aliens. He asked the two to share their thoughts and to make any other comments or request they might want to make.

General Tilman stood and said that he was finding it hard to get anyone to call him Lester or Les and he didn't mind being referred to as the General, but he hoped that over time he would earn at least the name Les.

He then added that he and his longtime friend Admiral Becker, who would like to be called Dennis or Denny, felt privileged to lead the team to study and understand the Aliens and what had occurred. He looked over and asked "Denny" whether he had more to add.

The Admiral stood up and said like his friend Les, he wanted to be called by his given name, Dennis. He went on to say that they had only been at it for a day, and it was very early on a journey that the two of them figured would take most of the rest of their lives. He said that the tour they had just taken had solidified his desire to help all three planets recover to where they had been before the Aliens destroyed their beautiful planets.

He shared that the footage that they had seen of the survivors was the priority and with Bram's push they already had two Marine volunteers preparing food packages that would go out to the alien survivors. The team was in need of at least twelve talented players. He asked for anyone interested to step forward, they were all wanted. But anyone coming forward only stood a chance of getting on if they referred to him as Dennis or Denny and to his friend as Lester or Less.

The last statement earned him a round of clapping as he sat down.

Bram thanked "Lester and Dennis" for stepping forward to lead the Alien Research and Restoration Team or the "ARRT." He smiled and said that he expected that team to paint a masterpiece that would make everyone on Mataia smile.

He was not expecting a Mona Lisa but a restored green landscape with the Aliens enjoying an outing that was framed by a blue sea.

Lester stood up and said that he would need to get a painter on his team so he could satisfy the Fold dreamer.

Bram smiled and said that yes it seemed like a dream at the moment, but he was certain that just as they had figured out how to move the Swooshians to a new water world they would put the Aliens on a path to a bright future.

He looked over at Lacy and said that she needed to wait a few months before discovering any more Alien messages because at the moment she had given them all the work they could handle.

He then said it was time to get back to work.

Pat stood up and quietly said that it was lunch time, and they should get to the cafeteria before it was packed.

Bram followed Pat and Amy who were leading the way to the main cafeteria. He was not as familiar with the way as when he was at the Fold Work Center. He knew that Chef D'Carluca would be doing something special, so he decided to quickly get the main course from the serving line and go sit down.

It was not long after that Chef D'Carluca came to the table and said that he had a most delicious treat he wanted Bram to try.

He had one of his helpers roll out a cart with a covered dish. He lifted the lid and pointed to an all-white frosted cake. He explained that it was a pineapple-banana spice cake with cream cheese frosting. He thought it was one of his better creations and would like to get the opinion of those willing to try it.

Bram took note that by the time the cake had been shared, there was nothing left.

Everyone commented on how good it tasted.

Chef D'Carluca smiled and commented that nothing was too good for everyone on Mataia.

Bram thanked him for giving him a treat and invited him to come to the kitchen in the Fold building where he could prepare his next delicious meal or desert.

Chef D'Carluca asked if the new Chef in the Fold Center building was preparing delicious food.

Bram reassured him that the new Chef was excellent and that he had only praise for the meals he prepared.

That evening as they were sitting together, Pat asked what Bram was planning with their departure from Earth.

Bram thought for a moment. Then he said he was not sure. Thomas was doing the forward history study and doing an excellent job, but he needed someone like her to assess the direction that Earth's politics and the world situation was going.

He needed forward looking eyes that could follow the thread back from the future to the present so that they could take action before a perilous fork in the road was taken.

He complemented her on the ability to do that evaluation very well.

Pat asked why he was complementing her.

He smiled and said it was because they both knew that Earth had survived out to at least a thousand years into the future. All she had to do now was identify those forks in the road.

Pat smiled and said that she would turn her focus from the past to the future.

The next day when he came in, he asked Linda to set up a meeting with Erica so he could get caught up on the departure of the Fold effort from Earth.

Erica came in a few moments later and said that she had been so busy with the Alien find that she had kept away and focused on what she needed to do.

She said that the site was down to only the homes that were visible from the highway. The other homes had been Folded to sites in Mexico and Argentina. She said that she had some very large trees planted where his house had been, and a beautiful lake made where the pool and apartment building had been.

The hill leading to the compound was now a series of trees of various sizes. The remaining few houses and the work center would be Folded out when the decision to disappear was made.

She added that she had all the trees, and any plants required to finish the park on the property. She made the point that the General had kept a skeleton crew of Marines working on transforming the Fold property into a park.

She then shared the fact that Ted was facilitating getting the property ready to present to the Dallas city. He had a lawyer friend working the title paperwork transfer.

She ended by asking how much longer the Fold facility would need to stay in place.

Bram said he was not sure. He said that Zoe was the one in charge of erasing the Fold information from any records, but she like himself had been pulled over to focus on the Aliens. The other element was the memory of any folks that knew about the Fold program and the Fold site.

He had checked with Senator Stately of Utah, who had agreed to come to Mataia once his term in the Senate ended. The Senator had said that he and David agreed that leaving Utah would be great.

He let her know that Senator Bascom of West Virginia had committed suicide shortly after losing his reelection run.

Charles Ford the science advisor that had been on the Senate Fold oversight committee would Fold up at the same time Jeffrey and his family did.

He said he talked to Senator Etaing about coming to Mataia and when he shared the fact the entire Fold program and information would disappear, she smiled and looked at him with her head to one side and said she was already forgetting who he happened to be.

So, the few people that might have known a little about the Fold program might still be around but if they were to talk about it there would be no record anywhere and they would be left wondering what had happened.

Erica asked if she should eliminate the final houses and the work center.

Bram shook his head and said they should wait one more year. Then they would decide whether to Fold the work Center to Mataia or to some other location.

Erica said that fit her plans. She wanted to get more involved in the work going on in Mataia.

Bram asked whether she would be interested in partnering with Pat in looking into the future political, social, and economic direction happening on Earth and then taking appropriate actions in the present to guide the Earth through any turmoil that might end up making it look like the three Alien planets they had just found.

Erica replied that it sounded like something she would enjoy and that she might even be good at. She said she would meet with Pat and see how they would work together.

Bram complimented her on the splendid work she had done in transforming the Fold site at Dallas and he would pull her back in when it came time to finish the job.

Once Erica left, Bram asked Linda to come into his office.

Linda came in the door as Erica left. She knew that something other than Bram's normal work was going to come on to her "to do" plate.

Bram asked her to talk to her father to get his thoughts about getting the land transferred to the Dallas city. He wanted to make sure it was low key and did not make the news.

He then asked her to set up a meeting with the General so he could negotiate a few of his Marines to finish the transformation of the Dallas Fold site. He wanted the park ready to transfer in the next few months and would like all evidence of their presence gone.

He asked to have a meeting with Remi, Luke, Lori, and Orlando to discuss the use of the existing Fold work center and warehouse. He was wondering whether a more appropriate location might be on Terimund.

He smiled and then asked if everyone was ready for lunch.

<u>Chapter 19: The Way Forward</u>

Bram asked Linda to arrange a meeting with the General and the Admiral. He made sure to ask her to use their first names.

He then entered his office and took Isaac, Ada and Einstein Jr. from their tunnel kingdom and placed them on his desk.

He told them that he needed their guidance.

He asked them if providing food was all the help that Mataia should provide the Aliens.

The three mice shook their heads in the negative.

He said asked them whether the Aliens should be helped to survive. He was pleased that they indicated that they should.

Zoe gave them some cookie crumbs and praised them for giving the right answer.

Bram then asked whether the Aliens should be provided the means to communicate with each other.

Once again, the three mice shook their heads in the affirmative.

He then asked whether they should be taught their language.

Again, the three mice shook their heads in the affirmative.

Zoe petted the three mice and complement them on their wisdom and compassion.

She asked if they should help the aliens improve the structures of their homes and to provide better clothing.

The three mice shook their heads in the affirmative.

Bram then asked if he should stop Zoe from spoiling them.

He and Zoe both laughed when the three mice shook their heads to indicate No.

After putting the mice back in their tunnel kingdom Bram commented that the last question was a test question to prove to himself that they were really answering his questions.

Eric had been watching and jokingly commented that he was now convinced that Bram had only achieved fame and fortune because he had met the right mouse out on the desert.

Bram said that he agreed because the guidance of the mice was something of which he had never dreamt.

Linda came in and let him know that the General and Admiral were on their way over from the Main Work Center.

Bram thanked her and asked her to set up a meeting with Mallica so he could see how the team working to learn the Alien language, alphabet and the shape of their characters was progressing. He suggested he meet them in the Viewing Room.

Linda replied that she would arrange it and walked out.

Bram asked if either Zoe or Eric had anything they wanted to ask the General and the Admiral. He let them know that he was going to ask the general to maintain the pretense of guarding the Fold compound on Earth for the next year. He would also like them to remove all the concrete or black top around the building and plant trees and grass on the lot area.

He asked them where he should be considering Folding the work area and hangar.

Zoe was the first to reply and said he should consider Folding it to Terimund.

Bram asked about her quick reply.

Zoe commented that she had overheard Orlando discussing the need for a facility there.

Bram said that he liked that idea and that he would engage Orlando and see what he thought of the idea.

Linda called in and said that Lester and Dennis had arrived, and she was bringing them in.

Bram went to the meeting table in the center of the office and greeted the two of them. He offered them coffee, tea, or some other drink from the refrigerator.

It was black coffee for both of them and after serving them the coffee, Bram sat down with a bottle of sparkling water.

He thanked them for taking time to meet with him and said he had three objectives.

One was to arrange for Marine guards to remain at the Fold compound at Dalles.

The second was to share his thoughts on how to lift the Aliens up from their current dismal condition to the point where they could be working together to restore their planet.

The third was that he wanted to learn more about the Alien past and to get Pat and Amy involved in using the past to accelerate the recovery of the current Alien planet.

The General said that all the objectives fit well with the thinking and discussions he and Dennis had been having.

The first objective was easy. He would ask for volunteers to continue to play being Marines. He was sure he would have no trouble getting that fifty or so people that would be needed. He would sweeten the pot by offering to pay the expenses of Fold vacations.

He asked what Bram had in mind to lift the Aliens up.

Bram replied that he would like to provide the capability and the means for them to make better shelters and better clothing. The next step would be to provide the means for the various Alien groups to communicate with each other. And the third involved both Pat and Amy Folding plants, animals from the past to the present to help the Aliens improve their environment.

Dennis commented that he liked giving the aliens the means to communicate. He asked what they were going to do about the huge quantity of ash that covered the land, was in the seas and even in the air.

Bram smiled and replied that he was not sure how to handle it all. He suggested they set up an isolated processing plant that was located on the planet that had no Aliens living on it and process the ash into building materials that could then be used in the rebuilding. They could also place several filtering plants in the ocean to remove the ash from the water. He had no suggestion about cleaning the air.

Lester said he liked the two ideas and would have his team work on the details. He added that the air would most likely clear as the amount of ash on the land was reduced. He would have the team locate where the winds were the strongest and begin removing ash in those locations.

He commented that the level of activity would be hard to be kept from the Aliens.

Bram said that when the Aliens had reached the point where terraforming was to be introduced, they should be contacted and informed that humans were helping them recover. He added that by that time their team should all be fluent in the Alien language.

He was not sure what the Alien reaction would be, but he felt that the ARRT team would be able to set up the situation that would ensure a positive outcome.

The General agreed that they should take the critical steps first and worry about Alien reaction later. He figured that they should at least learn what the planet was referred to by the Aliens and what they called themselves.

Bram nodded as said that he was meeting with Mallica later in the day to see how her team was progressing in deciphering the message and in learning the Alien alphabet. Her team would help the ARRT team to get a better understanding of the Aliens.

He suggested that ARRT enroll Mallica and her small team and have them extract the history of the alien population.

Both the General and the Admiral said they would love to have Mallica join their effort. They both commented in how pleased they were to get the help of everyone that had so far stepped forward. It allowed them to keep the permanent members of the ARRT small at the beginning. They felt that the team should grow as the actual implementation of the improvement work went into place.

They asked how they were going to continue to recruit people to come to Mataia.

Bram thanked them for the question and replied that he needed to take up that subject with Erica, Elizabeth, and Melisa. Erica was ready for new work and was a great recruiter. He was not sure how they would attract new blood but figured the three of them would come up with the way.

The General agreed and said that one of his Marines had been a recruiter for several years and might be of help.

Bram asked the General to connect that ex-Marine with Erica.

Ripples in Time

The General and Admiral both thanked Bram for getting them focused on how to handle the Alien Research and Restoration Team. In the very near future, they would contact him and schedule a review of their plans.

Bram thanked them and wished them a productive day.

Bram was quiet for a moment and then asked Zoe and Eric if they had any friends that they thought might be interested in moving to Mataia.

Zoe nodded and said that she had several and she was sure that both Bob and Thomas would have friends that would welcome the opportunity as well.

Eric said he like the idea of recruiting friends and maybe they should include the family members of those friends.

Bram agreed. He said he would work with Erica to set up a recruiting process so they could recruit people in a way that introduced new people into the Mataian society in a smooth even pace. It was clear to him that they needed many more people than they currently had.

Linda called him and gave him the ten-minute warning that he was scheduled to meet with Mallica and her team next and that the meeting was in the Viewing Room.

Bram got up and said that he thought the meeting might be interesting.

Eric said he thought it might because he had been in her Swooshian language class and Mallica was one of the few people that worked almost at Bram speed.

When he entered and Mallica began talking to him in a language that was very singsong but seemed to have an outward flow of air he knew that she had broken the code. He saw a strange cube enclosed in one of the retrieval bubbles and figured she had also retrieved an alien artifact. Linh and Duong were sitting with their Chinese friends, and they were all smiling and provided the rest of the positive atmosphere in the room.

Mallica said that going to the Alien School had given them all about a sixth-grade education. They had learned the name of the planets, the name of the city where the school was located. They had also learned the name of the planets because there was a mobile with all the planets hanging on it and all cities were shown on each of the planets.

Bram asked what the Aliens were called.

Mallica commented that the word human was first recorded in the mid thirteenth century and owed its existence to the Middle French humain that meant "of or belonging to man."

That word, in turn, came from the Latin humanus, thought to be a hybrid of homo, meaning "man," and humus, meaning "earth." Thus, a human is an individual firmly rooted to the Earth.

She said that the Alien equivalent seemed to have a similar connotation. Since the fourth planet was the origin of all the Aliens and their equivalent of Earth is Kutika. So, they are Kutikans.

Bram smiled and complimented the team in naming the intelligent beings. He said he felt much more comfortable talking about helping the Kutikans. He asked that the team share it broadly.

He pointed at the bubble with the cube inside and asked what it was.

Mallica shook her head and said that she did not know. She went on to say that the team had translated the Kutikan message, and it was a forlorn one saying that their world was coming to an end and that they had put all of the history of their race on to an information cube and had launched it toward their star in hopes that some intelligent race would make it to their system in time to intercept the cube and learn about a race that had achieved a marvelous way of life but had not learned to get along with each other.

Mallica said it was the story of Superman where his parents had sent their child toward Earth to give him a chance to survive but in the case of the Kutikans they only had the ability to preserve their history.

She had worked with Marcus to send out a capture bubble that had retrieved the history. She said that he and Eric ginned up a piece of software that guided a bubble to the cube. He was able to calculate how far the cube had traveled and from the speed of the cube and the location of the third planet they were able to determine that the destruction had taken place about one hundred Earth years ago.

She said that Linh and Duong had contacted Remi who had demonstrated that he could figure out how to power up almost anything and had asked him for help. Once the meeting was over, they were going to take the bubble to him and let him try to figure out how to power it up so they could retrieve the history of the Kutikans.

Bram said that Remi would most likely get it powered up and they should consider asking Marcus to figure out how to extract and copy the information. He commented that Marcus had become a master at leveraging the supercomputer to investigate other computers.

Mallica said she would certainly engage him.

Bram asked Mallica to learn what kind of food was eaten by the Kutikans. He asked her to get a wide variety of food samples and bring the samples back to the present. He would contact Marial in the far future and see if he could get one of the food generators and set it up so the surviving Kutikans could eat food that they would have eaten had they lived before the destruction of their worlds.

Mallica said that she would make that a priority and by the end of the week she would have as large of a food sampling as possible.

Bram said that he was going to see if Chef D'Carluca wanted to get involved. He could learn how to use the food generator and perhaps calibrate it for what he prepared and then send the settings to the future so that his creations could be duplicated in the far Mataian future. He could also learn how to prepare the food that the Kutikans used to eat. Once he did that, The General and Admiral could get duplicate food generators built and distributed to the surviving Kutikans. This approach would greatly accelerate giving the Kutikans a diet that would sustain them in a healthy way.

Mallica smiled and said that the Kutikans were about to experience the Bram speed at getting them back to a place where they would be enjoying their lives.

Bram nodded. He said that he would like to be living when the Kutikans established their first city in the sky.

<u>Chapter 20: Primeira</u>

A few days later he was meeting with Castor and Donna. He had asked them to give him a tour of the dry planet that they were figuring out how to transform.

The tour began with the bubble looking down at the huge pile of dirt that had been Folded there from Mataia by Pat and Amy.

Then it went out around the planet. He was surprised by how dry it was. It indeed was a desert world. There were quite a few oasis like water holes that had plants around the edge. The biggest plants he had seen so far were bushes that topped out at about two feet. There seemed to be small shrimp-like creatures swimming in the water. He asked if the creatures had been studied and received a no.

There were three very large lakes that were about the size of the Great Lakes, but Castor said that all the lakes were only twenty feet at their deepest. This meant that any slight breeze raised fairly large waves that sucked the water out from behind and bared the bottom of the lake. Then the water would flow back, and the lake would level out again. This seemed to have kept life from developing in them.

Donna pointed out the large amount of Mataian dirt that was neatly piled up in one spot. She said that it was really very good dirt as compared with the rest of the world that it had been deposited on. However, they were still trying to figure out how to use it.

Bram asked whether they had yet named the planet and got the reply that they had several candidate names and they wanted his input at to which name they should pick.

He asked for the list and got; Storskal, Dorren, Paaaole, Esteril, Pulvis and Miska. Bram laughed and asked what the two had been drinking when they had come up with the list.

Castor said they had gone online and researched names for dry land and desert.

Bram then rattled off several suggestions: Trezo, Triu, Tertia, Terimund and Trecera. He was aware that he and several others were referring to the planet as Terimund.

This time it was Castor and Donna that laughed and the said that Bram was throwing out different versions of three.

He said that indeed he was. The planet they were going to populate, and transform was the third dry planet.

Castor said he disagreed. He pointed out that the Earth and Mataia were eight percent water whereas the planet he and Donna had been cast out on was ninety percent desert. It was one of a kind. It should get a name such as: Prima, Primeira, Primisa, Primera.

Bram smiled and said that he liked Primeira because it was indeed one of a kind.

Castor let out a "Hurrah" and he and Donna repeated it three times.

Bram suggested that the two work with Pat and Amy to determine where they should start the transformation process.

He said that he had an idea how to stabilize the lakes. They could put in water breaks across the lakes and use the energy of the water passing through them to both generate electricity and control the size of the wave traveling across the lake. Then they might be able to populate the lakes with some rugged fish and plant life.

He then asked if they might be able to utilize the hangar and work center that was currently on Earth at the Dallas site.

Both Donna and Castor asked if he had someone monitoring them because they had been discussing how they could establish a work center on Primeira but thought they were daydreaming.

Bram asked how soon they could use such a facility.

Donna asked how soon it could get Folded into place.

Bram said as soon as they determined the optimal location and worked with Pat and Amy to get the footings excavated. They should work with Marcus to determine the Fold coordinates.

Castor said that he and Donna had already pick a location by the up-wind side of one of the lakes.

They would make getting with Pat, Amy, and Marcus a priority.

Bram said that they had just set the timing for the total disappearance of the Fold community from Dallas.

He was going to leave the meeting and work with Erica, the General and Ted to arrange for the final Dallas site final folds.

He asked if they were contemplating having people live on Primeira.

Donna replied that they had talked about it. They thought that getting firsthand knowledge about the weather, changes in the conditions of the environment, doing analysis of the water, air and land would be enhanced by having people living on Primeira.

Bram said that he agreed with them, and they should work with Amy and Pat on developing the living areas since the two of them had city planners on Earth that they were working with. He suggested they also establish Fold transportation on Primeira.

He would make sure they had adequate funding for their team.

Donna and Castor thanked him for helping them name the planet and for inspiring them as how to proceed.

Ripples in Time

Castor said that he had a ditty, though it was not necessarily pretty. He held up a note and he and Donna chanted.

> Thought we were lost in the desert.
> No water, no life, nowhere to go.
> Lost in the desert with nowhere to go.
> Hot sun, hot sand, hot water, hot damn.
> Wham, Bam and then there was Bram.
> Wham, Bam and then there was Bram.
> Not serving ice cream but serving a dream.
> A dream, a life, the way to survive.
> A dream, a life, the way to survive.
> A place to live, a place to work.
> And he made sure we would not go broke.
> Wham, Bam, Thank you Bram.

The two stood up and left at a fast walk reciting their ditty.

Bram smiled and went back to his office.

Linda asked what he had done to get Donna and Castor so pumped up.

Bram smiled and said that it was a mystery how he sometimes did almost nothing to get folks excited. In their case he had loaded them up with a lifetime of work.

He asked Linda to set up a joint meeting of the General, Erica, Melisa, and Ted. He said that she was welcome to sit in.

Linda asked what the focus of the meeting was about.

Bram said that it was the elimination of all trace of the Earth Fold Facility.

Linda said that she would arrange it, and she thanked him for the invitation, and she planned to sit in.

Bram went back into his office. He asked what Zoe and Eric had thought about the meeting with Castor and Donna.

Eric said that he was ready to go jogging off with the two of them. It had been a very up lifting session. He was now excited to work with them to get their buildings and homes Folded into position. He was going to ask Marcus to let him be the primary person to do the Folding of the buildings into place.

Zoe commented that she had also been energized. She said that eliminating all traces of Fold on Earth had gotten accelerated and she was very interested in moving on. She was now interested in working with Amy and Pat in helping restore Kutikan to its former glory.

Bram said that he was also interested in focusing a good portion of his effort in getting the Kutikans back to living a life that let them develop.

He said that he was going to ask some questions of their little advisors. He walked over to the little door and rang the doorbell and opened it. A few moments later the three mice came scurrying out and got in his hand.

He placed them on the desk.

Zoe came over and gave them some cookie crumbs.

Bram asked them if it was the right time to erase all signs of the Fold facility on Earth and got a positive head shake from the three.

He then asked if Eric should place the Hangar and Work Building on Primeira and again got a positive head shake.

The next question was if he should set up a series of trips for the people that had worked and lived on the Earth Fold compound to visit the park that their work and living area had been transformed into.

He got a third positive head shake.

He asked if Zoe should work with Pat and Amy to bring forward the past plant and animals to the current Kutikan time.

This time the mice shook their heads in the negative.

Zoe gave a little moan.

Bram then asked if Zoe should be involved in restoring Kutikan.

The three shook their heads in the positive.

He asked if she should focus on cleaning Kutikan of the ash.

The three mice gave a very energetic positive head shake.

Zoe smiled. She said it made sense. The plants and animals needed a clean environment to be able to survive in the present.

Bram pointed to the three mice as they shook their head in the affirmative. He commented that it was the first time he had seen them respond to a statement versus a question. He gave them another cookie crumb and said that he would give their advisors a break. He picked them up and put them at the door to their kingdom and watched them scurry in.

Linda said that in fifteen minutes they should be in the Viewing Room. She would have everyone online and on the screen.

Bram called Linda in and said that he wanted them to agree on the order of the meeting.

He went on to say that he was going to ask the General to get his folks ready to finish the park after Eric folded the work center and hangar out.

He was going to asked Erica to arrange the Folds of the remaining houses and to ensure that the fence to the apple orchard was in place.

He was going to ask Ted to arrange for a quiet transfer of the land to the Dallas City. He wanted the title transfer to occur at a quiet ceremony at lake side at the park. He was going to have Stetson Catering providing food and drinks.

And he was going to ask Melisa to manage the visits of any Fold community person that wanted to take a Fold Trip on a weekday to visit the park. The limit at any one time would be five people.

He would ask the General to have his folks put in a chamber where the Fold vehicle could deliver the visitors.

He asked if there was anything else that needed doing.

Eric commented that Folding out the facility would require that the power to the Hangar and Work Center was removed.

Zoe asked about the security fence around the facility and the gate.

Linda asked about the no-fly air space over the Fold compound.

Bram said that he was glad that he had held a quick meeting before getting online.

Linda pointed at the clock and said it was time.

Bram greeted everyone and let them know this was the Fold shutdown meeting that was to take place next year, but recent events had dictated a more aggressive disappearance.

He then said that each of them would play a critical role in turning the site into a beautiful park owned and maintained by the Dallas City.

He asked Ted whether he and the lawyer were ready to execute the transfer.

Ted replied that they could do it at any time. He added that the clause that offered to cover the cost of maintaining the park for the next ten years was the lever to making the transfer a quiet one.

Bram asked if arranging the removal of the no-fly zone might add some additional leverage to the deal.

Ted thought that might be more important than the maintenance cost. It would open up the sky for additional flights. He said he would work with his lawyer to add this to the transfer paperwork.

Bram then said he would like to have the transfer be a ceremony by the lake and that he would like Stetson Catering to facilitate a top end lake side picnic. He asked whether Stetson Catering was willing to do that.

Ted replied that he would only do it if the person asking would go fishing with him.

Bram smiled and said that he would love to go fishing and it was a deal.

He then asked if Erica would be able to work on getting the no-fly zone removed. He also needed to have all the power remove from the buildings being Folded out and the fence around the facility removed. The only fence to be left standing was the one separating the apple orchard from the park.

He asked if Erica could handle those items.

Erica replied that she had been using the supervisor that had initially managed the installation of the Fold power system, and he lived and loved Mataia. She said the power would be no problem. She said that if Lester supplied a work detail she would get the fence Folded out on some dark night.

She then commented that he had forgotten removing the road that led up to the compound. She would get it Folded out at the same time as the fencing. Then once again she would need help in getting the large trees Folded into place.

Eric spoke up and said that he would work with her to ensure that the Folds would take place at the times she specified.

The General said since she had correctly used his name he had no choice but to deliver the help she needed.

Bram said that he was going to ask one additional piece of work that Lester needed to supply manpower for. He would need a hole excavated where Amy and Pat could Fold a receive and transmit chamber that would be underground.

This would be the chamber where Melisa would allow four to five people who were willing to visit the park on a weekday to Fold in and out.

He asked if Melisa was willing to manage the weekday visit to the park.

Melisa said that she could and suggested just one visit per week so that it would not draw attention. She said that everyone was currently so busy that she had seen a significant drop for the weekend Fold vacations.

Bram thanked her for the heads up about the weekend vacations and said that he wanted to meet with her and figure out how to get the weekend vacations up to their past levels.

Linda asked about the team that had been originally started out as a Lacy team but had been transferred to Lester. She wondered where they were.

Lester smiled and replied that they were mostly on his current team that was focused on how to restore Kutikan. He went on and said that a couple had chosen to get under Chef D'Carluca wing and had found out that he was a tough boss. One of them had just become the Chef in the Fold Work Center and was experimenting on Bram.

Bram smiled and added that he was finding it hard to bear the pain of eating so well.

Erica commented that she had recently worked with Senator Etaing who had inquired if there might be a spot in the Fold organization for her younger brother the lawyer.

Bram said there indeed was room, but he wanted to discuss the opportunity directly with Senator Etaing's brother because there was not a traditional career spot for a lawyer. The opportunities were many. He said he recalled that her younger brother had a talented wife and two kids, and they were all welcome.

He asked that the two of them meet with Melisa to organize the approach to recruiting new people.

Melisa commented that she had multiple inquiries from a variety of people asking how they could get a friend or a relative onboard the Fold program. She added that the time to organize how to keep a slow steady flow of new recruits coming in was now.

Bram made the point that the meeting had gone past the original objectives. He asked Linda to set up two additional meetings. One to brainstorm the final disappearance of Fold from Earth. And the other to focus on setting up a recruiting strategy and process.

He thanked everyone for participating and it was now time for he and the people in the Viewing Room to go to the cafeteria and suffer their Chef's torture. He waved goodbye and cut the feed.

Linda commented that she was happy about Bram agreeing to go fishing with her Father.

Bram replied that if every bargain was as easy as that one, he wanted to bargain more often with her father.

248

Chapter 21: Weddings

Donna had reminded Bram about the upcoming Rushing River weddings and that she and Castor had both wedding parties ready. They were going to practice their wedding in the chapel on Mataia, but they were still ready to Fold to the Rushing River location for the Wedding. The folks who were Earth located on Earth would practice virtually but then would attend physically.

Mike and Mary were please to hold the wedding and pleased that once again the catering would be done by Stetson catering. They commented that the Fold weddings were keeping them in business.

The weddings reminded Bram that the fence with the laser shield needed to be removed and he would need a suitable Fold arrival and departure site near the Rushing River.

Bram contacted Ted and arranged to go fishing after the weddings. He asked if Ted was ready to list his fishing expeditions as one of the weekend Fold vacations. Ted replied that he thought it would be a great way to establish his fishing business. He asked how that could be arranged.

The answer was that he should get Melinda involved and let her set up Dallas as a Fold vacation site.

Zoe had heard the conversation with Ted and said that she was looking forward to go fishing with no gun battles on the horizon.

Bram said that such an occasion would be welcome.

She then shared the fact that both Thomas and Bob were getting to the point where they were going to be the next to get married. They both said that they wanted to be the first to get married on Mataia. They were working on getting their two brides to be cleared so they could migrate to Mataia before the wedding. They figure that would give the two a chance to experience the Mataian culture and then if there was an issue they could decide to back out.

Bram smiled and said that he was sure that both Bob and Thomas would make sure their two brides would love Mataia.

Eric piped in that he knew that the two had already set up three weekend Fold vacation each. They were hitting the locations on Earth that they knew their significant other had mentioned as places that were on their bucket list.

Bram said that those weekend vacations were a key element that had made the transition to Mataia an enjoyable one.

He would need to suggest to Erica that they get used as part of the recruiting of new people to Mataia.

Linda buzzed in and asked what he had done to get her father interested in working with Melisa to set up Stetson Fishing as part of a Dallas weekend vacation. She added that her father had said he had a new secluded river side home that would be a great purchase. It was a home built for a family of ten. The family was a well to do one and the home was gorgeous.

"I have done nothing other than agree to go fishing with him," Bram replied. He was pleased that Ted was acting so fast. He was sure that one of the catalysts was Rita, Ted's wife. She had often mentioned that she wanted him to set up a fishing business.

Linda then added that Luke had let her know about the Fishing business and that he was planning to use his weekends to Fold back to Earth and use his boat as one of those that was earning money.

Bram replied that seemed to be a terrific way to both relax and be productive.

Linda replied that Bram was having too much of an influence on her family. She then shared the fact that she was going to Fold with Melisa to Dallas on the morrow to tour the house in question. Melisa had commented that she figured she needed to move fast to get a large luxurious waterfront home.

Bram chuckled and said he agreed with her and said that he agreed with Linda that he was having too much influence on the Stetson family.

Linda replied that she was Mrs. Evender now and hung up.

Zoe asked if Linda was mad.

Bram shook his head and said that she had mentioned that she had often tried to get her father to set up a sports fishing business and had been turned down every time.

He called Melisa and asked her to find a house on the highway near to the Rushing River Resort. It didn't need to be fancy, but it should have a space where a Fold vehicle could deliver and pick up people. She might also consider making the place attractive enough to put it in her weekend vacation list.

Melisa said she would see if she could meet his request. She said that the purchase of the large luxury home on the Columbia River was almost in her pocket. She had made an offer and was meeting the Realtor and the owner when she visited. Linda knew the realtor and was accompanying her to facilitate the purchase. She said she would ask the realtor what might be available on the highway to the Rushing River.

Bram asked Melisa that if she made the purchase to contact the general and cancel the building of a Fold chamber at the park.

Melisa replied that she would do that.

He thanked her and hung up.

He asked Zoe if she knew how much Melisa's Weekend Fold vacation business made each year.

Zoe said that she had no clue.

Ripples in Time

Bram said that Melisa had let him know that the business was taking in close to three million a year. It had ten million invested in the stock market and the income that was currently coming in was at about two million each year. He said that Melisa spent several million each year to maintain each of the vacation locations.

Melissa also had the business gifting about two hundred thousand a year to a fund called the Fold Miracle Child that helped disabled kids and young adults.

He felt that he had the right person managing a well-oiled machine.

Zoe smiled and asked how the Fold Miracle child was doing.

Bram smiled and said that their miracle child was now a clamorous young woman who had just contacted her parents and let them know that she was engaged to one of the Marines who was residing on Mataia and working in Remi's lab doing analysis of materials coming from some place called Kutikan.

Zoe smiled and said that it would be good to have Zuri on Mataia and involved in an activity that interested her.

Bram agreed and he was wondering what activity there might be that would be challenging enough.

Linda came on over the intercom to say that her snoopy sister had just let her know that she had snooped out more aliens and was standing at her desk wanting to talk to him.

Bram told her to send Lacy in and that three people were eager to hear what she had to share.

Lacy came in and went to the fridge and got a bottle of water. She said that she had found the evidence of some intelligent aliens, but she was not sure what she had found. She said that the object was definitely a rocket or spaceship and was moving at close to the speed of light and headed toward a distant galaxy. She had identified the distant galaxy, and she had identified the potential starting point of the space going object. She said that she had come to see him because she was resource strapped and was looking for help in going to the objects launch location and the objects destination location.

Bram asked her if she was monitoring his office because she had arrived just in time to offer up a very unique opportunity for their miracle child that was coming home to get married and would be looking for something interesting to work on.

Lacy smiled, everyone in Bram's inner circle knew that Zuri was the miracle child. She asked who the lucky person was that Zuri was planning to marry.

Bram smiled and said that he was the Marine that had danced with her during the quadruple marriage.

Lacy said that figuring out what her team had just discovered would indeed be a unique opportunity.

Bram asked if there was anything that needed to be immediately done.

Lacy replied that she had assigned one of her team members to keep an observation bubble Folding along the same path as the spaceship so they could keep track of it but, even at close to the speed of light at which it was moving, it would be another few thousand years before it arrived at the solar system where it seemed to be going.

Bram nodded and said that she should continue to track the object, and he would work on staffing a team to develop the details of what her team had discovered.

He commented that it was now clear that other sapient life forms existed in the vast universe. They now had contact with two sapient populations. One that was as different from the human form as could be but was as intelligent and one that at a peak, was beyond what the human had achieved, had it not destroyed itself.

He went on to ask where in the discovery spectrum Lacy's new discovery would land.

Lacy replied that Zuri might tell them the rest of the story in the near future. She said she was relieved that her team could continue to focus on finding other life forms and that the follow up of the teams most recent discovery would be in good hands.

Bram said that he had to get refocused on weddings because he figured that one more would soon be added to the list. He knew that Zuri and her husband to be would most likely want to be married where they had first met.

A few days later Elizabeth came to his office and said that she was the liaison for a young ex-Marine who was afraid to go to the BOSS and asked her for her help in arranging for his wedding.

Bram smiled at Elizabeth emphasizing boss. He asked if it was the lucky guy that was marrying the person that had been their miracle child who she had coached through college.

Elizabeth smiled and said that "yes our miracle child is now a beautiful young woman." She said that the two wanted to get married where they had first met.

Bram asked if being part of a three-wedding ceremony might work?

Elizabeth nodded and said that it would be appropriate. She said that Zuri had one special request that after the wedding and the wedding dinner, she would like to go to fishing with Ted and his crew.

Bram said that fiction could not be any better than real life, he had just made arrangements to that effect with Ted. He commented that Ted would most likely say that he would be honored to take Zuri fishing as her first big step in her marriage.

He added that he was sure that Rita would insist on having a picnic in the park after the fishing trip.

Elizabeth asked who the other two getting hitched were and when was the date for their weddings.

Bram replied that Donna and Castor were the two getting married and the date was still fluid, but it was about a month away.

Elizabeth said that was close in, but doable. She said she would let, Zuri and her husband to be, Weylan know. She then added that the two wanted him to preside over their wedding.

Bram said he would be most honored to marry them. He then added that he would handle setting up the fishing trip. He asked if the two had selected a honeymoon location.

Elizabeth said the two were thinking about vacationing some place on Mataia.

Bram suggested she contact Pat and Amy who he was sure would come up with several suggestions and videos that would help Zuri make her choice.

Zoe excused herself for interrupting, but she wanted to share that she had been looking at the video's that Amy and Pat kept taking of the various places. They had just recently found a place where the Mataian Plate Tectonics had created one of the few water falls that existed on the planet.

She suggested that Elizabeth share that with Zuri.

She smiled and added that she wanted to make sure that the only other person who had a first name starting with the last letter in the alphabet would end up taking the best honeymoon on Mataia.

Elizabeth said she would make sure Zuri viewed Zoe's suggested honeymoon location.

Bram asked if Elizabeth would act in the same role as she had in the previous weddings.

She said that she had been asked to do so by Zuri, but she would need to see what Donna and Castor had planned.

Bram said he thought she was a shoe in.

Elizabeth nodded and said it was time for her to get going.

After she left, Bram was about to get ready to review the restoration work going on Kutikan when Zoe reminded him it was getting close to lunch time and it was their turn to go over to the Main Work Center and have lunch with Pat and Amy.

On the way-out Bram invited Linda to go to lunch with them.

Linda replied that she never missed going to lunch when it came to going to the Main cafeteria.

Bram called Marcus and Remi to let them know about the new Alien discovery and that he wanted to see if they could locate the home of the Alien. He asked if they would join him in Lacy's teamwork center.

Pat watched as Bran entered the cafeteria and commented to Amy that, by the look on his face, he was thinking about more than the wedding.

Amy asked why she though that.

Pat said if he was only thinking about the wedding he would be all smiles, instead he had a serious work face.

Bram looked over at Amy and Pat and smiled as he went to get his food.

Pat said that at least he had noticed them and come up from whatever the new focus happened to be.

Amy again asked how Pat knew that it was a new focus.

Pat replied that once he had organized a new focus area, he never got that deep faraway look. She was sure it was a new focus.

Bram sat down and asked how everything was going.

Amy commented that he should develop a way to clone people so they could continue to handle the work load he kept pushing at them.

Bram smiled and replied that as he recalled, everything that she and Pat were working on was work that they had each requested or volunteered to do. He added that he personally knew that self-control was extremely difficult, but it was the only remedy that he knew for her condition.

Linda laughed and said that she was pleased to learn that he was just as tough on his other good friends as he was on her.

Pat asked what was new with him.

Bram replied that the Stetson sisters were both trying to give him a hard time. The oldest was complaining about the fact that he had too much influence over the Stetson family and the other kept finding new Aliens.

Amy reacted first and asked if he were joking.

Bram said that he was not and that after lunch he was going to go to Lacy's work area to investigate it a little farther but in the long term he was going to see if Zuri would take on the longer-term investigation of the newly discovered aliens.

Pat commented that it would be a great assignment for Zuri. She added that she was really curious what Bram would discover.

He smiled and said that only the person willing to curl up with him on the recliner would learn every detail.

There was a chorus of voices volunteering to curl up with him.

Bram raised his two arms, laughed, and said he only wanted Pat to curl up with him, but he would share the details of what he found with all of them.

<u>Chapter 22: Amoral Aliens</u>

After lunch, Bram left Pat and Amy and headed to Lacy's work center.

When he entered, the work area went silent. Lacy immediately asked for the time.

Bram asked if he was arriving at an inconvenient time.

Lacy smiled and replied that someone in her group had just earned a paid Fold vacation because the work team had a bet on the time that he would come to their work area.

Bram asked if this was a standing bet or just on this day.

Lacy replied that the bet and the prize had been made on her return from her meeting with him.

Bram shook his head and said he was getting too predictable. He asked who the winner was.

Lacy turned to the person who had written down the time and asked him who had the closest time. He called out the time and one of the technicians jumped up and down whooping it up and said she was going to spend a weekend in Jamaica.

Bram congratulated her and said he would throw in a hundred for her knowing him so well.

He then asked who was tracking the new alien spaceship. As he got to her station, Marcus, and Remi both showed up and Lacy again asked for the time

Bram smiled and asked if the team always spent their work hours gambling.

Marcus looked confused and asked what was up.

Bram explained that he had just won someone in the room a prize.

When the person who had taken the time called out the winner, the person who was following the alien spaceship yelled out a loud, YES. She looked at Marcus and Remi and thanked them.

Then Lacy said there were several additional winners because the second part of the bet was that Remi would be with Marcus.

This time the person that had been logging the time read four names from the list and said they had all earned a day off or an extra days pay.

Bram asked if Lacy could afford to give anyone time off.

Lacy shook her head and said she couldn't but said that the time off would be held until there was some time available. She added that is why she had added the choice of a day's pay because they could all use a couple of extra dollars on the Fold vacations.

Bram complimented Lacy on running a fun work area then he asked the lady he was standing behind if her name happened to be Clair.

The young woman stopped and asked how he could possibly remember her.

He smiled and replied that she was one of the persons sitting by the pool on the day the three shooters had shot and almost killed one of the people at the pool. He said he had studied that situation and had learned who everyone was. He shared the fact that she had been born in Tennessee. Her mother was a technician, and her father was in the automotive business restoring, maintaining, and selling cars.

He went on to say that her family name was Alpharad, and it means queen of everything.

She shook her head and said that everything she had heard about him was true.

Bram smiled and asked what everything she had heard implied.

She shook her head and said that people claimed that he never forgot anything and knew almost everything.

Bram said that such talk was an over exaggeration and that in fact she probably knew just as much as anyone.

He asked if she knew the origin of the spaceship she was tracking.

She shook her head negatively.

He asked Marcus to back track the rocket path and see if he could locate the origin.

He asked Clair is she knew if the spaceship had passengers, and she again shook her head negatively.

He asked Remi to send a prob into the spaceship.

Almost immediately Remi said he had lost the observation bubble. It must have Folded into something solid. He said he was Folding a second one in toward the front.

It was obvious to Bram that the second met the same fate as the first one.

After the fifth loss Remi said that it seemed that the rocket was a solid and seem more like a very large missile than a spaceship.

Bram asked how large the missile happened to be.

Clair said that was something she did know. It was roughly six football fields in diameter and twenty football fields long.

Bram shook his head and said that if it was an explosive with the power of C4 they were looking at a planet killer.

Lacy said that if that was true then she and her team had bad news because they had just found three more planet killers all leading back to the same source.

Bram asked how far away each of the rockets were from the source.

After a moment someone in the room called out that the rockets were all about one light year from the source and two light years away from the targets.

Ripples in Time

Bram said that he remembered Lacy saying that the first missile was traveling at half the speed of light and that meant that the missiles were about two Mataian years from hitting their targets.

He announced that he was setting up a team to study and resolve the situation that had been discovered. It would be a separate team that he was going to call The Eliminators, and they would have two main objectives. One was to eliminate the four planet killing missiles and the second was to investigate the civilization that was so amoral that they would send the missiles to eliminate entire worlds.

He was asking Lacy and her team to get a closer look at what the four targeted planets had in common and let him know. Their primary mission remained to find additional intelligent beings and he would determine how each of the four planets would be investigated.

He then commented that they must be looking into a region of the universe that was closer to its center and older than they were. He pointed to the fact that Earth was at the edge of the Milky Way galaxy and that the Milky Way was at the edge of the Universe and traveling away from its center.

Mataia was in a galaxy almost one hundred light years closer to the center of the universe. Primeira was a light year away but at about the same distance from the center. Kutikan and the two other planets were again about fifty light years closer to the center.

He went on to say that he would not be surprised if the Amoral planet was only a few light years from the center of the Universe. He then asked what they thought might be on the side opposite from where they were looking.

Lacy smiled and replied that she would wait for him to answer that question and when he did she would ask him to share it with her.

Bram shook his head and said that they all had enough exploration that when their lifetimes were over, the next generation would wonder why they had explored so little.

Marcus spoke up and said that he had the galaxy and the solar system where the Amoran Aliens resided. He reinforced Bram's discussion by saying that it was in toward the center in what seemed to be a very old galaxy.

He suggested that they plan a visit for the next day.

Bram said that would be a good time. He asked Lacy if she planned to join in on the trip.

Lacy asked what time and where should she be.

Bram replied eight sharp and at the Negative Fold launch pad.

He then left Lacy's work center and returned to his office.

Linda smiled as Bram approached her desk and let him know that her sister had called to let her know that she was going for a ride with him the next day.

She asked who else he had in mind.

Bram replied that Marcus and Remi would be going with him. He added that he would also like to the get the General, the Admiral, and Mallica to go. He added that Zoe and Eric would also be going.

Linda asked whether she should include snacks and a lunch.

Bram said that she should since he did not know exactly how long it would take.

He looked around and realized that Remi and Marcus were not with him. He called Marcus and asked him to have the coordinates of the five planets that had been discovered with intelligent life on them.

He contacted Remi and asked him to have a twelve-person Fold craft ready to Fold at eight in the morning.

That evening Bram shared the events of the afternoon and asked if Pat wanted to ride along.

Pat responded with a negative shake of her head. She said that she and Amy had discussed the possibility of a Fold expedition to examine the new find, but they agreed that they had their hands full with the effort to provide food for the Kutikans and getting ready to bring forward the plants from the past.

Additionally, they were working with Donna and Castor to get started on getting the work center and the hangar from Earth into position and powered up on Primeira. She commented on the fact that structures would be powered up and managed just like the buildings on Mataia.

And for the short-term Mataia would be the location for the treatment of waste from the buildings on Primeira. The water use there would be processed and Folded to the top of the buildings at Primeira by some portable water preparation system that had been Folded to Primeira. The work was getting rapidly done but the list of things to do was extensive.

She shared the fact that Erica was just as swamped with the request coming from Donna and Castor. The big-ticket item was the across the lake wave breaks that he had suggested to the two of them. They felt that getting the lakes calmed would be a big step forward to getting on with terra forming the planet. She said that the two were referring to terra forming as Prima Forming.

Bram said he like the sound of the new term. Prima Forming was what it was and what she and Amy were doing on Mataia should be called Mata Forming. And what they would do on Kutikan should be called Kuti Forming and on Walelhan it should be Wale Forming and on Vultlhan it should be Vulti Forming. That way each one of the planet transformations the two of them was doing could specifically referred to and progress tracked.

Pat said that she would share the names with Amy, and she was fairly certain they would take up the names and begin reporting progress using the names. She admitted that the two of them had already gotten their actions confused because of the lack of not having clear names.

Bram said that the same was beginning to happen to him. They needed everyone to be able to clearly and easily distinguish where and what in the Universe they referring to.

He then shared the fact that the Amorans seemed to only be able to reach out some three hundred light years with their technology but evidently the technology was rigorous enough at that range to discern intelligent life. He was referring to them as Amorans because he felt their action were those of a coward and they were amoral. Their approach was not one of embracing other intelligent life but to eliminate it so they would not have to have competition in an infinitely large universe. He felt such behavior was the most despicable actions that any civilization could take. He said that he was going to ask the team that would study them whether the Amorans should be isolated and kept from using their technology in the way they were currently doing.

Pat said that by selecting Zuri to lead that team he had put the best person to determine if that was appropriate.

Bram agreed.

He then said that he wanted to set up four more teams to study the four new planets with intelligent beings on them.

Pat asked if he had team leaders selected for those teams.

He replied that he had not had time to think who was ready to lead those teams.

Pat suggested he ask the current team leaders to suggest individuals that were ready to be promoted and capable of leading the new teams. She said that she felt that asking the current team leaders would empower them and it was a good way to surface new talent.

Bram agreed and said he would put out the word after he got back from the upcoming Fold trip.

The next day as he jogged in to work he almost fell down when Zoe sang out a new ditty.

> There's dirt in Fold city.
> Amoral action, sinful and degrading
> There will be judgement in the waiting.
> There's dirt in Fold city.
> It ugly when things could be pretty.
> But Amoral actions, Judgement in the waiting
> Four victims unknowingly about to be hit.
> Being sent a wallop so devastating.
> It is Amoral action, it's the dirt in Fold City
> Action will be taken; Fold City has awakened.
> Fold city will react against Amoral action.
> There will be no dirt tolerated in Fold City.

They all entered the hangar and were surprised to hear the ditty being repeated by a chorus from other people at the Negative Fold center.

Bram knew that Pat had likely written the ditty and had sent it to Linda who had posted it in everyone's in box.

He thought about the atmosphere that was so positively charged and energized not only himself but everyone around him. He thought he would miss the jogs that he had so enjoyed on Earth when he went into work, but he now knew that he was having just as much fun on Mataia as at the Dallas site. The Dalles site that was now a lush green park for the members of the Dallas community to enjoy.

Linda asked what he thought of his greeting as he entered the hangar.

Bram thanked her for getting everyone that had made it to work involved. It had set a positive tone for him.

Linda said he should thank his mate because she had sent it over to her.

Bram said he would certainly do so. He asked if she knew if everyone was ready.

He said that he was going to take fifteen minutes to converse with his advisors and then head down to the launch area.

Linda replied that the General and the Admiral were in the cafeteria having breakfast. They had asked her to give them a five-minute warning. She added that Orlando was having breakfast with the General at the request of the General. She said the general had asked for him to be part of the Fold to Amoral.

Bram replied that Orlando was welcome, and she should pack an extra lunch for him.

Linda nodded and said that was easily done.

Bram went into his office and took out Isaac, Ada and Einstein Jr. and put them on his desk.

He asked them if he should ask the current team leaders for names to lead the new teams needed to study the newly discovered Alien planets.

He got the positive head shakes he expected.

He asked whether there was any hope at changing the Amoran culture.

This time he got two no head shakes, but Ada did not respond. A moment later she moved her head in a circle. The Isaac and Einstein Jr. joined her.

He asked if they meant maybe. This time there were three positive head shakes.

Zoe came over and gave them all some additional cookie crumbs and praised them for expanding the language that they shared. She received three positive head shakes.

Bram asked if he should destroy the missiles now.

He got three positive head shakes.

He thanked the three and carried them to the small door leading to their tunnel system.

Eric shook his head and commented that each time he watched the two of them converse with the mice he wondered about the world around him and if he really understood any of it.

Bram replied that all of them lacked the sensitivity and the ability to grasp the totality of the environment that surrounded them. They lacked the additional sensory organs that would give them a clear vision of the reality they live in.

He got up and led the way out of his office.

Ron Mueller

274

<u>Chapter 23: Amora</u>

When Bram got to the Fold area, everyone going on the expedition to Amora was ready and standing by.

Bram said good morning. He then walked over to Orlando and asked what his role was going to be.

Orlando smiled and replied that the General had asked him to come along so a proper ditty about the trip would be written.

Bram chuckled and said he was glad there was someone accompanying him that would find some humor in learning about Amora.

Marcus suggested that they first visit the four target planets and then approach Amora from the area of one of the planets. He pointed out that Amora had demonstrated that their sensing technology was a superior and long range one. He did not want them to be able to back track them to Mataia.

Bram agreed with Marcus and said that the four planets were already targeted and traveling from their location to Amora might frighten the Amorans, which he said was very appropriate.

He asked Marcus to make sure they were not detected by the four worlds they were going to visit first. He wanted to look and gain some understanding of the four worlds but did not want them to know about the visit at this point in time.

Marcus put them well outside of the solar system of each planet and then sent in some observation bubbles that Folded swiftly back in time like a rock skipping across the still water of a placid lake. He was able to capture the desired information and images in a matter of a few minutes. In less than an hour the team had visited all four planets and were ready to skip to Amora.

Marcus stopped and had the supercomputer back on Mataia received the information. He then had it do a comparison between planets.

He reported that all four planets were roughly the same size, had almost the same rotational velocity, traveled around their star at about the same rate and all had an advanced technical capability that had them exploring their solar system via rockets that were similar to the ones Earth was currently using. Their skies were full of flying airplanes.

Bram thanked Marcus for the quick analysis and the comparison of the three to each other.

He said he would like get the same information about Amora.

Marcus said that he would Fold to some location well outside the Amoran solar system and send his bubbles in.

Ripples in Time

He had no sooner Folded to the location he had chosen than his sensor warned that they were being hit by some sort of unknown rays.

Marcus immediately Folded. He announced he was Folding back one thousand years into the Amoran past.

This time he Folded to a thirty-thousand-foot altitude above the planet.

He sent in his bubble scouts and then began a series of one hundred year forward Folds. When he was within one hundred years of the present, he received a signal that he believed was a challenge and he immediately Folded back fifty years and waited to see if he would get a challenge as he reduced his Fold skips to ten second Folds that in essence kept them invisible.

He explained that the ability for the long-range sensing was about one hundred years old. He speculated that during the following hundred years the sensing technology was significantly improved. He reported that his scout bubbles had not recorded any flight ability nor any rocket action. He speculated that the Amorans had not developed flight or space travel. Their long ranging sensing technology was most likely exposing them to technology that they saw as a threat.

Bram thanked Marcus for his quick analysis. He asked him to remain in their past but send his scout bubbles to the present time and have them skip backwards in time long enough to get a complete picture of Amora.

It turned out that going back through time was the appropriate technique because they got challenged at each point of exposure, but no action was taken because the scout bubble was on to the next point in the past.

It was noon and they decided to relax for a short time before following Marcus's recommendation to return to Mataia.

This time Marcus said that he was already having the supercomputer process the data they had gathered, and he would organize it so they could have an assessment review in the late afternoon.

Bram complemented him for the rapid work. He thanked Remi for having the bubbles and the transport ready.

He then asked the General what Gary Tatum, Art Baratta and Matt were doing and for whom they were working. He said that he wanted to get those three to lead three of the four teams that he was going to create to investigate the four targeted alien planets.

Mallica spoke up and said that Matt had been working with her on translating the various alien languages and if Bram was asking about him to offer him a position, she would support getting him in the position to lead a team. She commented that translation work and learning new languages was going to take an upswing. It would give her an opportunity to recruit some new folks. She added that the translation work was irregular and more like part time work and most of her members were on other teams.

Ripples in Time

The General replied that he was not sure who each of the other three worked for. He was in contact with them, but they mostly discussed how much they loved living on Mataia when they had a beer together. He said that he encouraged them to keep the conversation away from work.

Bram nodded and agreed that keeping it social made for a more relaxed periodic meeting. He said he would follow up with Erica who kept track of everyone's assignments and made sure everyone's compensation was competitive versus their Earth counterparts.

The Admiral commented that he didn't realize that law enforcement personnel got such low pay.

Bram reminded him that the compensation was based purely on the take home pay minus the taxes the various governments extracted. What the Admiral was experiencing was what the typical worker on Earth experienced.

The significant difference was that on Mataia he had no expenses and the money he did earn was all his to spend as he saw fit. He could spend it all on Fold vacations or on Earth shopping sprees.

The Admiral smiled and said that life on Mataia was a phenomenal experiment in easy living.

Bram asked the Admiral what team he wanted to lead. He was surprised when the response was that he was ready for any additional work, and it did not need to be in a leadership role.

He asked if the Admiral would consider taking the role of coaching the four new team leaders and their members as they took on the study of the four new Alien worlds.

The Admiral nodded and replied that he would love to do something like that.

The General spoke up and said that he would like to add coaching to his resume.

Bram was pleased to have the two volunteers to coach the new teams. It would allow him to focus on the rehabilitation and fresh development of Kutikan and working with Zuri on studying and dealing with Amora.

On return to his office, he immediately put in a call to Erica and asked about the status of the four people he was interested in naming as leaders of the four new teams.

Matt Simple, working for Mallica, had already been selected and would hear about the opportunity from her.

Gary Tatum, one of the Marine divers, was now working for Amy and Pat in the capacity of feeding the surviving Kutikanians. Moving him over was just a matter of timing.

Art Baratta was a graduate Chef trained by Chef D'Carluca. This meant that he was really not a candidate.

The alternate name that popped up was Duong Tran. He felt that Duong would make an effective team leader.

The final name was Charles Ford the science advisor that had been on the Oversight Committee. He was currently under employed working for Elizabeth.

He put in a call to Elizabeth and asked her about Charles and learned that she though highly of him and enjoyed working with him. She commented that his partner was also a great fellow. Bram asked her if putting him in the lead of one of the new teams he was creating would be appropriate.

She said that it was a very good move. Bram asked her to attend the afternoon update that Marcus was holding at four and then afterwards she would be ready to let Charles know. She asked where she should be at four and then said she would see him there.

Bram then put in a call to Duong and invited him to attend the meeting that Marcus was having at four in the Fold Center Viewing room.

He then put a call into Amy and asked her about Gary Tatum and was told he was one of the leaders on their team. He asked her if she could fly her chopper without him. She asked what he had in mind. He suggested that she and Pat attend Marcus's meeting being held at four that afternoon in the Fold Work Center Viewing Room.

Amy hung up and asked Pat what Bram was up to. Pat shook her head and said that he had left in the morning to investigate five separate newly discovered Alien races. All she knew was that Marcus was having a meeting at the end of the day. She speculated that they would get an overview of each of the alien races. Other than that, she had no idea what Bram was up to.

Bram asked Zoe and Eric what they knew of the four people he was thinking about.

Zoe commented that Duong would be a great team leader.

Eric agreed with her and then said that Charles was exceptionally sharp and fun to work with. He also liked his partner who was a little less outgoing but pleasant to talk with.

They both said that they had not followed what Gary had been doing but expected that he would be well thought of by whomever he worked for or with.

And they both agreed that Matt, who was like a brother to both of them, was exceptional.

They both ended by saying that Bram could have picked a dozen other people that would be qualified to lead. They commented that there were no followers but only talented and capable people to pick from.

Bram smiled and asked if they were the critics or the endorsers.

Zoe shook her head and said that they had so little critique because everyone tried to follow his favorite saying to treat others as you wish to be treated.

Bram commented that he had seen the final draft of the Mataian Constitution, and it began with that phrase.

He then commented that thought had triggered the fact that the weddings were on the coming weekend.

Zoe asked how that would have triggered such a connection.

Bram replied that he did not know how his brain got triggered but what had happened, was that she had mentioned those words, and he had seen her catching a fish out on the Lake and he had seen Zuri sitting on the bow of Ted's boat and that had reminded him of her Wedding request to go fishing.

Zoe shook her head and said that it was time to go to the meeting and deal with reality and that as strange as that might be it was not as strange as trying to figure out how his mind worked.

Bram followed her and was still chuckling when they got to Linda's desk.

Linda got up and followed them. She said that if the meeting was making Bram chuckle, she was not going to miss it. She said that Lacy said she should not miss the meeting. She said she thought they would be the last to get to the meeting.

Bram did not reply but continued to follow Zoe.

They all went in and sat down in their seats.

Marcus stood up at his desk and welcomed them. He commented that he and some of them had taken a very successful trip out to five new Alien discoveries. He had a story to tell that he found uncomfortable and that went against everything that the Mataian society lived by. He asked Elizabeth what the first sentence in the Mataian Constitution was.

Elizabeth responded, "Treat others the way you wish to be treated."

Marcus then displayed four missiles and the four planets that were the targets and explained that Bram had labeled them Planet killers.

He then zeroed in on Amoral. He commented that he agreed with the name that Bram had given the planet and its society.

He then displayed what was a very pleasant world with a landscape that was similar in variety to what would be found on Earth. The land mases had different unique shapes, but it clearly showed that the planet had gone through the plate Teutonic activity similar to Earths and it had mountains similar to those on Earth.

The plant life was abundant and there seemed to be a variety of animals. The beings were bipedal and were similar to a human but looked more like the Denisovans but were amazingly like them than he had anticipated.

He highlighted the fact that they had not developed flight or any rocket capacity. Their major technical achievement had until just recently been their exceptional sensing capability. They had been able to discover and study four alien cultures that were three light years away. What they discovered must have alarmed them to an extreme. They had rapidly developed, built, and deployed the largest missile that he had ever seen. It was extremely large, but it was simple. It was an engine pushing a tremendous amount of explosive material and a guidance system.

He pointed out that Lacy's team had discovered the missiles and then he and Remi had found the location of Amora, and later the location of the four targeted planets.

This morning Bram had led them on an exploratory Fold journey, and they had visited all five planets. He commented on the fact that they had not done a close in Fold on the four planets. Remi and he had sent their scout bubbles in to get a closer look at all four planets and had the close ups that needed a lot of study. The top line was that they were all similar to Earth, they had developed flight and rocket technology and had cities and living areas.

He said that was all he had ready as an overview.

He asked Bram if there was anything that he wanted to add.

Bram thanked Marcus at having been able to give such a thorough overview so quickly.

He then said that Amoral would be the focus of investigation by a team that would be led by Zuri.

He was also naming four teams to study and analyze the four other Alien civilizations. He had identified the leaders for those teams and their bosses were all sitting in the room and would let those individuals know of their new roles.

He commented that the next couple of years was going to be exciting and that eventually they would communicate with the newly discovered intelligences.

He said that dealing with the Amoral aliens was going to be personal for him. That society had to change, or he would need to figure out how they could be isolated.

He called the meeting to an end and stood up and led the way out of the Viewing room.

Every time he thought about the actions that the Amoral aliens had taken; it shook his belief system. He knew they were going to test the limits of each of the principles he held dear.

Chapter 24: Mole

Pat was sitting next to Bram on their dual recliners when she asked him whether he was ready for the coming weekend weddings.

He jokingly asked whose wedding they were going to attend. Then he gave a small laugh and said that he was actually looking beyond that and anticipating the fishing trip. He said that he had asked Castor what he was looking forward to and he had answered the chance to go fishing and not having to carry his entire field kit and weapons.

Pat agreed that she was looking forward to fishing as well, but she was really happy to be the Matron of honor for Zuri. She felt like a younger sister was getting married.

Bram agreed that being asked to preside over all three marriages was an honor that he would remember for his lifetime. He felt that having been able to watch Zuri blossom was the sweet honey of life.

He said that he had lunch with Nuro and Jina and they were happy beyond belief. They said that Zuri had picked a mate that was very much in love with her, and the Marine Corps had made him strong enough to withstand Zuri's ways. She was proud that he was a Chef and was now the Chef that boasted of serving the smartest man on Mataia and soon he would be making the dinners for the smartest woman on Mataia.

He said that as far as Donna and Castor was concerned, the two of them had saved him so many times that he considered them not only very good friends but two people that had been and were still willing to take a bullet for him. He was pleased that Orlando was the best man for Castor. He was surprised that Donna's husband had chosen Duong to be the best man as the fill in for his best friend who would attend remotely.

The dinner and dance afterward was going to be close coupled to the Wedding as it had been for their wedding and then there was the fishing expedition and an early evening picnic at Celilo park. Zuri was honeymooning on Mataia.

Donna and Castor had chosen to honeymoon on Primeira. They said that some strange women had Folded in two beautiful homes to their lake side lots and had arranged for a yard crew to landscape the yards using the foliage available on Primeira.

Pat smiled and said that she and Amy had managed to expedite the two homes getting constructed on Earth. Erica had arranged for the interior decor. The General had arranged for the digging of the foundation. Amy and I determined the center coordinates of each structure and Marcus Folded the homes into place. Water and waste service was being handled by the system on Mataia.

This was their present to the two couples. They would be the first to honeymoon and live on Primeira.

Pat went on to say that the water wave reducers were considered Bram's gift that allowed them to live near the water.

Bram asked whether she and Amy had stocked any fish there.

She said that doing so was more difficult than it sounded because just throwing them in was not an option if they were to have food to survive. She and Amy were learning how hard it was to build an environment from the bottom up and had been working for some time to get some sea life for Mataia and had yet to get up to the fish level of the food chain. It was really a bottom-up system and there was no skipping steps.

She said that fishing with Ted and fishing on Earth was going to be happening for a long time and maybe when he retired, he might be able to go fishing on Mataia.

Bram said that he was in no rush and accepted the fact that there was no past to go get the natural stuff that existed before like on Kutikans that had brunt their world out of existence.

Pat nodded but clarified that even with the abundant availability of past resources, re-establishing the Kutikan environment was going to take a very long time. The Kutikans that were alive at the moment would be long dead before Kutikan would be reestablished. She estimated it would take several generations to reestablish the environment.

Bram asked if she knew what had happened to the environment. She shook her head and said the team was still looking into what triggered the doomsday weapon.

Pat answered her phone.

It was Jina calling to let her know that Zuri had just Folded in. She was wondering if it would be possible to give Zuri a tour of her home to be.

Pat said that after breakfast the next day she could meet Zuri and give her a tour and the keys to the house. She could also suggest what to stock up on so that it would be move in ready after the wedding.

She asked whether Weylan would be touring as well.

Jina said that neither of them was sure since her arrival was a few days early.

After Pat hung up, Bram commented that it was going to be hard to resist getting Zuri started but he was going to wait until after her honeymoon to get her rolling in her new assignment. He said that he was currently in the process of staffing her team so it would be ready to roll when she began.

Pat said waiting until after the honeymoon was a good idea. She was sure that Zuri would find out all she needed to know on her own.

Bram said that he was taking the next day off and going out to look in on Einstein and spend the day walking the desert.

Pat chuckled and asked what he was going to do the day after to avoid Zuri.

He laughed and said he might go visit Mike and Mary and do a little river fishing with the excuse of seeing if things were ready for the wedding.

And then on Friday he could tour the new house by the lake that should be in Melisa's possession and see if fishing off the pier was any good. And finally, he could inspect the house near the Inn that he had asked her to purchase.

Pat laughed and reminded him that he had a lunch date with her the next day.

He replied that he was going to lock himself in his office and have Linda refuse to let anyone in.

Linda laughed when Bram asked her to keep everyone away from his office. She said that rumor had it that Zuri was on Mataia, and she was eager to learn about her new assignment.

Bram said that it was not fair to put the Amoral assignment on her shoulders just before her wedding.

Linda shook her head and suggested that he leave the filtering to Zuri and that Zuri would be distracted by love and romance for the entire time she was on her honeymoon.

Bram said that he was not good at judging such things. His mind would be working both situations at the same time.

Linda commented that Zuri had mentioned that she did not have a warped nonlinear unconventional mind like his. She said she had a strong mind, but it was linear and hers to command.

Bram laughed and thanked Linda for describing a person on the verge of being taken away in a straight jacket.

She laughed and said that she was glad to be of help.

Bram went in and took Ada, Isaac, and Einstein Jr. out and put them on his desk.

Zoe came over and gave them a few cookie crumbs and warned them that Bram was going to unload his worries on them.

Bram said that Zoe was right. He asked if he should tell Zuri about the terrible action taken by planet Amoral.

All three gave a positive nod.

Zoe asked if Bram should visit the rock in the desert before the wedding?

All three gave a positive nod.

She then asked if he should tell Zuri about Amoral before going to the rock.

And she got three positive nods.

Bram smiled and asked if the fact that Zoe was giving them extra cookie crumbs had biased their answers.

The three mice shook their head in the negative.

Eric commented that the two of them had gone off their rockers.

Both Bram and Zoe laughed when the three mice shook their heads in the negative.

Bram picked up the three mice and returned them to their kingdom entrance in the bookshelf.

He commented that the reason that they never needed to see Dr. Windal was that they had three mice that regularly relieved their stress and erased all their doubts.

Eric smiled and said that maybe he should be the one going to sessions with her after all he was beginning to believe in mice that understood English.

Bram said that he was going to get a snack from the second most famous Chef on Mataia and asked who was going with him.

Zoe laughed and said that she should stay and work on her nails, but she would join him and took the lead while Eric took his usual spot behind Bram.

Bram had challenged the two multiple times about the fact that he thought their protection was no longer needed but they always responded, "someday."

It turned out that Chef Henslier was celebrating the arrival of his bride to be by making a special desert that he was giving out for free. When Bram walked in, he realized he was walking into an enthusiastic crowd that was in a celebratory mood. He was soon surrounded. Suddenly he saw one of the technicians with a gun in his hand. He stepped in toward him, grabbed the gun, and then realized that there was no place to aim it without the risk of someone being shot. He spun into the attacker's chest and brought the gun barrel to his chest just below his collar bone and pulled the trigger twice. The bullet went through him and hit the gun man twice in the chest. The gun man let go of his weapon and fell to the ground.

It was all over in less than a few seconds.

Bram turned and watched as Zoe examined the fallen technician.

Zoe shook her head and said that he was gone.

Bram walked over and sat down at a table. He looked at Eric and asked if Zoe was always right about the fact that danger was waiting to happen.

Zoe asked if he was bleeding.

Bram replied that he was not bleeding as much as he thought but he was sure that two bullets passing through most likely had done some damage.

The next thing he knew he was put in a wheelchair and rushed down the hallway to an examination room that also had an x-ray and cat scan equipment.

The Fold Work Center doctor did a quick external examination and sealed the wound and then put him in the cat scan.

A few minutes later he said that there was no internal damage. The bullets had traveled through and not hit any arteries or any organs.

Bram thanked him for his quick examination and said that he was going back to the cafeteria to have some of the goodies that the Chef had prepared.

The doctor suggested he take it easy.

Bram replied that he would walk slowly, chew carefully and refrain from laughing.

The doctor asked Zoe if Bram was always so nonchalant.

Eric replied that he was seeing Bram at his best.

Bram smiled and walked slowly out and back toward the cafeteria behind Zoe.

He saw a table open near the window and sat down.

A few moments later Chef Evender came out with a cart that had every dessert that had been made for the occasion.

Bram looked over the cart and asked if it could be left there because he was planning to ruin his lunch.

Chef Evender suggested that he save his stomach for a Spaghetti de Mare that was in the process of being prepared for him.

Bram nodded and replied that he would limit the amount of dessert, but he really could use a tall mug of coffee.

Zoe said she could go for a large mug of coffee as well.

The coffee had just arrived when Pat, Zuri, Amy, Elizabeth Donna, and Mallica came rushing in.

Linda ran in right after they had entered.

Bram smiled and asked if they had heard he had a cart full deserts prepared by the second most talented Chef on Mataia.

Pat shook her head and asked if he had really shot himself.

Bram nodded, and replied it was the only thing he could think of to prevent someone else from getting shot. He had not intended to kill the shooter, but he had intended to take him down.

Zoe shook her head and said that it all happened so fast that Bram had already killed the shooter before she or Eric had a chance to take their weapons out of their holsters.

Donna commented that both Orlando and Castor swore that in his previous life Bram was either a Barbarian or the first Marine hero. In either case they said that they never got to shoot when Bram was on the attack.

Bram replied that his Aikido coach had also claimed that he felt a presence of the past when watching him practice. But what he remembered most was what he had been told to do. It was to act then talk. In this case there was no one to talk to after he had acted.

Pat had listened and knew that Bram was himself and feeling fine.

Ripples in Time

She said that she had a ditty for the occasion.

> A mild man, a somewhat crazy mild man
> The hero of long ago was one today.
> He is a mild man who to shoots himself.
> To save all those around
> Saving those he enriches and cares for
> He sits and laughs enjoying sweets.
> And says its nothing, just two small holes.
> One in front, one in back, what, the heck
> The sweets are great and the coffee a strong deep black.
> Hey, let's celebrate the weddings, let's celebrate
> Zuri's back and her soul mate is no hack.
> He makes the best sweets and that's a fact.
> And there is a man, a somewhat crazy mild man.
> For sure a hero on this day as he is on every other day.

Donna took up the ditty and soon everyone in the cafeteria was repeating the chant and stomping their feet in rhythm to her cadence.

Zuri had come into the cafeteria and came to Bram and gave him a hug and quietly told him that she loved him like an older brother.

Bram replied that he was looking forward to the wedding, but he was really into going fishing with his younger sister.

He had just finished his desert when the attending Dr. walked in and asked how he was feeling.

Bram apologized about not having been more cordial and able to greet him earlier. He was about to ask his name when Linda introduced him as Dr. Edwin Marzurka who arrived two days ago.

Bram said that his arrival was well timed and that the handling of his first gunshot victim had been well handled.

Dr. Marzurka shook his head and said that he had been a trauma doctor for five years and had never met any gunshot patient that had walked out of his office and gone to have some sweets and a cup of coffee. He said that he had come in and listened to the ditty and then joined in. He said that a couple of words needed changing and that instead of mild man it would be more appropriate to say wild crazy man.

Bram laughed and asked if that was just a reaction or was, he giving a diagnosis?

Dr. Marzurka shook his head and said that he was really happy that he took Dr. Sewal up on coming to Mataia. His wife was in love with the house, the ease with which she was able to get the things she needed, and his two kids loved the school and all the new friends they were making.

He said that what had convinced him to accept was when Dr. Sewal read him the opening paragraph of the Mataian Constitution and now that he had met the person who repeated that phrase often enough for it to be the first line of the constitution he knew he had made the best decision of his life. He shook his head and finished by say, "even if that person is a wild and crazy man willing to shoot himself."

Bram thanked Dr. Marzurka and said that he planned to spend the rest of the day sitting on a boulder out in the middle of the desert with his mental phycologists and advisors.

He smiled when the Dr. said that he didn't think he had met them yet and asked where their offices were.

Bram replied that their offices were at a secret location out in the desert and only the most privileged ever got to meet with them.

Pat smiled and commented that she agreed with the suggestion that the word that should be emphasized was a crazy man.

Bram asked Linda to arrange for a Fold transport to take him to the desert after lunch. He said that until then he planned to relax and enjoy the scenery from his office window.

Ron Mueller

Chapter 25: Recovery

The Spaghetti de Mare lunch turned out to be served to a fairly large group. Pat, Amy, Elizabeth, Zuri, and Donna joined him, and the cafeteria was filled.

He found out later that a lot of other people had planned to come for lunch, but Linda had asked them not to.

When he found out he thanked her.

The flavor of the spaghetti was somehow enhanced. He had several servings and finally ask Chef Henslier what he had done to make his Spaghetti de Mare the most delicious that he had ever eaten.

Chef Henslier smiled and yelled, "Hurrah!, Hurrah!, Hurrah!," and he saluted Bram and then shouted he is not only a hero but also a top food critic with excellent taste.

Bram was all smiles and glad that he had praised the taste of the food. He was surprised at the reaction.

He thank the Chef again and said that he was off to his relaxing afternoon.

He followed Zoe back to his office where he picked up Ada, Isaac, and Einstein Jr. and then they walked down to the Fold Launch pad.

It turned out that Pat and Zuri were coming along.

Once they got to the boulder, he took the three mice out of his pocket, and they scurried down into the hole in the rock.

He noted that Zoe and Eric had each chosen to stand on opposite sides of the boulder.

While they were waiting, Zuri asked if they should postpone the wedding.

The three returned with Einstein and his mate and two new little ones who looked robust and normal in size.

Bram greeted them and said that they were looking healthy.

He pointed to Zuri and said that she was getting married on the weekend and had come to say hello before she went on her honeymoon.

Einstein seemed to understand and went over to Zuri and stood on his hind legs until she lowered her hand. He got in and curled up for a moment and then got out.

Bram explained that Einstein had just approved of her marriage.

Zuri smiled and thanked Einstein who shook his head up and down.

Bram said there was no need to postpone the wedding. His shoulder might be a little sore, but his mouth would work just fine. He would be able to officiate the three weddings.

Zuri smiled and said that he had really made Weylan's day by praising his signature dish.

Bram smiled and said that he realized that almost immediately and the spaghetti was the best that he could remember. He had outdone Chef D'Carluca.

He then said that he was taking a walk through the desert before going back home. He wanted to see if the plants on the island had adapted to Mataia.

Pat asked if she could walk along.

Bram replied yes, and said that Zuri should join in. He said that he planned to come back often to relax and think about how to guide the teams that were addressing problems that none of them had anticipated.

Zoe took the lead and said he could guide her by simply calling out right or left.

Zuri asked about the main problem with the planet and the aliens that her team would be focused on.

Bram replied that she and her team would be studying how an advanced society could be so amoral that they would launch four planet killing missiles at four civilizations that were at least three light years away and most likely had no inkling that Amoral existed.

Zuri shook her head and wondered if she were up to being neutral until she learned more.

Bram replied that it would be really hard. Additionally, the Amorals as he was referring to them had developed long range sensors able to reach out and study the details of planets at the three light year range. That would make studying them extremely difficult. He wanted to make sure they never located Mataia.

He suggested that her team begin their studies back before the Amorals developed their sensing technology. He let her know that Marcus had that time, and he had extensive imagery of the planet. Bram also said that they should learn the language and identify the actual name of the planet.

Zuri replied that she thought her team would have their plate full.

Bram agreed and suggested they go slow. One of the first tasks was to eliminate the planet killer rockets.

Pat brought the discussion back to the desert on the island and said that it seemed to be returning to full life like it had on Earth.

Bram asked why she thought so.

Pat pointed to several cactuses that were blooming and commented that the last time they had walked the desert those cactuses seemed to be having trouble. She said she would get one of her team to figure out what had changed.

Bram asked whether knowing that would help her with the rest of Mataia-forming the planet.

Pat said that she felt like it would.

Zuri commented that she had heard that the General and the Admiral were leading a team studying the planet Kutikan. She asked if that population had actually almost totally annihilated themselves.

Bram nodded and added that Pat and Amy were heavily into bringing the past environment forward in time in an effort to re-establish the planet.

They were working with Remi and the lab to figure out how to recycle all the ash that had been generated by whatever wiped out all living organisms and plants.

Zuri commented that it was hard to accept an advanced civilization committing seppuku.

Bram said he agreed and bet that it had all happened because of some accident and some sort of automated retaliation response.

Zuri agreed and said she was putting her money on a monumental planet killing accident. She added that it was one that the Earth seemed to be setting itself up for.

Bram stopped and said that it was time for him to get back to the office. He wanted to launch one of the four teams before going home.

Pat agreed that it was time to get back but that the two of them should go home and relax.

Bram knew that Pat was not making a suggestion and that she was insisting he call it a day. He knew instinctively that she was right.

Zuri said that she was having dinner with her parents. She said that Weylan was bringing a Lemon Meringue pie for dessert.

Bram asked if he could come over for dessert?

Zuri shook her head and said that Weylan was sending a blue berry pie over to Pat.

Zoe said that she and Eric would plan to come over and have some hot blue berry pie and a scoop of vanilla ice and asked Pat what time they should plan on arriving.

Bram stayed out of the exchange as Pat gave the time and asked Zoe to bring vanilla ice cream.

Pat looked at Bram and asked if having company for desert was OK.

He nodded and replied that once he got home he was going to sit down on their couch close his eyes and think for a while.

It was not long after they sat down when Pat smiled when it was clear to her that he had fallen asleep. She got up and went to the kitchen and decided that a cheese, lettuce, tomato, and egg sandwich would be supper. A large piece of blue berry pie and vanilla ice cream would be desert. She put a bottle of Spumanti into the refrigerator to cool and then returned to sit in the recliner.

Bram was breathing in a steady rhythm. She was glad that she had insisted they come home when he had wanted to go to his office to finish the day.

Ripples in Time

She shook her head when she thought about the fact that he had chosen to shoot through his body in order to prevent someone in the cafeteria from being shot by the gun man. She was amazed that he had done so with the intent to shoot his attacker. She knew Bram was the person that ran toward a problem when most would freeze or run. In this case he had done more than run toward a problem.

The doorbell rang and she realized that she had not awakened Bram for his sandwich.

Bram woke up and gave a light laugh and said that he had done a thorough examination of his eyelids, and they had no holes in them.

Pat got up and went to the door and let Zoe and Eric in, Bram asked if he had missed dinner.

Pat replied that she had made a large salad for them, and it had been waiting to make sure he did not find holes in his eyelids. She led the way to the dining room and then brought the salads in. She served coffee that was on the refreshment bar.

Bram realized that his body had chosen to focus on working on the bullet wound and that Pat had let him sleep through the normal dinner time. He looked at the size of the salad and said that he only wanted half of it.

Pat had left the dressing to the side, so it was easy to cut Bram's salad in half.

Zoe smiled and said she would cut his piece of blue berry pie so that it was only half as large as hers.

Bram smiled and replied that he was cutting down on the salad so he could double up on the blueberry pie and ice cream.

As he ate, he decided to get to bed early. He knew that the next day was going to be heavy. He wanted to work with Zuri to get her team set up and be functioning while she was on her honeymoon. He also wanted to get the four other team leaders in place and give them their starting goals.

He wondered whether Pat might like to stay an extra day at the Inn. He figured that getting to fish out on the lake and then doing some river fishing would be great.

He asked if staying an extra day at the Inn would interest anyone.

Pat nodded and said she thought it would be a great idea. She knew that if they returned Bram would be back into his intense work. She figured one more day of relaxation was what he needed.

Zoe replied that she and Eric would love that and if they had anything to do, they could do it from there.

Bram nodded then smiled and asked if shooting himself meant that she was going to start protecting him from himself.

Zoe shook her head and said that she did not possess the ability to provide that kind of protection. She pointed to Pat and said that that kind of protection came from her.

Pat was in the process of pouring a glass of wine for everyone. She said that she had an impossible responsibility in that area. She pointed to the sling that Bram was using and said that she lived with someone willing to shoot himself. She finished with the question, "How was she ever going to protect him from his mind?"

Bram knew that there was no answer he could give. Instead, he proposed a toast to a calm, great wedding, and the best fishing that they had ever enjoyed.

Zoe and Eric left shortly after they all finished desert. She commented to Eric that Bram probably should take the next day off, but she knew he would not. She suggested that they make sure that Linda arranged to have those that Bram planned to interact with come to his office.

Shortly after Zoe left, Bram said that he was going to go to bed early.

Pat let him know that she thought it was a great idea. She would be right up after getting things ready for the morning.

Bram did not remember falling asleep but when his eyes opened next the sun was shining through the window. He knew he was late for work. He shook his head and knew that his body had done what it had to do to recover.

The spot next to him was empty and no longer warm so he knew that Pat had been up for some time.

He got up showered the best he could without wetting the bandages on his right shoulder.

He then made his way toward the great smell of pancakes and sausage.

When he entered the kitchen both Pat and Zoe greeted him.

He asked Zoe if she had moved back into his house.

Zoe shook her head and said that he was so late that she had come over to make sure he had survived.

Bram smiled, poured himself a cup of coffee and sat down next to Eric.

He asked him if Zoe was on something or was, she always so hypomanic.

Eric replied that he refused to answer on the grounds that he wanted to remain married.

Zoe smiled and said that Eric wasn't answering for that reason but because he didn't know what hypomanic meant and yes watching someone shoot himself had taken her to the edge of her controllable level of stress.

Bram smiled and said that the only other person who he would have had a clear shot at was his most trusted female bodyguard.

Zoe laughed and said in that case she felt much better about the choice he had made.

Chapter 26: Guns and Bible

Bram arrived at his office an hour later than normal.

Linda greeted him and said that she had arranged for all the people that he had wanted to meet to come to his office. She asked if he wanted to have lunch brought in.

Bram knew that she was trying to ease the workload for the day. He accepted her arranging for folks to come to his office, but he felt like going to lunch was something he needed to do. He knew this time Zoe would be clearing the path if the lunchroom was crowded. He figured it was like getting back on a horse after getting thrown. Then he smiled at his analogy since he had never been thrown from a horse.

He thanked Linda and went into his office. He went to the bookcase, opened the little door, and brought Ada, Isaac, and Einstein Jr. to his desk.

Zoe had brought over some cookie crumbs and said that she wanted to ask the first question.

She asked if Bram should work that day? The three mice shook their head in the affirmative. She shook her head and called them little slave drivers.

Bram said the mice knew that it was better to keep going than to pamper oneself.

He then asked if he had picked the right leaders for all the new teams.

He was pleased with the affirmative head shakes.

He then asked if Zoe was too protective of him.

All the mice shook their heads in the negative.

This caused Bram to ask whether he would need her protection in the future.

He was surprised when the headshakes were all in the positive.

Zoe reacted as well. She said that she was going to alert Bob, Thomas, and Orlando. She said that she would also consider Castor and Donna, but it was their wedding weekend. She asked if the fence around the Inn was still in place.

Bram replied that it was. He asked if she thought something would happen during the wedding weekend.

Zoe commented that so far all of the weddings had been consummated with a gun battle. She was going to be prepared for it.

Bram asked her who would be instigating such an action.

Zoe said she would contact Lacy and see if she had any ideas. She then asked if she had actually been successful in removing all traces of Fold from Earth at the present time and in the future. She said that it had to be a miss that she had not foreseen.

Eric quietly asked if they knew how they sounded reacting to the headshakes of three mice.

Zoe replied that yes, they were reacting to the headshakes of three mice that had so far batted one thousand per cent.

Eric nodded and said he agreed but still wondered how the mice did what they did.

Bram said he had no idea and that maybe they talked to the wind and the wind gave them the answers.

He decided to have a talk with Orlando and get him to have all his Marine friends at the ready.

Linda called in to give him a ten-minute warning before the stream of people would arrive. She let him know that Zuri and two folks she had selected were ready to come in.

Bram organized his thoughts and then pulled his white board to the end of the meeting table. He always felt that the ability to write on it allowed him to concentrate better than working on his computer. He had an updated wide board version that automatically took in his writing and put it into his computer Word document.

He welcomed Zuri.

She introduced Jan Rattle who would act as the leader for the week she was on vacation. Then she introduced Valentina Vogler who preferred to be called Val and who had an engineering degree from Cal Tech and had attained the rank of Ensign in the Navy.

Bram welcomed them.

Zoe asked if they cared for any refreshments.

Bram waited a moment and then he shared his expectations of the team. He then let them know that he wanted them to deal with the fact that they were to determine how to manage an entire planet of beings that were intelligent and at the same time amoral. They were willing to kill four populations on planets that were three light years away and who had no clue that each of their planets had been targeted for annihilation.

He said that in the coming week he would work with the team to eliminate the missiles that were a third of the way to those planets.

Zuri interjected that she did not want the missiles destroyed. Instead, she wanted the missiles turned and to begin their return back to their launch origin. She asked if Bram could get that done and then prevent the Amorals from changing the return course.

Bram smiled and said that Zuri had the right thing in mind and yes, he would work with Remi to make sure that once they turned the missiles, they would not be able to be turned again.

He complimented her on choosing to use their own weapons against them. He suggested that she and the team step back in time to the point when the Amorals did not have the super sensitive sensing technology and study the planet in detail. They should focus specifically on what would make an intelligent society be willing to condemn another world to death with no provocation.

Zuri nodded and said she would be very interested in discovering that motive. She said that she could not imagine what it might be.

Bram then said he would like to suggest two more people to round out the team. He said that Linh had suggested that Simone Lisitsa, one of the IT specialists on her team be named to the new team. He then added that a recently recruited sociology student named Vasily Wit seem to be a good fit on her team. Both were ready to be interviewed that day.

Zuri said she would get them to come to a meeting where all of them could talk about the objectives, the strategies and outline an initial work plan that afternoon. Then when she returned from her honeymoon, they would finish their planning and get on the project full time, and she added with a vengeance.

Bram remined them that they should approach their effort with his favorite saying and now the lead in to the Mataian constitution.

Zuri nodded and thanked him for that reminder. She then stood up and said that it was time for her to get her team organized so he could easily guide them during the next week.

Bram asked if Linda could get the other four team leaders to come in together while he went to the cafeteria for a break.

Linda said she would agree if he stayed in his office until Zoe and Eric checked out the cafeteria first.

Bram gave a small a laugh and said that lightening seldom hit in the same spot twice, but he would wait in his office.

He had just finished preparing for the next four team leaders and whomever they might bring with them when Zoe returned and said that they would be early, and the cafeteria was relatively empty.

Zoe took the lead and they all walked to the cafeteria.

Bram was pouring himself an iced tea when one of the kitchen staff came out to where he was and said that he would take the drink to the table and bring whatever he wanted from the snack bar as well.

Bram looked to the kitchen door where Chef Henslier gave him a salute. Bram raised is left hand and waved. He then selected a bear claw and went to an empty table that was in the far corner near the windows. He sat down with his back to the wall.

He took note that Zoe sat facing the cafeteria entrance and Eric sat facing him. The chair that faced the window but had its back to the door was empty.

The kitchen aid put Bram's drink and bear claw down and said that if he wanted anything else he would be at the counter ready to respond.

Bram thanked him and after he had left, Bram asked Zoe what she was thinking about for the upcoming wedding weekend.

Zoe said that she was going to meet with Orlando, the General and the Admiral after work to decide how to prepare for an attack.

Bram shook his head and said someday he would like to understand what continued to fuel the desire to kill him. He wondered if there was such a thing as an undiscovered organ that was an attack magnet.

Zoe shook her head and then smiled and said that the attackers were just jealous that he had such a good-looking bodyguard.

Bram chuckled and said he would have replaced her, but he had never found a person more homely to do so.

Eric stood up and said that he thought it was time to get back to work and led the way out of the cafeteria.

Bram asked Eric what was bothering him.

Eric replied that every time there was a gun fight, he always ended up in back and Zoe ended out running in to the shooters.

Bram replied that he remembered very clearly that Eric was at Zoe's side as they both jumped the swimming pool fence in their skimpy swimsuits, and he remember very well that the two of them stood side by side responding to the incoming barrage of bullets coming from the speed boats bearing down on them and he remembered the two of them leaping into the hail of bullets when the future sent assassins back to kill him.

Bram stopped and asked if he remembered all the many times Eric had saved him or was it that the two of them talked to mice that irritated him.

Eric started laughing and said that as always Bram had changed his mood for the better. He said he was not sure what was bothering him. He figured that it was the fact that they were always fighting back and seldom did they attack or even suspect whom to attack.

Bram said that he could understand that situation. He too was constantly frustrated about getting attacked by people that he did not know and whom he had never negatively affected. It was hard for him to come up with the rational logic to clarify that situation.

Zoe said she kept it simple. She said she talked to mice and relieved her frustrations.

Eric said he was going to do that as well.

Bram stopped by Linda's desk and asked if things were set.

Linda said that everyone was going to come in after lunch.

He asked her to check with the General, Admiral, Lacy, and Orlando to see if they could meet online in fifteen to discuss the upcoming wedding situation.

Linda said that she would set it up.

Bram then went into the office. He asked Zoe if meeting with them early would be acceptable.

Zoe thanked him for freeing up her after work hours. She figured that everyone would feel better about getting it done earlier.

Bram agreed and he would feel better as well. He wanted to hear what each of them thought of the situation and to evaluate how they would determine the source of where the order and the munitions for the attack had originated.

He felt that the source had to be Earth bound and it had to be because of residue Fold information still existed somehow, somewhere.

Linda called in and let him know that she had everyone on and was ready to start the meeting with the folks he had requested.

Bram welcomed everyone and then stated his objective of setting up the defenses for the weekend.

The General smiled and commented that all they had to do was to provide him with enough ammunition so that when he shot himself through the body to kill the attackers, he would be able to keep firing. He then went on to say he was happy to see that Bram had recovered enough to think about and plan on countering any additional attacks.

He said that every ex-marine attending the wedding would have access to the weapons they were used to using.

Bram thanked him and asked Lacy if she could have the attack bubbles on call.

Lacy replied that they would be on call and would be using the latest weapons available. She said that she had the bubbles refurbished and rearmed with the latest weapons that her contact in the army had provided.

Bram thanked her and commented that she had always used the skill with her air attacks to confuse and defeat the attackers.

The Admiral said that he had six ex-Navy Seals that he had recruited and brought to Mataia. They would be arranged around the higher ground and provide sniper capability to the defense.

Bram said that the Admiral was providing a surprise capability. He commented that he had not been aware of the arrival of the six.

The Admiral nodded and said that he had planned to introduce them just before the discovery of the Amoral planet and the other four planets. Then he hesitated again when he learned that Bram had shot himself in the most amazing self-defense move that he had ever heard of. And now Bram was organizing for a potential attack at a wedding. He said he was lucky to be on Mataia where he did not have to explain the sequence of events to anyone else.

Bram nodded and said he would like to meet them before they provided their support.

The Admiral said that the six were anxious to meet the person that the ex-Marines were claiming that was tougher than any Seal would ever be.

Bram laughed and replied that he figured they were in for a disappointment.

Ripples in Time

Orlando smiled and said that he had greeted them for Bram and had shown him in action and the six had all agreed that they were looking at the mild-mannered person who turned into a toothed attack monster when it got into a fight. He said they were even more impressed when they learned that Bram was also a non-dimensional minister registered to perform marriages.

Orlando said that the six were calling Bram the pistol packing preacher that carried a bible in one hand and the instrument of death in the other, always offering to treat others as he wished to be treated but willing to give back better than what he received.

Bram smiled and said he should have kept Orlando busier, but he then thanked him for having his back and that it would allow him to greet the six without having to bring them up to date.

He said that he wanted to make sure they understood that he never initiated any of the actions when he had to retaliate against the attackers. There was no religious righteousness involved.

Orlando said that he had made the point that there had never been a time when the creator of the Fold effort had acted preemptively.

Bram thanked everyone for being ready and he added that he hoped that it was preparation that they would not need to activate.

He then said that it was time for lunch and afterward he had four team leaders and their members to meet with before the end of the day.

He asked the Admiral if the six new ex-Seal team members might be able to join him for lunch.

The Admiral replied that the six would be quite pleased to join him.

Bram thanked him and declared the meeting over.

Linda disconnected the feed and then asked Bram if there was any special order for his lunch.

Bram said since he was dealing with a bunch of Seals he wondered if the Chef had fish on the menu.

He asked Zoe and Eric how they felt about the meeting.

Zoe commented that she felt sorry for the potential attackers.

Eric said he agreed that the attackers faced certain annihilation if they attacked and did not immediately surrender.

Bram said that he agreed and hoped that the preparation was all it turned out to be. He then declared it was time to eat.

Chapter 27: The Inn and More

Bram kept the lunch with the six ex-Seals low key. He welcomed them and asked if they had any questions and asked what type of work they were looking for. He was glad to hear that they would work with anyone wanting their help. He said that they should make sure they found work that they would want to do in the long term. He suggested they work with the staffing folks that Erica led.

Zoe saw that the six were a little overwhelmed. She asked each where they were from and to share some high point in their life.

Without exception every one of the six said that their Navy stint was the highlight.

Zoe asked whether they had any girl friends or sweethearts back home.

Bram listened and knew that Zoe was doing what he would not have been able to do. She was drawing out what made the six valuable to Mataia. He would have to thank her later.

After the lunch back in his office, he met with the leaders that he was putting in place to study the four new civilizations that had been discovered. He gave them his initial objectives but suggested they organize their teams, and all together develop a strategy and detailed plans on how to study, learn and later engage the people of those planets.

He stressed the point that their approach to the four planets should always be from their past before the Amoral planet had developed their long-range sensors. After they were at the planets they could then come forward in time to the correct current time. He wanted to ensure that the Amoral planet never knew from where the Mataians were coming from.

That evening he once again fell asleep on his recliner. Pat had gotten an update from Linda that Bram had gone all out throughout the day. This time when Bram woke up, he said that he didn't feel like eating but Pat insisted that he at least have a bowl of pomegranate seeds and glass of milk. He asked about making it chocolate milk and Pat said that would be OK, but they did not have any and the local quick pick-up store was closed.

They both knew that no such store existed, and Bram said that he would settle for the milk.

<h1 style="text-align:center">Ripples in Time</h1>

The next morning the Fold to the receiving location along the highway that was about three miles from the Inn included Orlando, Castor, Donna, Bob, Thomas, Zoe and Eric and a large box that Orlando said carried a significant number of arms for the Marines who would come later and who would bring more weapons and ammunition.

Bram and Pat both asked about the would-be spouses.

Castor and Donna replied that they would be Folding down shortly, and they would all be ready for the afternoon wedding walk through. They added that Zuri and her Marine beau, Bram's personal chef, were escorting them down.

Bram asked when had Weylan become his "personal" Chef.

Their Fold happened and they were inside an old barn.

Bram said that they should unload and then proceed out the back door away from the highway and then call for the transport that Ted had arranged. He said that Ted had set it up so that it would wait in the Inn parking lot for a pickup call. Ted had stressed that the folks arriving should be outside and ready to get into the transport.

Once the process started, the driver would make a continuous loop that always started at the Inn. The driver knew nothing about the Fold system, and he might ask questions that most likely should not be answered.

Once they were all out and the weapons box was ready, Bram pointed to the call box mounted on a post and clearly labeled, "pickup call phone." He pressed the call button and asked to be picked up.

The pickup vehicle was a minibus that had a large back carrying space. It could easily carry twenty people and a significant amount of luggage.

When the minibus stopped and while Orlando and Castor loaded the large weapons box, Zoe did a quick inspection of the under carriage and the interior before allowing Bram to enter.

Bram went to the front door of the van so he could check out the driver. As soon as he saw who it was he started to laugh. He asked how long Cedric had been a minibus driver and did he have a license to transport weapons and ammunition. He knew immediately that Ted had set him up.

Cedric laughed said that he had started working at his new profession at about six in the morning when he had picked up the minibus from the rental car office.

Bram said he refused to ride in the front suicide seat and got in and sat down next to Pat.

Orlando got in the front seat and said that he knew exactly how Cedric drove and had no fear of sitting next to him.

The transport never stopped. By lunch time all of the wedding party and a healthy number of guests had Folded in.

Bram had positioned the laser shield so that it was above the top of the two fences but could be dropped down in just a few seconds. He had walked the fence to ensure that there were no obstructions that would be in the way when the barrier was lowered to the ground. He tested and an additional feature that had come to him from watching a movie depicting the defense of an ancient castle where the archers fired their crossbows through narrow slits called balistraria. He had programed the controls of the laser shield so he could raise the front part of the top cover from the wall section and raise the top up two feet and provide an opening that the snipers could shoot through. He had created a horizontal balistraria for the snipers to shoot from.

He then asked the ex-Navy seals to take up positions in the top floor of the rooms that faced the front. He suggested that if they were attacked he would activate the opening and it would open for two seconds allowing them to shoot and then it would close automatically, and they would need to activate it to be able to shoot again.

The leader of the six said he loved the idea of setting things up so they could lay to the side of the windows and roll into position as the shield went up and then roll away as the shield went down, and they all reloaded.

Bram said that the rooms were theirs and they should enjoy the best rooms in the Inn.

A few minutes later the Admiral came to Bram and commented that he had just made lifetime friends of the six ex-Seals.

Bram smiled and said the Navy was much easier to make friends with than the Marines.

Orlando was standing with Bram laughed and said that he had told his Marines not to trust anyone so brainy and handsome but when pretty boy out did him in the first major attack, he put out the word to give him a break and the Marines now loved him.

The Admiral laughed and said the General had told Bram so much that his men were trying to take Orlando's job.

Orlando shook his head and said that competition was about going to lunch with Bram who had Chef D'Carluca wrapped around his little finger and was always trying to impress him with some special lunch. It was a lunch that those guarding Bram got to share.

Bram shook his head and said that they needed to make sure that all the guests got into the Inn safely by six in the morning and anyone that was late would not be Folded to Earth. He said he planned to put the shield up during the practice and that everyone already at the Inn was to be inside the shield.

Mike came over and said he and Mary had just arranged to have some of the guests that were staying overnight moved away from the rooms he had arranged for the Seals.

He then let them know that Stetson Catering were done getting their food serving tables set up and they were ready for folks to get their lunch.

Bram used the portable microphone he had in his hand and let everyone know lunch was ready and it was a first come first serve event.

He watched as all the young men rushed over to form three lines in front of each serving table. He approved of the fact that the Stetsons had come prepared to handle a large crowd of eager eaters.

Pat waved to him from the table that she and Amy were sitting at.

He walked over and saw that they were holding a seat for him that had a plate with a little of everything on it. He noted that the plate was a heavy-duty disposable. He sat down and took a bite of the slice of pink roast beef and knew he was in for a great lunch.

Elizabeth had watched the arrival of all the wedding party and had talked to all three brides and grooms and had walked them through the wedding ceremony. She had made the point that Bram would preside but if there was any disruption, he would then take action in the manner he thought would be most appropriate and they should do as he instructed otherwise, she was in charge and would keep things on track.

The lunch was a leisurely one and Elizabeth hated to break it up, but she stood and gave everyone the ten-minute warning and asked that the food be removed from the Inn.

Bram watched as the Stetson crew transformed the main floor into the arrangement for the wedding. He noted that Orlando had moved the majority of the ex-Marines to the veranda and was giving them instructions.

He also saw Ted had his team put up a table at the end of the veranda and put the extra food and desert on it.

He would have to give him and Marial a hard time about spoiling the young men.

Elizabeth then called the wedding practice to order and had everyone walk slowly through it.

Bram took the three rings from the ring bearer. He realized that Elizabeth was using plastic copies for the practice.

He noted that Elizabeth had everything flowing smoothly. He looked out the windows to the veranda and realized that Orlando was still instructing the men on how to defend the Inn. He noted that they all had an updated version of the field weapons that they had previously used. It was clear that the General's connections with the gun industry was still strong.

Ripples in Time

Elizabeth declared the practice over. She reminded the wedding party that they would all go immediately to their tables after the ceremony and be served by Chef D'Carluca and his team. The rest of the wedding guests would be sitting at tables that would have a number on it that let them know the serving table and the order they had in the line to that table.

Bram went to the Veranda and asked about the new weapons. Orlando said that they were the latest version of the Marine field weapon. Bram asked where they would be stored in the long run.

Orlando looked at him and replied that he would make sure they were stored wherever Bram suggested.

Bram said that he wanted them to be stored on Earth and that the house down the road should be modified to have a vault that would hold an array of weapons.

Orlando nodded and said he would personally work on getting that done.

Bram saw that Pat, Mike, Mary, and Amy were sitting and enjoying an iced tea. He was also aware that Zoe, Eric, Bob, and Thomas were standing along the veranda wall looking like they were enjoying the scenery.

He walked over near where Mike was sitting and smiled as his former FBI bodyguards took new positions with two of them on one side and two around the corner of the Veranda that faced the Rushing River.

It reminded him of all the previous times that they had faced adversity.

This time he felt that by having developed the laser shield he was doing his part at keeping those around him protected.

Marcus, Mylan, and Marcus Jr. came out on the porch. Mylan smiled and announced that she had convinced her Dad to take Monday and Tuesday off and go on a two-day Fold mini vacation to Easter Island. She said that Melisa had just told them about having purchased and prepared a house on the island for Fold vacations. Melisa said that she was putting it on the list on Monday, so I ask Dad to be the first to go there.

Mylan said that she was going there to evaluate the guide that Melisa had hired.

Bram looked at Marcus and said that there was no way to get out of going with his daughter on a business trip. He said they should all have an enjoyable time. He then asked if they were going to stay after the wedding to go fishing and got a resounding yes from all of them.

Marcus Jr. immediately said that he had refused to go to Easter Island if it meant missing the fishing trip. He said it was great to come to the wedding, but the fishing trip was the real reason that he had come.

Bram asked if the two of them knew the flower girl and the ring bearer.

Mylan reminded him that the school on Mataia had a small population, and it was taught similar to a Montessori school with everyone in the same room and often working on the same projects. They all knew each other well.

Bram smiled and said he envied them. They were getting the best schooling possible, and they had a dad that went on many vacations with them.

Marcus said they were going to watch a movie in the television room and guided the way back inside.

The six ex-Navy Seals came out to where Bram was standing and said that they wanted to thank him for arranging for them to have such great rooms. They commented that they were impressed with the Marine band and the Pop Music group. It was great to dance and enjoy a drink at no expense. One of them said that Mataia had to recruit more young women so that the women wouldn't have to dance so much and get worn out.

Bram pointed to where Erica had just sat down and said that they should go and let her know that she had to do a better job recruiting young women.

One of the young men shook his head and said that he was afraid to do that. She had interviewed him, and he figured that he was lucky to have made it to Mataia.

Bram walked over to where Erica was sitting and asked her if she had been tough on the young man standing with him.

Erica nodded and then pointed at each one and said she would introduce each one of them to Bram.

She began by introducing Dan Karajin that started off with her on the wrong track by saying the Admiral had approved him to come to Mataia and wondered why she was interviewing him. She said that his attitude had made the rest of his interview much more intense, and she had almost refused him. She said that she had called Dennis and let him know that she was considering rejecting him.

She then went down the list, Art Solti, a Bostonian who had earned a metal of merit for his service. Easy to get along with and a person who did not seek to use an Admiral for cover.

She then named Herib Hahn and said that what stood out was his love of skiing on the small family ski slope in the Rockies. She admired the fact that he had worked on the slopes while still going to school. He admitted joining the Navy was his way to see if he could get out to the bigger world.

Leo Barenbon, the lion of the six. She described him as the quiet leader who seems to also be the thinker. He impressed me with his careful answers. He grew up in the rural south but has a liberal view of race and gender.

Then there is Coro Atemis, the shy one but willing to risk his life for what he thinks is important. Erika made the point that he felt that having a just government was important.

Finally, Krys "the black Seal" a quiet hero that had only praise for the other five of his team. He made the point that they had always stood up for him whenever color entered negatively into the picture. She said that his support of Dan was why she had finally decided to accept him because she was not satisfied with the Admiral saying he would have a talk with Dan.

Bram smiled and pointed at Erica and made the point that she was not so tough she was just thorough.

Someone spoke up and said that she had saved his Naval career, and he had come back to her and pleaded his case so he could get on Mataia. He said that he had turned down a promotion to Lt Commander.

Erica smiled and greeted Stanley Lecter who was standing with Gerry, who had been a part of what Bram called the Magnetron Romance and was now Erica's husband.

Stanley went on to say that he looked back and was lucky to have met someone who told him to treat others the way he wanted to be treated.

Bram said that he was glad to see the US Navy so well represented.

He then pointed at the six and said that they wanted Erica to recruit more young women so they would be able to dance with them.

He said he was going to go inside tind see who was dancing and make sure the wall flowers got off the wall.

That evening Pat listened as Bram shared his thoughts about who might be the instigator of any attack.

Bram said he was confident that Zoe and her team had been thorough in erasing the Fold information. He said that the only way the history of the Fold program would resurface was if one of his attackers had prepared an information time capsule and left it for his children to find. That child now grown would be given the time capsule and learn about the enemy that had killed their parent. They in turn might be able to organize and get the funding from others that might have been named in the time capsule.

Pat smiled and said that she would leave getting the proof for his theory of how an attack might be staged. She said that she was thinking about the wedding of the miracle child. She said that she and Jina had spent time sharing how the Fold program had changed not only Zuri's fate but also Nuro and her life for the better. Jina felt that it was providence that the person who had developed the Fold technology was the person who would perform the marriage of their daughter.

Bram said that was a good note on which to get into bed and get re-energized for a busy wedding day.

Chapter 28: Amor and More

The next morning Bram had a quick breakfast with Mike, Mary, Pat, Elizabeth, and Amy. His bodyguards were standing around the room. Each had prepared a plate with waffles and had a cup of coffee nearby.

Mike had made enough waffles and fried sausage links that there was plenty for everyone. He had plenty of butter, a variety of jams and maple syrup.

They were all quiet as they ate breakfast. The plan was to get dressed after breakfast.

Pat broke the silence and asked about all the guests and where they had all stayed.

Bram said that the new house where they had arrived had more than fifty of their former Marine personnel. The wedding party had all stayed at the Inn. The other guests had stayed on Mataia and were in the process of arriving as they spoke.

He said that Chef D'Carluca, his crew and the dinners for the wedding party had arrived and were in the viewing room that had been taken over to hold their meal.

Elizabeth said that she had made sure the wedding party members were up for breakfast that was being catered by Stetson Catering. Who had already positioned all their food against the wall of the Inn's ballroom.

Mary smiled and commented that once again she and Mike could take it easy since Chef D'Carluca and the Stetsons were doing all the catering. She said that it didn't get much better than that.

Mike said that it did because he had gotten an invite from Ted Stetson to go fishing in the afternoon.

Orlando came into the kitchen and let Bram know that all the marine guard were on the veranda enjoying a hearty breakfast. He said that the Minibus was making a constant circle, and all the guests were arriving form Mataia early as they had been requested.

He asked Bram what else he could do.

Bram stood up and took out a controller. He showed it to Orlando and said that it was the activate and deactivate controller for the laser shield. At the moment the laser shield was activated but he had raised it so that the bottom was currently at the height of the top of the twenty-foot fence. He explained that once the shield was down, there was not much that needed doing. He felt it was better for Orlando to hold the controls while the ceremony was underway.

Orlando nodded and said that he would hold it but if anything needed to be changed he was counting on Bram to do that.

Bram said that it would be no problem. They would both be at the altar.

Cedric came in and let Bram know that he had just completed the last run of the shuttle. He had checked with Linda to make sure all the guests that were coming were here.

She had reassured him that no more Folds would occur.

He added that she had shared the fact that the auditorium in Mataia was set up to broadcast the wedding and that those on Mataia would be watching.

Bram asked Orlando to ensure that everyone was inside the fenced area.

He followed Orlando out.

He asked Cedric to park the minibus at the opposite end of the parking lot as far away from the Inn as possible.

Cedric did one better and parked the minibus on the other side of the bridge across the river. He then jogged back to the lodge.

Once Cedric was in, Bram lowered the laser shield. He walked out to the fence and made sure that the bottom of the shield was all the way down in the two-foot-deep cement trench by throwing a few pebbles down into the trench to see them sparkle and get folded into the negative Fold realm.

He then walked up to the six rooms and made sure the six ex seals were awake, and in position. He verified that the leader understood how to activate the raising of the top of the shield and that they had three seconds to shoot.

He was reassured that they could get two shots off in that amount of time and if they could see their targets clearly they would have two hits each time.

Bram then went and got dressed and went down to the hall to the lectern. He had everything written out. He didn't need what was written, he had everything memorized but should the action distract him he would be able to get reoriented quickly by using his notes.

Elizabeth approached him and let him know that the wedding party was ready. She walked over to the leader of the group providing the music and let him know that she would signal him when it was time to bring out the brides.

Bram saw that Lacy was sitting at the back and she had her headset on and knew she was in communication with her Fold attack team located back on Mataia but controlling attack bubbles located somewhere high in the sky and taking small Fold skips in time so they would be invisible to any sophisticated monitoring group on Earth.

He wondered if any movement of people, drones or other means of attack had been spotted.

The thought that maybe all of their precautions were for naught crossed his mind.

But Elizabeth's signal for the processional music to start brough his attention to the fact that bridesmaids and the groomsmen were coming up to the stage.

Elizabeth then walked up and stood at a podium set up at the corner of the stage and greeted everyone and then smiled and said that she was simply going to advise them in simple Mataian of two facts. One they should each have each other's back and they should apply the first sentence of the Mataian constitution and change the words slightly and "treat each other as you wish to be treated."

That brought an unexpected cheer from those in attendance. She then wished them a lifetime of happiness.

Then the music change to "here comes the bride"

Bram turned his attention to the brides being escorted in. The General, wearing his formal Marine uniform escorted Donna in. Castor's bride was Escorted in by Orlando, who was wearing a Dark Green suit with a white hanky and a white boutonniere.

Then Zuri appeared Nuro was beaming as he brough his daughter up the aisle. Zuri was stunning in her plain white wedding dress. A blue sapphire necklace on a gold chain accented her chest and matching dangling earrings accented her ears. He knew that her husband to be had spent a small sum to purchase her the matching sapphire engagement ring. He and Pat had gifted the necklace and Nuro and Jina had gifted the earrings.

The hush in the room spoke volumes as he watched the Fold miracle child, now a woman walk up the aisle to take the hand of a young ex-Marine, now a graduate Chef from the Chef D'Carluca school.

Bram had each of them read their marriage vows.

Then as Zuri finished exchanging vows, the sound in the hall changed and it sounded as if it was raining. Then several explosions above them seemed to accent Bram shouting out that he declare them all married, and the bride and groom should kiss. The sound of rain intensified and the explosions around the Inn intensified.

Orlando had rushed out to the veranda and realized that the attackers had bullets that were penetrating the screen, but they were being evaporated down to dart sized needles.

Bram realized that the bullets were made of some superior kind of metal. He increased the power of the lasers. He knew that this would be a drain on the batteries that powered the laser shield but figured he had about twelve hours of power. If needed he would replace his bubbles.

He watched as the six snipers were firing and saw that they were taking out twelve attackers every time the shield opened.

The rockets being fired hit the laser shield, sent up huge sparklers and blew up. A couple got through only to fall on the ground and explode. The explosions shattered the windows.

Lacy came out to the Veranda and said she was losing a considerable number of bubbles. She said that the drones being used against her were very sophisticated. She had taken out twenty drones and had lost twelve bubbles.

Bram asked if she had enough fighter drones.

Lacy replied that it depended on how many of the sophisticated drones the attackers had.

Bram said that he was going to join the snipers and add a little more pain to the attackers.

Orlando, Castor, and Donna said that they were going to join him. Orlando handed Bram one of the new sniper rifles he had in the gun case.

He then led the way to the second floor.

Bram began slow but in a few moments every time the shield opened; he was able to get three shots off. It seemed to him that the battle was going on forever.

He noted that Pat, Amy, Marial, and Linda had set up an ammo delivery service.

The General had made some calls and suddenly the sky seemed to be full of helicopters firing their Vulcan gatling guns.

Bram continued firing and watched as it became apparent that the attackers were being defeated.

Lacy's fighter bubbles were no longer facing the sophisticated drones. She had broadcast the command that the attackers lay down their weapons and surrender or they faced certain death.

Orlando shouted that he was going to lead his men out and round up the enemy.

Bram followed him down to the shield and opened the gate and watched fifty fully battle armored men follow Orlando out toward the attacker's position.

He was pleased to see the sky fill with at least fifty attack bubbles that laid down laser fire in front of Orlando and his men. The laser then took out a couple of attackers that had chosen to fire their weapons.

Lacy once again announced it was surrender or die. This time she had use a deep based voice that sounded like the voice of God from one of the biblical movies.

He was surprised how effective it was. He saw hands go up and fighters go down on their knees.

Orlando had his men bring the attackers into the parking lot and lay face down. They then zip locked their hands behind them. There were close to one hundred prisoners.

Bram asked what they were going to do with one hundred prisoners.

The Admiral smiled and said that he was going to send them on a slow boat to some island in the Pacific and drop them off.

Bram nodded and said that would be a great way to handle the situation. He then asked about the dead ones.

The general asked if there was a way to Fold them to a location where they could be buried or left for eternity.

Bram nodded and said that they could be folded in to the very distant past long before the human existed.

Elizabeth announced that it was time for the wedding party to have their reception dinner.

Ripples in Time

Mike and Mary had brought out the brooms and cleaning equipment and the General had asked a number of his ex-Marines to help him sweep the glass off the floor.

Bram asked Lacy to work with Marcus and Amy to move the dead to some ancient time. He then went in and joined the Wedding party and for the meal that Chef D'Carluca had prepared.

Pat sat down next to him and put her hand on his and asked if he was OK.

Bram nodded and said that he needed to follow up and learn who had instigated the attack.

He watched the three brides and grooms get up for their first dance.

Once they had the floor and everyone cheered, he took Pat's hand and led her to the Dance floor and soon the dance area was full.

Lacy finished her dance with Ray and then came over to Bram and said that all the bodies had been, ID'd photographed, and Folded to a distant past of the Earth. She had the weapons, the ammunition and the personal belongings stored in the barn of the house down the highway.

The Admiral had used his connections and had called in some transport and the prisoners were on the way to the coast where they would be put on a US Navy ship and taken to some remote island in the Pacific and dropped off.

She said that Linda had limited the fishing trip to ten fishing boats that were all full and ready to go. Those Folding back to Mataia would have until six in the evening to take a Fold.

Bram thanked her for the update. He said that he was ready to go fishing.

He looked around at all the people in the room and felt good about the fact that he had been proactive in preparing for the attack.

Pat saw Bram relax. She knew that he had spent a great deal of time working on the attack scenario. She also knew that he would be relentless at finding out who was behind the funding and organizing of the attack and would not relent in the search. Those organizers would rue the day they had decided to challenge Bram.

Bram spent the rest of the afternoon and early evening fishing and thinking through how to move forward on his personal journey.

He knew that he had unfinished work in learning and embracing new beings and intelligences that would enrich everyone.

He was determined to end the attacks from those on Earth, though he was not sure that it would be possible. He was aware that he had improved his technology but so had those who had attacked.

Ripples in Time

He smiled as he remembered the day he had been pulled over for speeding through a small town and the officer that had stopped him was bubbling with enthusiasm because he had just caught his first speeder with his new radar system that could accurately clock a car while he sat on a side street. The officer had been so happy that he had only written him a warning ticket.

Bram felt that way, he had been given a warning about the improving technology and knew that his current laser shield would need to be improved.

He smiled as he thought about time. In his world it did not stand still. In the Fold world it existed in both the positive Fold and the negative Fold realms but in the negative Fold realm it was not linear and in that realm all of history was fluid. He had stepped in several times, and he was sure he had created ripples in time.

He planned to remain active and affect both past history and future history in as positive of a way possible, but he knew that he would not always have control of the size of ripples he would create.

The End

Ron Mueller

About the Author

Ronald E. Mueller

remwriter95@gmail.com

Ron grew up in what is now Flint River State Park in Southeast Iowa. The 170-year-old house Ron lived in is built into a hillside. It faces a 125-foot-high cliff towering over the little Flint River. The house and the land talked to him about; the passing of time, the struggle to conquer the land, the struggles people faced and the wonder of nature.

He climbed the cliffs, crawled into the caves, dove from the swimming rock, collected clams from the bottom of the pond, gigged and skinned frogs for their legs. He trapped muskrats for fur, hunted raccoon in the dead of night, and with only a stick hunted rabbits in the dead of winter.

His young life was outdoors, and nature tested him.

He walked to a one room stone schoolhouse uphill both ways. A stern but warm-hearted teacher, Mrs. Henry was instrumental in shaping his character as she shepherded him from the fourth to the eighth grade. A Montessori before its time. It was a wonderful way to grow up.

His experiences inter-twined with snippets of fantasy lend themselves to the adventures he leads the reader through.

Ron Mueller

Published by: Around the World Publishing LLC.